Kiss Me at Willoughby Close

Kiss Me at Willoughby Close

A Willoughby Close Romance

KATE HEWITT

TULE
PUBLISHING

Chapter One

"I'M SURE YOU understand."

Four words, Ava Mitchell decided then and there, that were code for *"you're screwed and I don't care"*. So she did the only thing she could in response and lifted her chin a little, curved her lips in a small smile, and said, "Of course."

Nigel Farraday, her husband's solicitor, a man she and David had had over to dinner several times, gave her a quick, answering smile of apology before dropping his gaze. Bastard. Not that there was anything he could do. He was just the messenger. It was David, her husband of five years that had left this world a week ago, who had really screwed her over.

How could he have done this?

"I hope," Simon said, clearing his throat, "you don't have any notion of contesting the will."

Ava swiveled to give her stepson—not that either of them would have ever referred to their relationship that way— what she hoped was a scathing look of disdain. It was one she'd mastered a long time ago, practicing it in the mirror, making sure she got it right. Mouth pursed, eyes electric before the lashes swept down, dismissing the person in question. It was important to have a look like that in her arsenal, to be able to dismiss someone before he or she dismissed her.

But now, for some reason, she couldn't quite manage it. She did the downward sweep of her lashes and felt her eyes fill. *No.* No, no, no, she was not going to cry here, not in front of Simon and Emma, who had hated her from day one of her marriage to their father. They'd probably given each other a victory high five when they'd found out about the will.

Or maybe they'd already known? No, Ava didn't think they had. Otherwise, she would have sensed it over the years—the smugness, the certain knowledge that all would be made right in their eyes. They just had to wait for their father to die first.

"Ava?" Simon sounded impatient now. "I'd advise against taking legal action, if you're thinking about it." He pressed on, an iron edge to his tone. "The will is watertight. Isn't it, Nigel?" He glanced back at the solicitor, sounding so smug it made Ava want to choke.

Next to him Emma sat ramrod straight, her hands clenched together so tightly her knuckles were white. She hadn't said a word to Ava since she'd entered the room ten minutes ago and had been lobbed this emotional grenade.

The solicitor shifted in his seat. "Ah… yes, I would say

that it is. More or less…"

Ava almost felt sorry for him, squirming in his chair. He obviously didn't want to be party to Simon and Emma's—and David's—ruthlessness. Or maybe it was just uncomfortable for him to feel so much hostility in the room. Either way, Ava didn't have the energy to pity anyone else—her own situation was too dire.

She blinked rapidly, willing her eyes to clear, and then lifted her chin. Again. "I won't contest the will." She didn't have the money for a court case, and she had no doubt Simon and Emma would fight tooth and nail to make sure she didn't get another penny, a penny they didn't think she deserved. Brother and sister, they were a perfect pair, each as bitter and resentful as the other, at least when it came to her.

The trouble was, she had no idea what she *was* going to do. How she was going to survive. After five years of fidelity, loyalty, and, yes, love, David had left her with ten thousand pounds, her clothes and jewelry, her car, and her Yorkshire terrier, Zuzu.

She supposed it could be worse. A lot worse, if she thought about it. He could have left her with nothing, although, was that even allowed? They'd been *married*.

Unfortunately, she had no idea of the legal ins and outs of wills and inheritance and, even if she did, she didn't have the resources, financial or emotional, to do anything about it. It was just… she'd expected a bit more.

Simon cleared his throat again and Emma recrossed her

legs. Nigel shuffled some papers and, in the ensuing, expectant silence, Ava realized they were waiting for her to leave. She wasn't needed here anymore. She certainly wasn't wanted. She'd been given her payoff and now she was meant to get out. She pictured them going over the rest of the will, dividing up all of David's assets. The sprawling house on the outskirts of Wychwood-on-Lea, the chalet in Switzerland, the timeshare in Majorca. The bank accounts and the ISAs, the stocks and the savings, all the *money.*

She hadn't expected all of it, not by a long shot. Of course she hadn't. But she *had* expected a little more than what she'd got. All right, a lot more. She'd been his *wife,* after all. She'd expected David to see her provided for, to let her stay in the house for as long as she wanted or to leave her with enough money to buy her own modest place. Was that too much to ask? To expect? Apparently, it was.

Ava rose from her chair unsteadily, a wave of dizziness crashing over her. Only yesterday she'd been standing in Wychwood-on-Lea's little parish church, shaking the hands of strangers and managing stiff pleasantries after what everyone said was a lovely funeral service. Ava had thought it had been pretty bog standard—the usual hymns, a vicar who had never met David and bumbled through a vague-sounding eulogy, and a hundred people in attendance who knew him from business or golf, and didn't have all that much to say besides he'd been taken too young. Sixty-six, these days, was dying in his prime.

"How long can I stay in the house?" Ava asked Simon, giving him as unflinchingly direct of a look as she could. She figured it was better to ask him here, in front of Nigel, rather than when they were alone. Surely, in front of his father's solicitor, Simon wouldn't have the balls to boot her to the curb as soon as he could, which was what he and Emma surely wanted to do... with gloating smiles on their faces, no doubt.

"How long do you think you need to find alternative accommodation?" Simon asked, a slight curl to his lip.

Ava was under no illusions about what Simon and Emma thought about her. *Gold digger* had hovered in the air during more than one tense interaction over the last five years. Emma had mouthed it at her silently once while David was looking the other way. Simon probably thought she was going to surf the high street now, looking for a new sugar daddy. That option might have appealed, once. Once a long time ago.

"A week?" She suggested, because she had literally nowhere to go but she didn't relish the idea of staying in David's house while Simon and Emma hovered, waiting for her to leave, stopping by to make sure she hadn't been light-fingered with their inheritance.

"That seems reasonable," Simon answered with a grudging nod. "You can have a week."

Nigel made a small noise of protest and then fell silent. He'd always been a pushover.

"Thank you," Ava said, channeling a mixture of Scarlett O'Hara and Blanche Dubois in an attempt to be gracious.

No one replied and with nothing left to say or do, she walked out of Nigel's office in Chipping Norton and stood on the slate pavement of the market town's high street, breathing in the warm May air as people ambled by, and she wondered what on earth she was going to do now.

Well, first she would go home, for as long as she could call it that. Although, if Ava were honest, she'd never considered Carleton House to be home. It wasn't her style, and David hadn't let her touch so much as a teaspoon. He'd explained that early on, right after their whirlwind wedding, when he'd brought her back there.

"This is Simon and Emma's childhood home," he'd told her gently. "The home their mother decorated, and the best memory they have of her. I'm sorry, but I can't let you change that."

Ava had been both chastened and touched by David's thoughtfulness towards his children. Her own father wouldn't have cared less, had barely glanced at her after her mum had scarpered. And she'd thought David's request was reasonable—until she'd realized how utterly and completely he meant it.

She'd put a framed photograph from their wedding, on Moreton Beach, with her short veil whipping around her face and David holding her hands, on the windowsill in the dining room, and the next day it had been moved to their bedroom. David hadn't mentioned it, and neither had Ava. The message had been plenty loud enough. She hadn't touched anything else, not the 1980s-style drapes that she loathed, or the patterned carpets that looked like they belonged in a Yorkshire pub. Sometimes, she felt as if she were trapped in a museum, or worse, a shrine.

But she still hadn't expected this. Ava unlocked her car and slid into the cherry-red Mini convertible that David had bought her for her thirtieth birthday, a couple of months after they'd married. She'd felt spoiled and loved then, but now she wondered if he'd been indulging himself rather than her. She'd never asked for such a car, or even any car, but she'd always felt he enjoyed the idea of his young, glamorous wife tootling around the village in her bright red convertible.

Ava threw her leather bag onto the passenger seat, glancing at it in faint apprehension. Inside was an envelope with her name written on it—part of her legacy from David. Nigel had handed it to her at the beginning of their meeting, before the will had been read. Ava hadn't wanted to read it in the office, with Simon and Emma scowling and straining to see what their father had written to his second wife, so she'd slid it into her bag.

Now she wondered at its contents. Would he explain why he hadn't left her more? Permission to live in the house for as long as she wanted, or a savings account with her name on it, to keep her comfortable for the rest of her life? Or was she being far too demanding, expecting such things? What was a second wife of five years to expect from a marriage? If they'd divorced, she would have got more.

With a sigh, Ava started up the car and pulled out onto the high street. She'd read the letter when she got back to Carleton House, and she had a cup of tea and several decent biscuits to comfort her. Or maybe a glass of wine. Who cared if it was only eleven o'clock in the morning? She'd had a shock.

Ten minutes later, she pulled into the large, circular drive in front of Carleton House, a modern monstrosity that had been considered cutting edge architecturally in the 1980s, when it had been built, but now looked dated and a bit silly, with its box-like roof and jutting windows that had far too many angles. The fact David refused to redecorate since his first wife Marian had died in 1996 didn't help matters.

The beat-up Fiat of the part-time cleaner, Marina, was also in the drive and Ava steeled herself to make small talk, because, while she generally liked Marina, she wasn't in the mood to talk to anyone.

She opened the front door and breathed in the scent of lavender polish that permeated the air the two days a week Marina came, mainly to dust and polish, because two people in an enormous house made very little mess. And now just one person, and not for very long.

Mixed in with the smell of polish was that of lilies; there was an enormous bouquet from David's financial firm on the hall table. The smell was cloying and sweet and made Ava feel nauseous.

"Mrs. Mitchell?" Marina came scurrying around the corner, her round, friendly face creased into a smile. Ava had told her many times to call her by her first name but Marina always refused.

"Hello, Marina," she said tiredly, and eased off her black Manolos.

"Mr. Mitchell, he is so kind." Marina clasped her hands together as she beamed at Ava. "The solicitor, he call me this morning to say Mr. Mitchell has left me something in his will!"

"Did he? I'm glad."

"Ten thousand pounds! I cannot even believe!"

Ava stared at Marina for a moment, caught between the urges to swear, scream, or laugh hysterically. So the part-time cleaner, who had only been employed by David for the last eighteen months, got the same amount of money as Ava, his wife, did? Now she really knew where she stood.

She took a deep breath, telling herself not to be petty. "I'm so glad," Ava murmured, because Marina could use the money. Hell, so could Ava.

While Marina hoovered the living room's wall-to-wall cream carpet, Ava went into the kitchen and switched on the kettle. Staring at the maple cabinets and clumsy modern art she'd never liked, she knew she wouldn't miss this house all that much, huge and luxurious as it was. But she'd miss having somewhere to live.

She made a cup of tea, took a packet of custard creams out of the cupboard, and went to the conservatory, her favorite room in the house, with its airy lightness and view of the garden and fields beyond—and one where she hopefully wouldn't be disturbed.

Tucked up on one of the rattan sofas, its bold floral print always making her wince a little, Ava sipped her tea and munched through half the packet of custard creams before she finally reached for her bag and the envelope inside.

She slit the envelope and pulled out a single piece of paper covered with David's bold, slanting handwriting. Just the sight of the familiar way he shaped his letters—the too-long "t"s and scrawled "s"s—gave her a little pang. He really was gone. And while she didn't miss him quite as much as perhaps she should, she still did miss him. She still wished he was here, giving her the wistful smile, raising his eyebrows as if he was asking her a silent question, one they both knew the answer to. Except maybe she never actually had.

Ava took a deep breath and unfolded the letter.

Dear Ava, if you're reading this then I've packed it in and I hope you're not grieving too much. I'm sure you won't be. I know the terms of my will might surprise you, but I also know you'll understand. I couldn't have it any other way, not with Simon and Emma. We had a good time together, though, didn't we? And you'll land on your feet. You always do. Love, David

Ava read through the all-too-brief letter three times before she balled it up, scrunching it up as much as she could. But even that wasn't enough and so she flattened it out again, smoothing the many creases, before ripping it into tiny pieces that fluttered all over the floor. She'd have to clean those up later. The last thing she wanted was Simon or Emma figuring out that she hadn't liked the contents their father's letter.

But what had David been thinking? *You'll land on your feet?* What the hell was that supposed to mean? Except Ava had a feeling she knew exactly what David had meant, and the realization made bitterness burn through her gut. Their marriage had had its practical uses for both of them, but she'd believed she'd meant more to him than... than *that.* More than Marina, at least, but then he had given her the car and the clothes as well. And Zuzu.

As if on cue, Zuzu whined and pawed the door to the conservatory. Feeling old and aching, Ava uncurled herself from the sofa and went to the door. She scooped up the Yorkshire terrier, nuzzling Zuzu's friendly little face, closing her eyes as her dog licked her cheek. Zuzu licked her again, something Ava normally didn't like, and then she realized why. She was crying, and Zuzu was licking away her tears.

With a shuddery sigh, Ava returned to the sofa, cradling Zuzu like a baby. It wasn't the amount that bothered her so much, although that did sting a little. Ten thousand pounds when David had millions... well. It was still something.

Amounts aside, it was the *deliberateness* of it all that chafed her so raw. Ava had a horrible feeling David had intentionally given her the same amount of money as Marina. They'd both provided him with a service.

Or was she being horribly cynical, and he'd just picked a number that seemed fair? Maybe she was reading way too much into it, assigning coldhearted motives to David when he'd felt… what? That was the question, what *had* he felt?

And what had she?

Ava buried her face in Zuzu's silky fur and drew a quick breath, willing the tears back. She didn't want to break down. She hadn't broken down in the eight days since Brian, David's golf buddy, had rung from the club, sounding more surprised than grief-stricken as he told her David was being rushed to the hospital after collapsing on the eighteenth hole. That had been fodder for several jokes during the funeral, how David always finished a golf game. Each time Ava had smiled stiffly. She hated golf, didn't see the point of it at all, and certainly not then.

When he'd rung, Brian had called her Amy, but that had been, no pun intended, par for the course. She'd been married to David for five years but plenty of his cronies hadn't seen fit ever to remember her name or call her by it.

The threat of tears having passed, Ava lifted her head. Zuzu clambered off her lap and sniffed about the custard cream crumbs and bits of paper on the floor.

Ava stared straight ahead, her mind starting to tick a little faster, going into practical mode. She had one week to come up with a plan and then enact it. She had ten thousand pounds, a working if rather ridiculous car, a wardrobe of designer clothes, and a small amount of not-very-expensive jewelry. For being a trophy wife, she didn't possess that many trophies.

Still, it was more than she'd had eighteen years ago, when she'd run away to London with a hundred quid and a bus ticket. She could do this. The realization both calmed and strengthened her. David's death had left her spinning, and his will and its lack of provision for her had given her another dizzying push round. Now she was determinedly coming to a stop, looking around her with clear eyes and a level head.

She would survive, because that, at least, was one thing she'd always been good at.

Chapter Two

"WELCOME TO WILLOUGHBY Close."

Ava gave the letting agent who had introduced himself as Darren a distracted smile as she stepped out of her car, blinking in the bright spring sunshine. The converted stables of a manor house, Willoughby Close managed to be charming without edging into twee. A cobblestone courtyard with wooden benches and potted plants was surrounded on three sides by four attached cottages, two of which the agent had told her were occupied. Today she was looking at number three, a two-bedroom that was, temporarily at least, in her price range.

Ava had spent the last two days sorting through her options, trying to figure out a way forward through the hazy mess of shock and grief. Where to go was the most pressing question she needed to answer, and she'd debated hightailing it back to London, where she'd met David while she'd been temping, or even slinking back to Wolverhampton, where she'd grown up. Neither option appealed in the slightest.

She didn't know anyone in Wolverhampton anymore,

thankfully, and she'd lost touch a long time ago with her few London friends, plus city living was expensive for someone with finite resources.

And, the truth was, she liked Wychwood-on-Lea. She might not have made many friends—that had never been one of her strengths—but she liked the village, its cozy quaintness, and she didn't think she had the energy, emotional or otherwise, to start over, even though some kind of new beginning was both imminent and necessary... eventually.

Besides, didn't the experts say one shouldn't make any big decisions after a bereavement? She could stay in Wychwood-on-Lea for a few months, at least until she figured out her long-range plan. And she rather liked the idea of living in the same village as Emma—Simon lived in Oxford—and discreetly thumbing her nose at her stepdaughter, refusing to be cowed or chased away.

"The caretaker has the key," Darren explained. "We're waiting for him."

Ava nodded, noting the way his gaze dipped to her cleavage before returning to her face. "You're new to the village?"

"No, I've lived here for five years." She smiled politely, giving him the kind of steely gaze that let him know she'd seen him checking her out.

Not that she could blame him. Her pale pink sundress was both tight and low-cut, as were most of her clothes. Clothes David had bought her, because he liked everyone knowing what a babe he'd snagged.

Ava hadn't minded, not really, because that was who she was and she understood it was part of the deal. She didn't marry a man who was thirty-one years older and not expect him to gloat a little. But with it came a host of other inconveniences and assumptions, some of them unfortunately true.

Slipping her sunglasses back down, she strolled around the little courtyard, inspecting the baskets of flowers in front of two of the four doors, the cheerful pots of clematis and trailing ivy. Yes, it was all very charming. And private, at least from the rest of the village. Willoughby Close was surrounded by the manor's sprawling estate, the crenellated towers of the house visible in the distance.

"Does anyone live in the manor?" she asked Darren, who looked to be about twenty-two. He looked startled by her question; he'd been checking her out again. This time her butt. Inwardly, Ava sighed.

"Um, I don't know, actually. The cottages are owned by the estate…"

Obviously. "Right." She eyed him dispassionately; he wore a shiny gray suit, a lilac shirt and a deeper purple tie. He had a rash on his neck from shaving. Ava folded her arms, a slightly chilly breeze rippling over her and causing goose bumps to rise.

She felt tense, and she wasn't entirely sure why. Perhaps it was simply the strangeness of everything. Just a little over a week ago she'd been in her Pilates class, about to text David to meet her for lunch at The Three Pennies. He'd had the Welsh lamb; she'd had a salad. Life had ambled on as normal. Now she turned back to Darren, who had got out his smartphone and looked to be checking his Instagram account.

"So where is this caretaker?"

"He said he'd meet us here..." Darren made a show of looking at his watch.

Ava sighed again. She wasn't in a rush; she had nothing to do today but look at this rental and then start packing her things. But she was so very tired, everything in her still aching, and she'd rather not be on her feet, in high-heeled sandals no less, making small talk with strangers.

"Ah, here he is."

A beat-up pickup truck pulled into the courtyard and Ava stepped back instinctively as the door opened and a man stepped out. She blinked slowly, taking in the long, jean-clad legs, the faded denim hugging muscular thighs and an impressive arse. Now she was the one checking out some-one's butt. She looked away, but not before her gaze had traveled up an equally impressive chest, clad in a gray t-shirt, and then clashed with the laughing eyes of a man who clearly knew just how good-looking he was. Ava could tell, because she knew how good-looking she was. Like seeing like.

Stupidly, a flush rose to her face, and she willed it down. She was not someone who blushed. And she had nothing to blush about it, in any case. She hadn't actually been checking him out. Just… inspecting. Admiring, perhaps, because he was quite the specimen. But nothing more than that. The last thing she wanted to do right now was flirt, and he wasn't her type anyway.

"Um… Jace Tucker?" Darren cleared his throat and held out one hand for what Ava suspected would be a limp, damp handshake.

"That's me." Jace Tucker had a low, rumbly voice, chocolate poured over gravel.

Of course. Did he practice that, along with the sexy, knowing smile? It all seemed a bit calculated. A bit too practiced and pat, like a party trick he pulled out at will.

"And you are?" he continued, and reluctantly Ava looked back at him, right into his laughing eyes the color of whiskey, framed by a square jaw and dark brown, rumpled just-climbed-out-of-bed hair.

"Ava Mitchell. I'm here to look at number three." Which he already knew.

"Good thing, because that's the key I have." He fished a key out of his back pocket and ambled towards one of the doors in the middle of the close, one without a hanging basket or pot of pretty flowers. Ava followed, slipping her sunglasses up to her forehead as Jace Tucker opened the door and then moved to the side to let her through.

It shouldn't have annoyed her, the way he did that. It was a gallant gesture, and yet one that seemed suspect since she had to squeeze by him, her breasts brushing against his chest. Ava fought another flush as she angled her face away from him and stepped into the little hallway of number three.

From behind her, Darren started reading the cottage's details from a printout he'd brought.

"Two bedrooms… lovely views of the Lea River… wood burning stove in the sitting room… dual aspect…"

Ava tuned out his monotone as she walked around. The downstairs was open plan, the galley kitchen separated from the living area by a granite-topped breakfast bar. French windows overlooked a tiny postage stamp of a garden, with rolling fields and the glint of the river beyond. Everything smelled new and slightly plasticky, the white walls pristine, the wood-burner still in its foam wrapping, the manual for the cooker on the kitchen counter.

It was small, but she was only one person. It was also empty, and Ava didn't possess a stick of furniture. Simon and Emma certainly wouldn't part with so much as a throw pillow, and to buy the bare necessities, even on the cheap, would cut significantly into her ten thousand pounds, but the one furnished rental in Wychwood-on-Lea had been little better than a bedsit, smelled of boiled cabbage and stale cigarette smoke, and had been far too depressing. She might be poor, but she wasn't quite that desperate. Yet.

And, Ava realized, she wanted to live here. She was surprised by how strongly she felt that. She'd never had her own place. First living at home with her dad, and then six hellish months of kipping on her best friend's floor. Then to London, sharing a squalid flat with a bunch of anonymous girls whose names she didn't remember, and then Carleton House.

Number three, Willoughby Close would be her first proper home. The first place she could call her own, could decorate. Not that she'd be staying all that long, because she still had no idea what her life was going to look like, where she was going to go, how to get a job. But she'd tackle those problems another day. For now…

"Is there any possibility of renting this cottage furnished?"

Darren stopped mid-monologue and gaped at her, looking, with his bulgy eyes and open mouth, a bit like a gormless fish.

"Uh… I'd have to ask the owner…"

"Not furnished as such," Jace interjected in an easy tone that Ava suspected was his default, "but I'm sure I could rustle up a few bits and pieces if you needed them."

She eyed him narrowly, wondering just where his bonhomie came from. In her world, people, and especially men, didn't offer something for nothing. And she usually knew exactly what they expected in return for their so-called generosity.

"Bits and pieces?" she repeated, skepticism audible in her tone, her gaze making it clear that Jace Tucker was suspect.

Jace shrugged one impressive shoulder. "I've got some

things lying around in various barns and sheds. It won't be out of some style magazine, but if you're needing furniture it should do you." He raised his eyebrows in silent challenge, as if daring her to admit how desperate she was. Did she want some moldy old sofa lying forgotten in a barn? Did she have any choice?

"I might have a look at any furniture that's available," Ava said, all haughtiness now, "if I decide to proceed with this rental."

Jace's eyes were laughing at her as he nodded towards the ceiling. "Why don't you have a look upstairs?"

Upstairs there were two bedrooms, one clearly a master with built-in cupboards, and a smaller one that would be adequate for guests... if Ava ever had any guests, which of course she wouldn't. The smallness of her circle of friends would depress her if she let herself dwell on it, so she didn't. She noted the spacious bathroom, the lovely, sunken tub, the glassed-in shower. She did want this place.

Downstairs, Darren was checking his watch and Jace was lounging against the breakfast bar, feet, in their worn work boots, crossed.

Ava avoided his amused gaze and turned to Darren. "I think I'd like to proceed."

"Oh." He looked surprised. Ava wondered if he'd ever made a sale before. "Brilliant. Um... if you want to come back to the office in Chipping Norton, you can fill out an application form..."

Ava turned to Jace. "How soon is the cottage available?"

His smile was slow and knowing as he answered, "As soon as you'd like. Tomorrow, if that suits?"

She swallowed a tart reply she couldn't afford to give. Jace Tucker was rubbing her the wrong way. It would be unfair to call him smarmy, but there was something about those glinting eyes, the sure smile, that made her grit her teeth. She didn't need another man in her life who thought she was a sure thing.

"I couldn't possibly be ready by tomorrow," she lied. "Saturday will be fine."

"Would you like to come by and see what furniture I've found before then?" Jace asked.

Ava hesitated. Yes, she would, and yet... this man made her scalp prickle and her hackles rise. She was pretty sure she didn't want to be alone with him.

"Thank you," she finally relented, struggling to sound gracious even though she knew she should be. He was offering her free furniture, after all. "When would be a convenient time?"

"Tomorrow? Two o'clock?"

She had no plans. Nothing to do but pack a few suitcases and get out of Carleton House. "Very well," she said with a little nod. "Thank you."

An hour later, she'd filled in the forms at the cramped real estate agency on Chipping Norton's high street, and then was driving back to Wychwood-on-Lea.

As she pulled into the drive of Carleton House she groaned out loud. Simon's BMW was in the drive. She'd managed to avoid David's children since the reading of the will three days ago, but she supposed it was too much to hope for that she could avoid them for the entire week.

She walked slowly into the house, steeling herself for Simon's particular brand of overt hostility. She dropped her bag by the door, poking her head in various rooms to see where he might be lurking only to finally find him in the dining room.

"Good heavens, Simon," she said dryly, folding her arms as she gazed at him crouching by the sideboard. "Are you actually counting the silver?"

Simon looked up from the open, velvet-lined drawers, the guilt that flashed across his face quickly replaced by irritation. "Just making sure everything is accounted for."

"Are you worried I'm going to slide some of your mother's sterling down my sleeve?" Ava raised her eyebrows, determined to stay light. She would not let herself be hurt by stupid, simple Simon and his moneygrubbing ways. If anyone was a gold-digger, it was him. "That would feel most uncomfortable, you know."

"Like I said, I'm just checking things." Simon eased the drawer closed and straightened. "But, if it helps, Emma and I made a complete inventory of the house and its contents awhile back."

"How forward-thinking of you. Anticipating this exact

situation?"

Simon's face began to flush. "You can never be too careful."

"Indeed."

They stared at each other, a standoff, and one Ava felt too tired to prolong. She didn't care about Simon. She never would. She'd never tried to win him or Emma over; it had been all too obvious from the start what a pointless endeavor that would be.

At their first meeting, during dinner at a Michelin-starred restaurant in London, two days after she and David had married, Simon and Emma had sat across from her stony-faced and silent, arms folded, neither of them willing to adhere to the most basic of courtesies. Halfway through the meal Emma had stormed out, theatrically, as if performing to an audience.

An audience of one, Ava soon surmised. Everything Emma did was for her father's benefit, whether it was tears or pouting or long-suffering silence. More than once, Ava had seen Emma give her father a sly, sideways glance, to see if her latest tactic was having some effect. Inevitably it was.

Ava had tried to feel sorry for the pair of them. Even when everyone in the restaurant was staring, Emma having slammed the door on a sob, she reminded herself Simon and Emma had lost their mother at a vulnerable age—Simon had been fifteen, Emma twelve. Ava had been between them both, fourteen years old, when her own mum had left home, never to return. She understood grief. She knew it made people act in ways they wouldn't normally, that it left them feeling raw and wounded even when they looked whole and happy on the outside, and so she cut them some slack. She also accepted they would never like her. Never, even, be polite to her. And David never seemed to mind.

"It's hard for them," he said once, when Emma refused to come into the house while Ava was present. She sat outside in her car, arms folded, a thirty-two-year-old woman having a tantrum. "You know that."

Ava had ignored the faint note of accusation in his voice, as if this was somehow her fault, and went for a walk so Emma could visit with her father in peace.

And now here Simon was, glaring at her with the familiar mixture of hatred and ill-disguised lust. Just like poor Darren earlier, Simon liked to sneak looks at her cleavage. Ava could only imagine what a quandary he was in, both despising and desiring his father's wife. It was something out of a Greek tragedy, or perhaps from a page of Freud's book. Not that she would know these things. She left school at sixteen with a handful of mediocre GCSEs, intent on an entirely different kind of life.

Too bad that hadn't worked out.

"Go ahead and count it all," Ava said tiredly as she turned from the dining room and Simon's bristling affront. "I haven't touched the silver in the five years since I married your father." Apparently it had been too special, along with everything else.

Simon started to bluster but Ava tuned it out. She was way too tired to deal with his histrionics. In the kitchen she scooped up Zuzu and nuzzled her face against her silky fur, closing her eyes and trying to summon the strength to see through the rest of the day. All she wanted was a large gin and tonic and about eighteen hours of sleep. She'd never felt so utterly weary.

"Any progress with finding another place to stay?" Simon asked as he walked into the kitchen. Ava could tell he was trying to sound neutral but the sneer came through anyway.

"Yes, actually." Ava cuddled Zuzu, her back to Simon. She wouldn't prolong the conversation by turning around.

"Where?"

"None of your business." She kept her voice pleasant as she finally did turn around. Time to end this. "Now, if you're done counting the silver and whatever else, perhaps you could leave me in peace? Because this is my home for another four days."

She walked out of the kitchen without waiting for him to respond.

Chapter Three

AVA PULLED INTO the courtyard of Willoughby Close, trying not to feel uneasy about her meeting with Jace Tucker. She'd keep the mood brisk and businesslike and they'd be fine. What was she worried about, anyway? Jace didn't seem like the type to make a play. He'd just flirt and try to make her feel uncomfortable, and she could certainly handle that.

Another car was in the courtyard, a beat-up Discovery in front of number two. Judging by the books, toys, and crumbs scattered in the back of it, it looked to be one heavily used by children. Ava wondered about who lived in numbers one and two but decided she wouldn't ask. She didn't really do neighbors.

She'd just parked and got out of her car when Jace rattled up in his truck, sliding out with a smile.

"Hey."

"Hello."

Ava had chosen her most conservative outfit for today's little trip—skinny jeans, a designer white t-shirt—admittedly tight—paired with a cashmere cardigan, also tight. A scarf had toned down the overall busty look, but she still looked exactly like what she'd always looked like, which was a sex kitten. She'd kept her cat-flick eyeliner, the tumbled golden-brown hair, the sultry look she couldn't avoid because that was how God had made her. She was usually fine with it but, for some reason, with this man she felt like he saw through her, although to what, she had no idea. She didn't think there was all that much to see underneath the glamor and the pout.

Jace was wearing pretty much what he'd worn yesterday, although the t-shirt was a different color. He looked good in faded jeans and work boots, and he so obviously knew it. How Ava could tell that she wasn't sure, because Jace didn't strut or sashay. No, if anything, he played down his looks, and yet… it was there. The smolder, the sexiness that was as part of him as it was of her. Ava gave him a stiff smile and then avoided his gaze.

"Why don't you hop in my truck?" Jace suggested. "I've put the most decent stuff in one of the barns, and you can have a look. Anything you like I'll throw in the back of the truck."

"Thank you." Ava clambered into the passenger side, breathing in the not unpleasing scents of coffee and leather. Jace slid in next to her, and even though there was a foot of empty space between them, he felt too close. Ava turned to look out the window. She really was going to have to get over her reaction to this man. Either that or figure out a way to use it to her advantage.

He started up the truck and soon they were bumping down a rutted dirt track, away from Willoughby Close. Ava watched gently rolling fields stream by, the manor house visible in the distance.

"Who lives in the big house?" she asked after a few moments.

"Dorothy Trent, otherwise known as Lady Stokeley," Jace answered. "Her husband was the Earl of Stokeley, but he died a long while back."

"Does she have children?"

"No, a nephew from London will inherit the title and the estate. Henry Trent."

Jace slid her a considering look, and Ava wondered what he was thinking. Assuming. That she was going to make a play for the next in line? Or was she being ridiculously cynical? Simon and Emma, and even David, had made her suspect everyone, even herself. Because who knew, if Henry Trent was single... well, that was one way to figure out her money problems. The thought just made her feel even wearier.

Jace pulled up in front of a stone barn that looked as if it had seen better days about a hundred years ago. Ava opened her door and slid out, breathing in the spring-like scents of freshly mown fields and damp earth. The air was full of birdsong, the field by the barn dotted with wildflowers. Ava couldn't see another building anywhere, and the peacefulness of the spot, along with the loneliness, tugged at her. She was feeling absurdly emotional about everything lately, a hard, hot lump in her chest that she'd been unable to dissolve in the nearly two weeks since it had lodged there.

"I've never heard birds chatter so much," she remarked as she followed Jace towards the barn.

"Goldcrests and long-tailed tits," he answered, without any innuendo at all. "They never shut up."

He opened the door to the barn; held on by rusty hinges, it looked half-rotted and it creaked ominously as it swung inwards, revealing a dim interior, the floor covered with bits of old straw.

Ava hesitated, suddenly conscious of how isolated they were. No one knew where she was, not that there was anyone for her to tell. If she was about to be murdered by a sexy caretaker Simon and Emma would be thrilled rather than alarmed.

Jace took a torch out of his pocket and flashed it around, revealing a pile of furniture pushed together, all of it looking old and dusty.

"I know it's not much, but these are the best bits I could find." He reached out and hauled one piece closer to the door and the sunlight for her inspection. "This is a bureau. Genuine antique."

Ava stepped closer, and saw that underneath the dust and grime, the bureau looked to be a very nice piece of furniture.

"Comes with a mirror," Jace said. "I can attach it, if you like."

Why are you being so nice to me? Ava swallowed down the question. She didn't think she wanted to hear the answer.

"Thank you," she said instead, and Jace proceeded to show her the rest of the furniture—a double bed frame with an ornately carved headboard, a settee from the Victorian era with velveteen upholstery rubbed to nothing in parts, a lion-clawed table with four mismatched gilt chairs.

"I know none of this is probably your taste," Jace said with a little grimace.

"Shabby Gothic," she quipped. "It's going to be the next big thing."

He smiled, whiskey eyes glinting even in the dim interior of the barn, and Ava's toes curled. Her stomach fizzed. Good grief, she needed to keep that under control. She'd only been a widow for ten days. And yet her marriage to David had foundered a long time before his death. She could acknowledge that in the privacy of her own thoughts, if nowhere else.

"So you want it all?" Jace said. "I'll haul it into the truck."

"It looks heavy…" Ava began and he tossed her another smile, like a party favor.

"I think I can handle it."

Arrogant. He was definitely arrogant. But with looks like his, not to mention the muscles, perhaps he had the right to be.

"Do you want me to help…" she began as Jace started to drag the furniture out to the truck piece by piece.

Another glinting glance. "Nope."

She leaned against the truck and watched as he maneuvered each piece of furniture, heavy, dark, old, into the truck. Muscles rippled and sweat beaded on his forehead. Every time he heaved a piece into the bed of the truck his t-shirt rode up, revealing a glimpse of toned abs. Ava looked away.

The wind rippled through the long grass in the field and the birds—goldcrests or whatever—chattered and chirped. Although she'd lived in Wychwood-on-Lea for five years, Ava hadn't spent much time out in the countryside. She tended to frequent the gym, the beauty spa, and a few nice restaurants and pubs. Now she tilted her face to the sun and closed her eyes.

Her body still ached with tiredness but she also felt a little upward lift of hope. She really was going to live here.

"All done."

Ava opened her eyes; Jace had managed to heave all the furniture into the truck and secured it with bungee cords.

"Thank you," she said, because no matter what he might expect in return, she'd needed his help and he'd given it. "I really do appreciate it."

The words were heartfelt but also reluctant, because now was the perfect time for Jace to drop his gaze meaningfully and say something like, *so how about a little favor in return?*

Except he didn't seem the type. No, he'd probably just make a play for her at some point, and then act indifferent when she turned him down.

Except… that didn't seem his style, either.

"Ready?" Jace asked, opening the passenger door of the truck and, confused by her own thoughts, Ava clambered in.

They drove in silence back to Willoughby Close, and then Ava was getting out of the truck and Jace was starting to unload the furniture. Feeling a little too surplus to requirements, Ava helped him carry some of it into the house.

"Table and chairs here?" he asked, nodding towards the living area closest to the kitchen.

"Sure."

They didn't talk as they moved the furniture; it was that heavy. Ava felt herself start to sweat, and that was a look she did not do.

Twenty minutes later, it was all in, even the big frame and headboard for the bed upstairs, which had not been easy.

"Do you have other stuff?" Jace asked as he swiped his forearm across his brow. "Mattress, dishes…?"

"I'll get them."

He hadn't asked a single question about her circumstances, where she'd come from or why she had nothing. Ava was thankful, but also surprised. She'd expected a little bit of digging, but Jace appeared to be the kind of man who respected silence.

"I forgot to ask," she said with a sudden lurch of panic. "Are dogs okay?"

"Fine. Both Harriet and Ellie have them."

Harriet and Ellie. Her neighbors. Their names hung in the air, as if waiting for questions. It would be normal to ask about them. What they were like, the ages of their children. Ava stayed silent.

"What kind of dog do you have?" Jace asked after a moment when the silence had stretched on, started to turn awkward.

"A Yorkshire terrier."

"Pocketbook dog."

David had said the same thing. He'd wanted her to put pink ribbons in Zuzu's hair, making Ava wonder if he had some sort of weird fantasy, or just the image of what a sexy, young, trophy wife should look like. Tight clothes? Check. Bright red convertible? Check. Toy dog? Yep.

She hated when she started thinking this way. It diminished everything she and David had had, had shared, and yet she couldn't keep herself from it, especially considering the will and that awful letter. *You'll land on your feet. You always do.*

Well, here I am, David, flat on my arse, or so it feels like.

Ava took a deep breath and then managed a smile. "Thanks again. I suppose I'd better start packing."

Jace nodded slowly, his gaze considering and yet revealing nothing. "See you Saturday," he said.

❄

PACKING DIDN'T TAKE long, just as Ava had known it
wouldn't. Four bin bags of designer clothes—the matching
set of Louis Vuitton suitcases were not, technically, hers—
and a small bag of jewelry and personal items. She took the
wedding photo of her and David, and a couple of books and
DVDs she'd bought herself. A bit defiantly, she grabbed a
pair of pottery mugs she and David had bought in France.

The will had only mentioned clothes and jewelry, but if
Simon was going to quibble over a couple of cups Ava
thought she might slap him. That would feel very good.

Two days later, having ordered some basics to be delivered to number three, Ava packed up the car, put Zuzu in
her carrier in the backseat, and locked up Carleton House for
the last time.

She stood on the doorstep, staring up at its big, boxy
proportions, those angular windows, everything looking like
what people thought modern was forty years ago.

It had never felt like home, but it was still hard to walk
away. She'd been happy here, more or less. Lately it had been
the latter, but still. She'd made her choices, made a life, and
she'd been willing to live with that. Would have, if David
hadn't gone and died.

Ava took a deep breath and then pushed the key through
the letterbox. At least she wouldn't have to deal with Simon
or Emma ever again. Their relationship was officially over.

Ava let out her breath and then resolutely turned to the

car. Seconds later she was speeding away from Carleton House forever.

When she pulled up to Willoughby Close she saw a commotion in the courtyard; the beat-up Discovery she'd glimpsed earlier was parked in front of number two, the boot and roof box both open and boxes and carrier bags of stuff scattered around.

A man was attempting to fold what looked like an enormous tent and put it into the roof box and, as Ava pulled in front of number three a woman appeared in the doorway, squinting in surprise at her as she turned off the car.

Ava would have much preferred lugging all her stuff into her new home without an audience, but there was nothing for it now. She checked her reflection in the rearview mirror and then opened the door.

Both the man and the woman stared as she got out of the car and then opened the back to get Zuzu. With her dog's carrier looped over one arm, Ava turned to them with a smile. "Hello," she said. "Are you my new neighbors?"

"What…" The woman looked flummoxed. She was attractive, the typically yummy mummy that villages like Wychwood-on-Lea specialized in, although upon a slightly closer look it seemed that she'd let herself go a bit. Her hair needed a trim and touch up and she was sporting a stone more than most of the mothers Ava saw parading down the high street with their over-privileged offspring.

"Yes," the woman continued, "that is, if you're moving

into…"

"Number three, yes." Best to cut this short. Ava glanced at her new home, and the woman kicked herself into gear with a bright smile.

"Oh, well, then. I'm Harriet Lang, and this…"

An awkward and somewhat interesting pause, and then the man chipped in, "Richard. The husband."

"Right." Ava felt herself go brittle as she clutched Zuzu's little crate closer to her body. "No husband here, I'm afraid." Harriet's eyes narrowed. Ava should not have offered that information. "Ava Mitchell," she added, meaning it more as a farewell than a greeting. "Nice to meet you."

She shook both their hands and with a perfunctory little smile she headed for number three. She felt them watching her as she fished for her key and then, with a tiny sigh of relief, unlocked the door, opened it, and then closed it firmly behind her.

Zuzu was yapping with excitement and, after flipping the lock, Ava let her out of her carrier. Her little dog trotted around, sniffing everything in quivering excitement.

The cottage still smelled new and plasticky, but with an overtone of lemon polish that hadn't been there before. Ava looked around and saw that the dust-covered furniture she'd helped carry in yesterday was now clean and gleaming. The wood burning stove had been taken out of its wrapping, and a neat pile of birch logs was now stacked next to it.

Further examination revealed a bag of freshly ground

coffee and a loaf of bread on the kitchen counter, and a half dozen eggs and a pint of milk in the fridge. Unless Willoughby Close had a welcoming committee, Jace Tucker had been here, and Ava didn't know how she felt about that. The more he did for her, the more suspicious and unsettled she felt.

But she could use the food, along with a million other things. Ava had bought a mattress and a set of dishes online, both being delivered later that day, but standing in the near-empty house she realized how much she hadn't bought. Didn't have. No pots and pans, or a coffeemaker, or a toaster. No towels, no sheets, no pictures for the walls beyond her one wedding photograph, and right now Ava wasn't even sure she wanted to display that.

It was eleven o'clock in the morning and all she wanted was to go back to sleep. Too bad she didn't have a mattress. Ava heard a car start up outside and from the window she watched as three children trooped to the Discovery, Harriet chivvying them into it with a bright smile on her face even though she looked about as tired as Ava felt. A puppy scampered about her feet.

Ava watched the kids clamber into the car, and then Harriet handed the dog in and went to check that the front door was locked. Finally she got in the passenger seat and the Discovery backed out of its parking spot before disappearing down the drive.

Ava was glad for the reprieve from prying eyes and small

talk, but standing there by herself, in her empty house, watching a family of five go on holiday, left her feeling lonelier than she wanted to feel.

She gazed out at the empty courtyard for another moment, wondering if she would put a hanging basket in front of her door, fill the empty planter with flowers and ivy. Would she make this place a home, or would it simply be a brief stopping point to wherever she'd go next?

And she had no idea where that would be, or how she would get there.

Ava let out a weary breath and then turned from the window. She might not be able to make this place a home quite yet, but she could at least unpack her stuff.

Chapter Four

A VA WOKE THE next morning to the sound of someone knocking with irritating persistence on the front door, and Zuzu yapping shrilly in response. She thought they'd go away if she simply ignored the sound, but after what felt like an eternity she finally stumbled out of bed—she'd slept on the mattress, delivered yesterday afternoon, in the middle of the sitting room floor, with nothing but a cashmere throw for covers. She'd have to ask someone's help to move it upstairs, probably Jace's, even though she didn't want to owe him any more favors. She could imagine the innuendo she'd see in his eyes, or at least think she'd see, as he hauled her mattress upstairs.

Ava rummaged through a bin bag of clothes before she found her dressing gown—a short Japanese kimono David had bought her—and thrust her arms into the sleeves. Zuzu danced around her, having worked herself up into a frenzy by all the excitement. The knocking continued, albeit more intermittently.

Finally Ava went to the door, undid the bolt, and opened

it to a frizzy-haired woman with a friendly, open face. "Hello?"

"Oh, sorry." A flush swept across the woman's face as she took in Ava's bedhead and skimpy robe. "I didn't realize you were asleep."

"It is morning," Ava pointed out as mildly as she could.

And she'd been knocking for what felt like hours. Zuzu poked her little head between Ava's ankles and gave the woman a good sniff.

"Actually, it's a little past noon," the woman said, smiling, "but whatever. I'm glad you answered. I wanted to introduce myself. I'm Ellie Matthews. I live in number one with my daughter, Abby."

"Ava Mitchell." Past *noon?*

Ava couldn't remember the last time she'd slept in so late. She really was tired. Not that she'd done much yesterday to warrant such a phenomenal lack of energy. She'd lugged her stuff in, unpacked a few of her clothes into the huge bureau upstairs, and then fallen asleep on the settee, only to be woken by the delivery man with her mattress and dishes. After she'd unpacked the dishes she'd had a makeshift and rather sorry supper of bread and butter and a glass of milk, and then fallen asleep again. She was a regular party animal.

"Well, it's nice to meet you." Ellie was starting to look awkward, and Ava knew she wasn't acting friendly enough. The trouble was, she never knew how to do these kinds of moments. Relationships with women had always mystified her. Men, for better or worse, were so much more straight-forward. "Sorry if this was a bad time…"

"Not at all." Ava pushed a hank of hair away from her face and tried for a smile. "Actually," she said, surprising both of them, "would you mind helping me with a little something?"

Ellie brightened as if she'd been waiting for such a request. "Of course—"

"I just need to move my mattress upstairs." Better if she didn't have to ask Jace Tucker for anything more.

"Oh. Right. Sure."

"Move out of the way, Zuzu," Ava said, nudging her dog gently out of the way.

"What a cutie," Ellie remarked. "Yorkshire terrier?"

"Yes."

"We've got a Golden Retriever Rottweiler mix. Marmite."

Ava couldn't think of a suitable reply, and so she just murmured, "Right." Then she turned to the mattress. "Hopefully this won't be too heavy."

They both started to heave the mattress together, while it flopped around like a dying fish. Mattresses, Ava discovered, could be annoyingly unwieldy. Plus Ava was only wearing her short kimono with very little underneath, and she was conscious of its gaping front, the hem barely covering her butt as she bent down to lift the mattress. Not exactly the impression she wanted to give her neighbors, but Ava supposed it didn't matter much anyway. People tended to think whatever they wanted no matter what she did.

They took turns lugging and dragging the thing up the narrow stairs, until they finally were able to heave the mattress onto the frame.

"Sorry," Ava said as she brushed a strand of hair away from her eyes. She was sweating, and so was Ellie. "That was more difficult than I expected."

"I was happy to help." Ellie smiled, her face shiny and red with the effort of moving the mattress. "You need somewhere to sleep."

"And now I have one. Thanks."

"I love all the antiques," Ellie commented once they were back downstairs, and Ava let out a rather hollow laugh.

"They're not mine. Jace Tucker is loaning them to me. I don't have a stick of furniture, actually." Why had she admitted that? She had some kind of Tourette's syndrome, offering personal information she didn't want to give out.

"Oh, do you know him?" Ellie asked. "Jace? I mean, from before?" Her eyes were bright with curiosity and no wonder. Jace was a hottie, and Ava had just inadvertently given her a juicy little titbit of gossip.

"No, I met him two days ago," Ava said a bit stiffly. Ellie's mind was sure to race now. "I'd offer you coffee, but I don't actually have a coffeemaker yet. But thank you for helping me." She'd meant it as a dismissal, but Ellie didn't take it as one.

"Why don't you come over to mine?" she suggested. "I have coffee and a coffeemaker. You look like you could use a hit of caffeine."

She could, and it was for that reason alone—or at least mainly—Ava accepted. "That's very kind of you," she said. "Just let me get dressed first."

She questioned the wisdom of accepting Ellie's invitation as she pulled on a pair of jeans and a t-shirt, both tight. Perhaps she'd spend a little of her money on some looser clothing. Either that or find someone who appreciated her tight clothing. That was the option she'd taken in the past, but right now the thought made Ava wilt inside. She was far too tired to make the effort that kind of endeavor required, the styling and strutting, the small talk and the flirting. Ugh. No way could she even think about that, and certainly not with David barely cold.

Unexpectedly, Ava's eyes filled with tears and she blinked them away as fast as she could. She did not want to fall apart. Not now, and maybe not ever. She'd keep soldiering on for as long as she could.

She thought about standing Ellie up, but it seemed too mean and she did want the coffee. As for the accompanying chat… Ellie seemed nice enough, but she also seemed curious to the point of nosiness, taking the good neighbor shtick pretty darn far. Ava wasn't sure she had the energy to deal with a bunch of good-natured but prying questions. In fact, she was sure she didn't.

She'd just have to deflect everything Ellie said. Fortunately, she was good at that. Usually. Her defenses might be a little low after David's death but she could build them up again. After running a brush through her hair and putting on a slick of lip gloss and her usual cat flick eyeliner, Ava headed over to number one.

A dog set to barking before Ava had even pressed the doorbell, and the creature howled when she did. Ellie opened the door, breathless, her wild hair in a frizzy halo around her face as she bent down to grab the collar of a dog that looked like it belonged in Greek mythology.

"Goodness," Ava murmured, stepping back out of harm and dog's way. The thing was huge and slobbering.

"He's really friendly." Ellie assured her. "A bit smelly, that's all."

What a recommendation. Ava edged past the enormous dog and into the cottage, which looked identical to hers in format, if not in décor or lack of it. While her place still looked barely lived in, Ellie had made a home. Admittedly, it was a shabby home done on the cheap, but Ava still admired and, yes, envied the coziness of the place, from the framed posters on the wall to the assembly-line pine table and four chairs by the breakfast bar, the bowl of fruit on top.

"This is nice," she said as the dog lumbered up to her and started to sniff in awkward places. Ava moved back. "How long have you lived here?"

"Only a couple of months, since early January." Ellie moved around the kitchen, taking out a cafetiere and spooning coffee into it. "We lived in Manchester before."

"Ah." Why, Ava wondered, was small talk so hard? Everything felt stilted and forced and, as for her own life… she didn't want to reciprocate by telling Ellie where she came from or what she'd been up to. "Who is the we in that?" she asked after a pause while the kettle started to boil and Ellie got out two mugs.

"My daughter Abby and me," Ellie said, and belatedly Ava remembered she'd already mentioned her daughter. She was so not good at this. Ellie gave her a quick, wry smile. "No husband in the picture, but I do have a boyfriend." This was said with a kind of quiet pride, and Ava thought it must be quite a new relationship.

"What's his name?" she asked dutifully.

"Oliver. He's a professor of history at Oxford."

"Impressive."

"He is." Ellie smiled and blushed, and Ava wondered if she'd ever felt giggly about a boy. Not since she'd been about fifteen. A lifetime ago, in other words. "What about you?" Ellie asked as she handed Ava a cup of coffee. Ava took the first grateful sip with her eyes closed.

"Boyfriend? I don't have one." She felt too fragile to talk about David, although she recognized not mentioning her recent bereavement would seem like a huge oversight once it was discovered, which it would be because Ellie was curious and Wychwood-on-Lea was a small place. Not today, though.

"Are you new to the village?"

"No." Inwardly Ava sighed.

She could tell Ellie was the kind of person who kept on with the questions, saw it as making conversation, and so it was. Ava was the one who had a problem with small talk, who felt as if every question was invasive, demanding, asking her to peel away layers she'd spent years acquiring. "I've lived here for five years, but I recently had a… change in circumstances."

"Ah." Ellie nodded sympathetically, and Ava knew she was thinking breakup or divorce.

Ava didn't enlighten her.

"Willoughby Close is a lovely little place. It's so wonderful to have neighbors—Abby and I were here on our own for two months before Harriet arrived, and now you. It's filling up quite nicely."

"There's no one in number four?"

"Not yet."

Ava smiled and nodded. That was something of a relief. "And what about the manor house? Lady Stokeley? She lives there alone?"

"Yes… she's quite a character, Lady Stokeley. Very stately and dignified."

Ava raised her eyebrows, waiting for more, because Ellie clearly wasn't finished.

But Ellie just fell silent with a shake of her head. "Abby's quite close to her, actually," she continued after a moment. "Somehow they hit it off and became friends, which was a surprise but really quite nice."

"Oh. Well." Ava took another large sip of coffee and Ellie brightened, so that she braced herself for another question.

"Do you work?"

"Not at the moment." Before David she'd done a lot of office temping, which was how they'd met, but she had no real desire to go back to that world. Couldn't even imagine it, really. "I'll need to find something, though."

"What kind of job are you looking for?"

"I don't know." Ava gave Ellie a breezy smile that she hoped was also repressive. "Something different, perhaps." Although what, she could not say.

Ten minutes later she managed to escape, feeling guilty because as inquisitive as she was, Ellie was also very nice, one of those people who was so transparently kindhearted it felt like you were kicking a puppy if you didn't reciprocate. And Ava hadn't, deflecting every question until Ellie had finally seemed to get the message and talked about the weather.

She'd also promised to have her over for dinner, and offered to walk the dogs together, a possibility Ava couldn't envision. Marmite could swallow Zuzu whole, and looked likely to do so.

Back in her own quiet cottage, Ava breathed a sigh of

relief, only to feel the emptiness echo around her and then the loneliness settle in. Damn. She didn't want to feel lonely. Maybe that was why she was sleeping so much. When she was unconscious she couldn't feel lonely. Unhappy. And awake Ava was both, which was annoying.

She didn't do lonely. She didn't need other people. She'd told herself that time and time again, and yet here she was, feeling at a loss in so many ways.

With a sigh, she went to take a shower, only to realize as she stepped dripping wet onto the tiles that she did not have any towels. Or bed sheets, for that matter, which were kind of important.

There were a lot of things she didn't have, far too many to buy, especially if she wasn't planning on staying here for all that long. But the lack merited a trip to Witney for at least the essentials, and it would get her out of the house. Maybe even get her out of her lonely funk.

It was a lovely day, the sky fragile blue and wildflowers dotting the fields as Ava drove down winding country lanes from Wychwood-on-Lea to Witney with the top down on her convertible. She didn't often go to Witney, save for the occasional shop of luxury items at Waitrose. She and David went to London for any major shopping, and they mostly ate out or had meals delivered.

Her life had been one of deliberate decadence… on David's part. He'd always insisted he hadn't married her to see her chained to the cooker, or cleaning toilets, and Ava had been fine with that. More than fine, really, because who wanted to slave over meals or cleaning bathrooms? She'd enjoyed all the luxury, believed David was spoiling her. But now that he was dead she couldn't keep doubts from creeping in. Fears that she *had* been chained, even if the bonds had been gilded.

But she didn't want to think about that now, with the top down on her Mini and the breeze blowing through her hair. The sun was shining and she had an afternoon of shopping to do. Maybe she'd even treat herself to a cappuccino afterwards.

Witney was a quaint market town, not quite as upmarket as some places in the Cotswolds, but Ava liked it better for it. She browsed the charity shops of the high street, looking for bargains. Between the tat and the mothball-smelling clothes, she found a few deals—a coffeemaker, a couple of pots and pans, an old framed movie poster of *Gone with The Wind*, which was one of her favorite films. She took it all back to the car and then went to Next and splurged on some decent sheets, a proper duvet, and even some throw pillows. Then a whip round Waitrose, filling her trolley with readymade meals, some good wine, the necessary custard creams and a few dog treats for Zuzu.

By the time she'd finished in the late afternoon, having enjoyed the promised cappuccino at a coffee shop in Woolgate, she was feeling both pleased with herself and a little melancholy again. There was no one to share the excitement of her purchases with—no one to make a coffee for, or show the oriental-patterned duvet cover, or chat about anything with. Her future yawned in front of her, utterly barren.

Of course, she could knock on Ellie's door and have another coffee and a chat, but Ava didn't feel like it, which was a rather contrary sentiment considering how lonely she felt.

But she wanted to be with someone who *knew* her, who made her laugh, who shared a joke, who gave a hug. Unfortunately, that person did not exist. The realization felt like a sucker punch to the gut. She did not have a single go-to person in the world, and that was her own fault, for the way she'd chosen to live her life. She'd put all her eggs into one basket and that basket was gone.

"Snap out of it, Ava," she muttered as she pulled into Willoughby Close. The courtyard was empty of other cars. "You've been here before."

Long ago she'd told herself friends were overrated. They turned on her, they let her down, or they were too much work. She operated better as an independent agent. Solitary. Strong.

It was just that she was feeling particularly vulnerable right now, what with David gone and having to move to a new place. She'd get over it. She'd get back to being her old self, and she'd figure out her future.

Because the alternative was too bleak to contemplate.

Back inside number three, Ava unpacked her possessions, which should have cheered her up but instead made her realize all the things she'd forgotten to buy. She couldn't hang up her framed poster because she had neither hammer nor nail, and so she ended up merely propping it against the wall. Almost defiantly she plugged in her toaster and coffee-maker, and then made herself a cup of coffee just because she could.

She took it out to the garden, the grass overgrown and weed-filled, and then realized she didn't have a lawnmower. Or any garden tools. Or for that matter, any garden furniture. How did people *live?* Where did they get all this stuff that suddenly seemed so necessary?

Of course, there had been plenty of stuff at Carleton House. It was just that none of it had been hers.

Ava sat on the steps by the French windows and cradled her cup of coffee in her hands, enjoying the warm May sunshine if nothing else.

Bees buzzed and birds chirped and a butterfly flitted near her head before drifting away. Really, it was all so bucolic, it should have been healing. Except Ava didn't even know what she needed healing for. Missing David? Wondering if her marriage had been built on anything real? Missing money?

And she still didn't know what she was going to do. She supposed she should start scouring the want ads. Either that or find another husband, fast.

Unfortunately, neither option appealed.

With a sigh, Ava rose from the steps and went back inside. Maybe she'd just go to sleep. Life was so much easier when she was unconscious.

Chapter Five

PART-TIME CLEANER. PART-TIME receptionist. Part-time cashier at a sandwich bar. Ava flicked through the classifieds in the back of the *Oxford Mail*, feeling more dispirited as she read each one. She didn't want any of these jobs, and worse, they all paid peanuts.

She'd been living in Willoughby Close for five days, and it was all starting to feel rather endless. Her neighbor in number two, Harriet Lang, was still away, and Ellie had popped over a couple of times to see how she was but other than that Ava had spent every day on her own, sleeping, mooching around, or walking Zuzu.

She needed to get a grip, get a move on, but she felt both lethargic and overwhelmed, and it was hard to know where to start. The cottage still looked barely lived in, but there was food in the fridge and at least today she'd managed to drag herself to the post office to buy a newspaper. Hence the help wanted ads.

Ava turned the page, scanning a further half dozen advertisements, none of which appealed. Then the doorbell rang, sending Zuzu into a fit of barking. That in of itself was a surprise, since Ellie had already popped by earlier that morning for a quick chat. No one else had come to her door; Ava had seen Jace in the distance a couple of days ago but he hadn't stopped by since she'd moved in, and perversely she found she was a bit annoyed by that. He was Mr. Helpful before she arrived, and not so much after. Her annoyance was annoying in itself; she didn't want to become chummy with Jace Tucker, after all.

"Ellie." Ava stared at her neighbor in surprise as she opened the door and Zuzu clambered for a sniff of her unexpected caller. "Is everything okay?" Two visits in one day was a bit much, even for Ellie, and her newfound neighbor looked a little more frazzled than usual.

"Yes, sort of, but I need to ask you a favor. A massive favor, actually." Ellie smiled, hopping from foot to foot, clearly running on adrenalin.

Ava didn't like the sound of that, but considering how kind Ellie had been to her, she felt she had no choice but to say, "Of course. What is it?"

"It's Lady Stokeley. I'm meant to drive her to Oxford today, but I'd completely forgotten that I'd booked Abby for a filling at the dentist's, and you know what they're like if you cancel, you can't get an appointment for months and months." Ellie drew a hurried breath before plunging on, "I tried to ring Jace to see if he could do it, but he seems to have gone missing, which is really strange. He's almost always here, all the time, but he's been gone all day. Anyway." She smiled distractedly. "Would you mind terribly? It only takes about twenty minutes, plus the driving time, of course."

Ellie had been speaking so fast Ava was struggling to keep up. "So you want me to drive Lady Stokeley to Oxford?" she said slowly, and Ellie nodded.

"Yes. If you don't mind."

Did she? It wasn't as if she had anything better to do, and she was slightly curious about the resident of Willoughby Manor. "Where in Oxford?"

"The hospital." Ellie looked vaguely guilty as she explained, "For her treatment. She... she has cancer, but I don't think she wants people knowing. She told me she'd tell people herself, so…"

"Okay," Ava said. "I'll try not to mention it."

Ellie perked right up. "So you'll do it?"

Had she just said yes? Ava shrugged. "Sure."

"Oh, really?" Ellie looked so relieved Ava thought she might pass out or burst into tears or both. "Thank you, thank you, thank you. I really appreciate it—"

"Ellie." Ava cut off her exclamations with a wave of her hand. "It's fine. When do I need to go?"

"Er… well, right now, actually."

"Oh. Okay."

Ava was feeling a little nonplussed about the situation as she quickly brushed her hair, put on the minimum of makeup, and then got in her Mini and drove up to Willoughby Manor.

It was a beautiful house, if a bit austere and looking slightly neglected. Ava couldn't imagine living there on her own.

Swinging between trepidation and curiosity, she mounted the steps and lifted the heavy and tarnished brass lion-shaped knocker. The thud reverberated through the whole house, and even after waiting a good minute, no one came to the door.

Ava hesitated, and then, since time was ticking and she knew from Ellie that Lady Stokeley's appointment was in less than an hour, she tried the massive handle. The door swung open with a creak worthy of a horror movie and Ava stepped inside.

It felt like stepping into a tomb. The air was dank, musty, and still and, as she blinked in the gloom, Ava saw the faded glory of the foyer—peeling wallpaper, old oil paintings, and lots of dust.

"Hello…" she called, her voice echoing through the emptiness. "Hello, Lady Stokeley?"

Nothing. Ava hesitated. She didn't like just barging into the old lady's place, but… needs must. And she was kind of curious.

"Hello?" she called again, injecting a bright, friendly lilt to her voice as if she was merely popping in for a chat. "Hello…" She poked her head into several enormous rooms downstairs, but they were all shrouded in dust sheets and looked as if no one had put a toe in for decades.

There was nothing for it but to head upstairs. "Lady Stokeley?" Ava called again. "Hello? Are you here?" She went up a few steps, each one creaking alarmingly. Around the corner and then a voice, quivering with both age and affront, stopped her in her tracks.

"Who, may I ask, are you?"

It was even gloomier up here and Ava had to squint to bring Lady Stokeley into focus. She stood at the top of the staircase, barely reaching five feet, her frail body painfully erect, her blue eyes blazing even in the dimness of the house. She held an ivory-topped cane in one beringed, claw-like hand and wore a twinset and tweed skirt that looked seriously vintage.

"I'm Ava Mitchell," Ava said after a tiny pause. "Your new tenant."

"And what are you doing in my house?"

"Taking you to Oxford. Ellie couldn't make it, I'm afraid." Ava kept her voice light and friendly, but inwardly she wilted at the stricken look on the old lady's face. It must feel pretty terrible to have things rearranged without her notice or consent, especially at a time when she already had to be feeling vulnerable. "I hope that's okay," she added, although if it wasn't she didn't know what she'd do. Go home, she supposed, and let Lady Stokeley miss a day.

Lady Stokeley drew herself up even further, eyeing Ava

up and down, making her conscious of the rather revealing chiffon blouse she was wearing, paired with a pair of figure-hugging capris. Ava widened her smile, giving it a bit of steel. If this old bird didn't like the way she dressed, too bad. Ava made a point never to apologize for who she was or the choices she made.

"Shall we go, then?" Lady Stokeley said and with something like relief Ava nodded and headed back downstairs. Moments later they were driving through the village, the sun shining down benevolently, Wychwood-on-Lea looking like it belonged on a postcard or the top of a biscuit tin.

Improbably, Ava's mood started to lift. Driving someone to chemotherapy was hardly meant to be a laugh a minute, but she was simply glad for the chance to get out of her house—and her own sadness.

"I was not aware I had a new tenant," Lady Stokeley remarked after a few moments when they'd driven in silence. "Jace did not inform me."

"I only moved in a few days ago. Number three. They're cute cottages."

"Are they? I haven't seen them." Lady Stokeley spoke in a chilly, formal tone that Ava suspected was her default for most situations.

"You should," she said impulsively. "See what your money has bought."

"Ah," she replied, turning to look out the window, "but it's not my money."

"Isn't it? Whose is it, then?"

Lady Stokeley turned back to her with a gimlet stare. "Young lady, do you not know it is extremely ill-mannered to discuss money?"

"I can't remember the last time someone called me a young lady. And you brought up the money first."

Lady Stokeley bristled. "Actually, you did, by referring to what my money has bought. I was merely correcting a false assumption."

"But we're not really talking about money, are we?" Ava pressed. She was enjoying this acerbic banter, and despite the still-chilly tone, she thought Lady Stokeley was too. "Since it's not even yours."

"You are impertinent," Lady Stokeley said, but her thin lips quivered in what Ava thought—or hoped, anyway—was a smile.

"So I've been told," Ava responded blithely. In for a penny, as they said. And she was enjoying this—goodness knew it felt far, far better than sitting home alone trying not to throw a pity party for one.

Lady Stokeley was silent, staring out the window again. Ava risked a glance at her, and saw that beneath the wrinkles, bags, and liver spots, Lady Stokeley possessed a flawless bone structure.

"I bet you were a real looker in your day," Ava mused out loud, and Lady Stokeley turned to her, shocked.

"I beg your pardon?"

"Beautiful," Ava clarified, in case she wasn't familiar with the slang. "I bet you were beautiful."

"Are you implying that I am not now?" Lady Stokeley shot back, and Ava laughed out loud for the first time in ages.

"Now *that* would be impertinent."

To her surprised delight, Lady Stokeley let out a chuckle. At least Ava thought that was what it was. It was a rasping sound that resembled the rattling of dead leaves, but Lady Stokeley was smiling as she did it.

"The money belongs to my nephew, Henry Trent," she said after a moment. "The house and all its belongings as well. Everything."

Now that was a familiar story. Ava thought about Simon and Emma denuding Carleton House of everything valuable before putting it on the market. They accused her of grubbing for money, but they were no better. Once she'd seen Simon Googling the price of one of his father's modern art atrocities on his phone.

"Well, that sucks," Ava said baldly, and Lady Stokeley let out another one of her funny laughs.

"Yes," she agreed after a moment. "Rather."

"Is that because of some *Downton Abbey* type law?"

"*Downton Abbey?*"

"Show on the telly."

"I am not familiar with it, but I suppose I can understand the gist. It's not a law, per se, since the entailment laws were abolished in the 1920s, but it amounts to the same thing. Everything is kept in a trust that passes to Henry. I've grown used to it," she added after a pause. "I knew about it long ago."

"When you didn't have your own children?" Ava guessed, before she realized she was being terribly nosy, and more impertinent than was called for.

"Precisely," Lady Stokeley answered, and her tone made Ava decided to drop the subject.

"Well, if I were you," she remarked after a few minutes had ticked by, "I'd spend as much as I could before old Henry inherits. Throw a party every weekend. Travel. Eat off gold plate."

"How perverse of you."

"Aren't you tempted?"

Lady Stokeley sighed. "No," she said, but Ava sensed a story behind the single word, and one the old lady didn't want to tell.

"Well, I would be," she said, although she wondered if she would have done things differently if Simon hadn't been counting the silver. Maybe Henry was as well; maybe he had an inventory just like Simon and Emma did, making sure his aunt didn't take any liberties. Judging by the state of Willoughby Manor, she most certainly hadn't.

They didn't speak again until they were pulling into John Radcliffe Hospital, and Lady Stokeley told her to head for the oncology ward. Ava made no comment, keeping up the pretense, pointless as it was, that she didn't know about the cancer.

The oncology ward seemed a dismal place. The waiting room was pleasant enough, with sofas and houseplants, but the feeling in it was suffocating with hopelessness and fear. At least it felt that way to Ava. How did anyone sit calmly and flick through an old magazine while the cells in their body were multiplying crazily, disease spreading with every second? She would not make a good cancer patient, but then would anyone? How did they all stand it, knowing time was running out even as they sat still?

"How long have you been in treatment?" she asked Lady Stokeley in a low voice, dropping the pretense. Everyone in the waiting room was either silent or whispering, by seeming mutual agreement.

"A few weeks. I'll get a week off soon, which will be a blessed relief." Lady Stokeley sighed and tossed the *Country Life* she'd picked up aside. "Two years old. I'd actually read it, and that, I assure you, is saying something."

"Is it very hard?" Ava asked, curious now, and strangely moved.

There was something unbearably poignant about being in a room with people who were facing death or life crises. One woman wore a colorful headscarf over a completely bald head; she didn't even have eyelashes or eyebrows. She looked weary but accepting, at peace even, a state of mind Ava thought she should perhaps adopt.

"Hard?" Lady Stokeley repeated, and then actually snorted. "What a ridiculous question."

And, with a pang of embarrassed shame, Ava realized it was. Of course it was bloody hard. It didn't bear saying, and certainly not asking.

"Sorry," she muttered, and Lady Stokeley had the grace not to reply.

Her name was called then, and Ava waited in the reception area while Lady Stokeley walked to one of the treatment rooms, moving slowly but looking, as Ava imagined she ever did, dignified.

Twenty minutes later, she came out again, looking the same, just wearier. And that was it—Ava asked if there was anything more to do, any people to see, forms to sign, but apparently, there wasn't.

"It seems they've done some tests," Lady Stokeley announced when they were back in the car, heading towards Burford on the A40. "I don't know what. Sticking me with a bunch of needles and such, but it seems this wretched chemo is actually working."

"It is?"

"You don't," Lady Stokeley informed her with a sniff, "have to sound so surprised."

"Sorry." Ava gave her an abashed smile. "That's great news. Absolutely brilliant."

"Well, who knows what any of it means." She leaned her head back against the seat and sighed. "But the doctors seemed pleased, and I suppose, by association, I should be, as well."

"Damn right," Ava announced, hitting the steering wheel for emphasis, and Lady Stokeley gave her a look of regal disdain. "Sorry," she said, not at all sorry.

Lady Stokeley needed a little pep in her life. Ava had the distinct impression people had been tiptoeing around her for years. Decades, even.

"You should celebrate."

"I'm not about to break out the Moet '97 just yet."

"Why not? If not now, then when?"

Lady Stokeley simply sniffed. Back at Willoughby Manor, Ava pulled up by the front steps and then came around to open the passenger door. She thought Lady Stokeley might have dozed off for a few minutes, but she roused herself as Ava opened the door and then slowly, painstakingly, climbed out.

Ava followed her inside, not quite willing simply to leave her to it. Lady Stokeley didn't protest, which made Ava think she was even more tired than she'd let on.

Lady Stokeley headed for the stairs, faltering on the first step so Ava came forward to take her arm, which felt light and fragile. "That chemo takes it out of you, doesn't it?" she murmured, and Lady Stokeley sighed.

"I am afraid it does."

Ava led her upstairs and to the bedroom, a moth-eaten room if there ever was one and completely depressing. Lady

Stokeley needed to splurge a little on some interior decorating. Make her last years count, or at least bearable.

Lady Stokeley gently shook off her arm and headed towards the bed. "Thank you," she said, all stiff formality. "I'm quite able to manage on my own now."

"Okay." Ava thought about asking if there was anything she could do, but Lady Stokeley was giving off vibes like she wanted to be alone and, really, the house gave Ava the creeps. It was so dark and dank and moldy. She'd take her pathetically empty cottage any day.

"Bye, then," Ava said, the words somehow seeming inadequate, and Lady Stokeley just nodded.

Not knowing what else to do, Ava turned and walked out of the bedroom, down the stairs, and through the front door, closing it behind her with a gusty sigh of relief.

Chapter Six

SOMEONE WAS KNOCKING on her door again. Incessantly. What *was* it with the people in this place? To add to the clamor, Zuzu started to bark shrilly. Her dog had never had so much excitement, with all these people knocking on the door.

Ava heaved herself up from the settee where she'd been flicking idly through a beauty magazine, trying to stave off the ever-present boredom and uncertainty, and went to the door, expecting an ever-persistent Ellie and finding Jace Tucker instead.

"Hello, stranger," she said, and then wondered where on earth that flirt had come from.

Jace's slow, toe-curling smile was, of course, the expected response, and Ava felt her insides fizz in answer. Hopeless.

Zuzu started to sniff around and Ava explained, trying to do some damage control, "All I mean was you were AWOL yesterday when Ellie was having kittens about taking Lady Stokeley to the hospital."

Jace's smile dropped, replaced by a surprisingly ferocious

frown, those whiskey eyes narrowed to slits. "What do you mean?"

Ava shrugged, suddenly tired of him, of Ellie, of everything. She'd been in a bad mood all morning, everything made worse by boredom, loneliness, and, yes, grief. She was trapped in the endless circling of her own thoughts, the narrowness of her life, and she had no idea how to break out of either. She'd thought about going to visit Lady Stokeley but she doubted the old lady wanted to see her and she didn't feel like facing the rejection or, for that matter, the moldy old house.

"No, seriously." Jace caught her arm in a gesture that was more commanding than concerned, and made Ava's hackles rise. He was *touching* her. "What are you talking about? Why did Lady Stokeley have to go to the hospital?"

"For her chemo treatment."

Jace stared at her, his face expressionless, his jaw tight. Quite a sexy look but then everything about him was sexy.

"Chemo treatment?"

Way too late, the penny dropped with a thud, and all thoughts of sexiness vanished. "You didn't know?" Ava said, still hoping she hadn't put her foot right in it, stiletto heel and all.

"No."

"But… Ellie said…" Ellie had said, Ava remembered now, that Lady Stokeley was keeping her condition private. Damn.

"What did Ellie say?"

"You'd better come in," Ava said.

Jace was looking rather poleaxed. She hadn't known he was close to Lady Stokeley, but it was obvious from the stony, stunned expression on his face that he was. Or maybe he was just concerned for his job? If Lady Stokeley died and Henry Trent sold up, Jace might be out of work.

He shouldered past her, pacing her downstairs as if searching for a way out, his hands jammed into the pockets of his jeans, which did impressive things to his already impressive shoulders and abs. Not that she was actively looking. It was just hard not to notice.

"So what did Ellie say exactly?" he asked, turning around to face her.

Ava folded her arms and leaned against the door. "That she couldn't drive Lady Stokeley to her chemo treatment yesterday, and so she was hoping you might do it, but you were gone all day."

Jace shook his head slowly, his expression tight. "I knew she was hiding something from me."

"I didn't realize you were close."

He gave her a narrow look. "You just moved here."

Ouch. When Jace wasn't putting on the smolder, he was pretty intimidating. His broad shoulders definitely seemed cold right now.

"I'm sorry I broke it to you that way," Ava said after a pause. "I assumed you already knew."

"What kind of cancer?"

"I don't actually know." Jace looked at her disbelievingly and Ava lifted her chin. "She's not the chattiest person, you know? And, as you pointed out, I just moved here. I think I went above and beyond my neighborly duty driving her."

"Sure." The sarcasm was as thick as treacle.

Ava looked away, trying not to show her hurt. She didn't even know this guy. And she didn't know Lady Stokeley. Ellie might persist in being friends because she was the human equivalent of a Golden Retriever but, essentially, everyone here was a stranger and all Ava wanted was to be left alone. Sort of.

"Did you knock on my door for a reason?" she asked eventually.

"Yes. I just wanted to make sure everything was okay with the cottage."

"It's fine." She glared at him, then decided that was showing too much emotion, and dialed it down a notch, giving him what she hoped was a cool, level look.

Jace sighed, those impressive shoulders sagging a little. "Sorry. I didn't mean… this hasn't been one of my better moments. I wasn't expecting the news about madam."

"Madam? Seriously?" Ava raised her eyebrows. "You call her that? What are you, a footman?'

A smile tugged the corner of his mouth. "It's a bit of a joke between us."

"Right." So Jace and Lady Stokeley had a thing going.

Cute. "Like I said, the cottage is fine." Realizing she was still sounding kind of hostile, she added, "and I'm sorry about Lady Stokeley but, if it makes you feel any better, the doctors seemed pleased with her progress. They ran some tests and it seemed like they were positive."

"It seemed…?"

"I didn't ask for details, and Lady Stokeley wasn't offering any."

"Okay." Jace raked a hand through his hair, and it flopped back onto his forehead. "I should have realized it was cancer," he said, almost to himself.

Curious, despite every intention not to be, Ava asked, "Why? I mean, besides the fact that she must be getting up there?"

"Eighty-six. She had pneumonia a couple of months ago and she told me she was fine but I knew something was going on. And Harriet was driving her to the hospital a lot, several times a week it seemed…"

Harriet, the neighbor she'd met so briefly on her first day. The Discovery had pulled up in front of number three a couple of days ago and Ava had watched several rumpled-looking kids pile out, and then the sheepish dad. Harriet had seemed wound up, and Ava had wondered what was going on between them all. Not that she'd ask. And not that Harriet had offered. Unlike Ellie, she didn't seem interested in being neighborly. Which was fine.

"So you knew Lady Stokeley had been ill and was going

regularly to the hospital," she said slowly, and Jace gave her the glimmer of a smile.

"I'm thick, is what you're saying."

"Not in so many words." Ava smiled back. "No one wants to assume the worst, do they?"

"No." His gaze turned considering and Ava knew he was wondering what her story was. Her worst. And for a second she had the crazy urge to tell him.

"So how do you know Lady Stokeley?" she asked, determined to banish that mad impulse, and cut off any questions Jace might be tempted to ask her.

"Well, I work for her."

"Yes, but like I said before you're obviously close." Ava waited, her expression inquiring. Deflect, deflect, deflect. Plus she was curious.

"I don't know if I'd say we were close," Jace said slowly. "But she did me a…" He paused, seeming to choose his words carefully. "A great kindness."

Ava stared at him, both nonplussed and even more curious. *A great kindness.* It sounded like something out of a Dickens novel.

"Really," she said, and too late she heard the note of skepticism in her voice.

It seemed like any conversation she had with Jace Tucker was going to be fraught. She was prickly around everybody, but especially him, and she didn't want to put her finger on why.

"Yes, really. And I'm very grateful." His voice sharpened slightly, surprising her. The lazy, laughing façade had dropped again, revealing that that was just what it was—a façade. A mask, just like she wore. The realization that maybe, just maybe, both were pretending was deeply uncomfortable. Time to deflect once more.

"So, I'm looking for a job," Ava said breezily, and then wished she'd chosen something more innocuous to mention.

Jace's eyebrows had risen; clearly, he was surprised by that admission, as well he should be, considering the convertible, the clothes.

"What kind of job?"

"Any job, really," Ava replied with a shrug. She couldn't pretend she had some impressive career on the backburner. "I used to temp in offices."

"I know The Drowned Sailor needs bar staff." He said it almost like a challenge, to see if she'd rise to it and be grateful. Ava winced at the thought of pouring beer for barflies.

"Maybe something else."

He shrugged. "I'm not sure what else is going in the village. Not many offices here."

"No." She pursed her lips. She didn't even want to temp, anyway. She didn't know what she wanted to do. "Well, then."

"How badly do you need a job?"

"I'm not going to default on my rent, if that's what

you're asking."

Jace shrugged. "Not my business. But if you need money, you might consider selling that Mini out there. Get something cheaper, or rely on public transport."

Ava knew he didn't mean it as a rebuke, but it felt like one. Because surely and not-so-slowly the way of life she'd got used to over the last five years was trickling away. It was over. And she was back to scratching and scraping by as best as she could. There wasn't much choice for a girl with a handful of mediocre GCSEs under her belt and a CV that had nothing but temporary secretarial jobs on it, none of them lasting for more than a couple of weeks. She got bored easily. Plus she wasn't even that good a secretary.

With an indifferent shrug Ava decided to end the conversation. "I like that car." Although she didn't like it that much, actually. It felt like David had bought it to make a point, and it was one she didn't need hammered home again and again.

Jace shrugged right back at her. "Needs must."

"Maybe." She tried for an insouciant smile. "Maybe not."

Jace folded his arms, giving her far too considering a look. A look that swept from the crown of her head to the tips of toes and would not make her blush. Ava met that long, assessing gaze, with a cool one of her one, chin tilted, eyes level. Goodness knew she'd been checked out before. She was well used to male admiration, but it felt different coming from Jace.

Once again, it felt like he saw beneath the kittenish pout, the smoky lavender cat's eyes, the tumbling, golden-brown hair, the form-fitting clothes, the curvy figure poured into them. The whole package that she'd worked damned hard to keep looking good. What he saw beneath all that Ava didn't want to begin to guess.

They stayed that way for what seemed like an endless moment, and then Jace nodded slowly, which irritated Ava even more. Why was he *nodding?* It was as if he'd figured something out, and she had no idea what it was.

"Okay," he said.

Okay? Okay what? He nodded again, and then he walked towards the door, and then he was gone. And even though she'd wanted him to go, of course she had, Ava felt the loneliness rush back in and wished he hadn't left quite like that, or maybe even at all.

Not wanting to stay cooped up indoors with the endless loop of her own discontented thoughts, Ava wrenched open the French windows and stepped out into the small garden. The day was warm, the sky cloudy but with a hint of sun, and the air was full of birdsong and blossom. She sat on the steps, hugging her knees to her chest, as Zuzu scampered around in the long grass. She was going to have figure out how to get her hands on a lawnmower, or how to operate one, for that matter.

In the garden next to hers the doors opened and with a

burst of laughter and chatter two children tumbled outside, along with a puppy. From her position on the steps, Ava could watch them over the low stone wall without them seeing her.

She stayed where she was, silent and still, as the two children—a boy and a girl—tussled for a bit, seemingly at the boy's instigation, and then started tossing a tennis ball for the puppy, who could barely fit it in her tiny jaws but gave a good try.

It was a lovely, bucolic scene, the kind of thing she'd see in hazy, slow motion, for an advert on television—for yogurt or laundry detergent or something silly, but it would make her long for the whole picture, the easy, simple happiness of it.

Of course, life wasn't really like that. At least, Ava's life hadn't been. She rested her chin on her knees and watched as the children continued to toss the ball, until the boy grew bored and decided to wrestle again. The girl screeched in what Ava guessed was a well-trodden response, and then their mother, Harriet, came to the door, a smile on her tired face.

"You two," she said, her voice equal parts exasperation and affection, and amazingly that made them stop.

"Mum," the boy said, "can we have fish fingers for tea?"

"That doesn't seem too big a request," Harriet replied, coming forward to ruffle his hair.

"And chips?"

"Ah, now you're pushing it."

But she was teasing, and both knew it, and Ava watched in a mixture of fascination, bewilderment, and deep, deep envy as the boy tussled with his mother, clearly taking care not to hurt her, while the little girl screeched in excitement. She really was a screecher.

"All right, all right," Harriet said with a laugh, extricating herself from her son's grip and then holding up her hands in laughing defeat. "I give up. Let me check if we actually have fish fingers, never mind chips."

"Chips! Chips!" The boy chanted as he followed her inside. "Please, Mum."

"We'll see what's in the freezer..." she called back, her voice growing faint as she went further into the house. And then they were all gone, and Ava was all alone, and somehow she simply couldn't bear it.

It didn't make sense. She'd been alone most of her life, in one way or another. Even her marriage... but no, she wouldn't think about that. Couldn't yet pry open the door to all the unresolved issues and emotions that seethed beneath her determinedly placid surface.

She just hated feeling so lonely now. So lonely and so damn tired. She couldn't remember the last time she'd felt so tired, so weary it hurt her bones even to get out of bed. Actually, she *could* remember, and it had been when she'd been...

Ava stilled, realization icing through her. *No.* No, she

couldn't be. She *couldn't* be. She was tired because grief made people tired. Didn't everyone say that? Wasn't it a thing? *That* was why. Not because…

Restless now, and panicky, she got up from the steps and went inside, Zuzu trotting happily behind her. Ava paced the downstairs, just as Jace had done a short while ago, her mind racing just as his had been. Zuzu scampered around her, dodging her determined steps.

How long had it been? About four weeks, she estimated, when David had come back from a golf game high on his victory against his usual golf buddies. Ava remembered because things hadn't been all that great in that department lately.

But it couldn't be possible. It just couldn't. And yet Ava couldn't escape the sure and certain knowledge that the last time she'd been this tired, this utterly weary, she'd been pregnant.

Chapter Seven

PREGNANT. SHE WAS pregnant. She *couldn't* be pregnant. The thought went around Ava's mind in an endless reel, going nowhere. If she were sensible, she'd buy a test, make certain. She wasn't sensible. She felt paralyzed by indecision, by shock, by fear. Pregnant. *No.*

Ava spent the rest of the day inside, sleeping, reading, and trying not to think. Her usual, except now she had so much more not to think about. Eventually she fell asleep for the night, only to wake late in the morning when someone was yet again knocking on her door. Good *grief,* but people around here needed to get a life just as much as she did.

She grabbed her dressing gown and, pushing her hair out of her face, went to answer the door, completely nonplussed to find not Ellie or even Jace there, but her immediate neighbor, Harriet Lang.

"Oh. Hello."

"Sorry, did I wake you?" Harriet looked startled and rather disapproving by such a possibility, so Ava decided on a half-truth.

"Sort of. I was lying in bed wondering if I should bother getting up." Too late she realized how lazy and depressing that sounded.

"Oh. Well." Harriet pinned on a bright smile. "I wanted to welcome you to Willoughby Close—"

Seriously? "Are you the welcoming committee, then?" And now that sounded bitchy. Oops.

"No, not officially." Harriet's smile was becoming strained. "Anyway, perhaps you'd like to…" She paused, seeming to debate whether she wanted to continue. "Come for dinner one evening? It's a bit mad at my house, but we'd love to have you." This was said with such a lack of genuine enthusiasm that Ava almost wanted to laugh. Almost.

"Perhaps," she said. "When I've settled in." Whenever that was. She paused and then added dutifully, "Thank you for the invitation."

Harriet looked surprised that she hadn't tripped over herself to accept. "Oh, well, sure. Okay."

With a little nod of goodbye Ava closed the door, not even caring if she was being rude. She was still so tired, and the fear that had kept her pacing last night had crept back. Pregnant. What if she was pregnant?

She stood there for a moment, one palm resting against the cool wood of the door, and took several calming breaths, or tried to. She needed to get out of the house. Out of her own head.

After having a quick shower and then throwing on some

clothes, Ava clipped on Zuzu's lead and stepped outside into a fresh spring morning. The courtyard was empty, everyone off doing their own thing. Ava glanced up at the big manor house, wondering how Lady Stokeley was faring. Perhaps she'd brave a visit up there, just to check on her.

In the meantime she decided to head into the village and go to the one place where she had a friend—if she could call someone whose name she didn't know a friend.

The little tearoom on the high street was a peaceful haven as Ava stepped inside, Zuzu giving a joyful bark of recognition—and because there were cake crumbs on the floor. The proprietor, a friendly-looking woman Ava had chatted to a bit over the years, came in from the back with a smile.

"I haven't seen you for a while."

"Life threw me a bit of a curve ball," Ava said. If death and grief could be considered curve balls. More like a bat upside the head.

"Ah." The woman looked at her in sympathy. "I'm sorry."

"Thanks." Ava felt how brittle her smile was becoming.

"The usual?" the woman asked, which was a skinny latte.

Ava hesitated and then glanced at the blackboard above the counter. "Not today," she said slowly. "Today I think I'd like a hot chocolate with the works. Whipped cream and marshmallows." She was, perhaps, eating and drinking for two, after all.

"I'm Olivia, by the way," the woman said when she returned with the largest hot chocolate Ava had ever seen, the top crowned with whipped cream, marshmallows, and a dusting of cocoa powder.

"Ava." She smiled her gratitude, ridiculously touched that the woman had introduced herself. Now they really were friends.

Olivia left her alone as Ava sipped her drink in the empty shop, Zuzu lying across her feet. Outside, a few people walked by—a couple of young mums with fancy pushchairs, a middle-aged woman power-walking with weights strapped to her wrists, an elderly man with a wheelie bag and a grumpy expression.

She needed to buy a pregnancy test, Ava decided resolutely, even as she backed away from the thought. Just the thought of being pregnant stirred up all sorts of memories and emotions she didn't need stirring up at this point in her life. But surely it was better to know…

Except, what if she was being ridiculous? She was on the pill, after all, had been for years. Decades. It had suited David perfectly, because he already had two children and, of course, he didn't want hers. Ava hadn't had much say in the matter.

Except, she'd missed a couple of pills. One or two at most, because there had hardly seemed to be any point anymore. David hadn't been feeling very amorous and, well, she'd never been great with routines.

The fact was, she could be pregnant. Just a slim chance, but until she knew…

With a sigh, Ava drained her hot chocolate and went to pay. Olivia emerged from the back again, smiling as she wiped flour-dusted hands.

"Sorry, I'm in the middle of making scones. Two pounds fifty, please."

Ava paid, and Olivia gave her a sympathetic smile. "I hope life straightens out for you."

"Me too," she answered with a gusty, heartfelt sigh, and then she turned from the shop.

Wychwood-on-Lea's high street was awash in sunlight, shop windows glinting, as Ava strolled down towards the village green, Zuzu trotting beside her.

She wasn't about to buy a pregnancy test from the village's one post office shop. Even if she didn't know many people in this place, she still didn't want them gossiping about her. And if the news got back to Emma or, God help her, Simon… Ava shuddered. The last thing she wanted was those two involved in her life again, in any way.

She paused on the village green; a young mum, about fifteen years younger than her, was pushing a chubby-cheeked, snot-faced toddler on the swing. Ava watched them discreetly for a moment, trying to imagine herself in the same scenario and finding it nearly impossible.

The woman noticed her watching and frowned, and Ava wondered how she looked. Creepy and stalkerish, or disdainful and contemptuous? Or just dazed and reeling, which was how she felt? Something not good, anyway, because the woman's frown deepened and she hauled her toddler, who screeched in complaint, out of the baby swing and stuffed her into her pushchair.

Ava watched her buckle the complicated-looking straps before she realized she really was starting to be stalkerish and she headed down the narrow lane that led to Willoughby Manor.

By the time she reached the rutted track that led to the converted stables, her energy—what little she'd had—was well and truly gone. Her footsteps dragged and Zuzu whimpered her canine concern, or perhaps just annoyance that Ava was walking so slowly.

Then they came to an apprehensive halt as she stared at the most unwelcome car parked in the courtyard. How on earth had he figured out where she lived?

"Ava." Simon emerged from his Beamer, dressed in a flashy suit for work—he did something in the City, Ava didn't know what. He checked his watch, an equally flashy gold-and-silver Rolex. "I've been waiting for nearly an hour."

"I didn't know you were coming," Ava returned levelly as she walked past him to her front door. "If I had, I would have baked you a cake," she quipped, but Simon only looked confused.

"What?"

Obviously, he wasn't a connoisseur of vintage movies

and music the way she was. "Never mind." She turned around, arms folded. She had no intention of letting him inside her house. "What are you doing here, Simon?"

"You know why I'm here, Ava," Simon returned in a near-growl and, for the first time since knowing this tosser, her heart tripped in alarm.

Simon wasn't a threat, of course he wasn't, and in any case, she could handle him. Yet standing in the sunny courtyard with Zuzu frisking by her heels, Ava felt a strange little frisson of fear as she realized he was very angry, and he'd had an hour to sit and stew in it. It wasn't something she felt she had the energy to deal with now.

"Actually, I have no idea," she replied, keeping her voice light and faintly mocking. "I was hoping to never see you again."

"Likewise," Simon gritted as he strode towards her, and Ava raised her eyebrows.

"Are you sure about that, Simon?" Awareness flared in his eyes and Ava's heart tripped again.

She should not have said that. What was her problem, prodding a bull with a stick? She was trying to show how strong she was and usually it worked, but right now she felt vulnerable and more than a little scared—and she *hated* being scared.

He took a step towards her, his contemptuous and, yes, lust-filled gaze raking her from head to foot. "I'm not as easy a mark as my father."

"Oh, please." Ava raked him with a scornful glance of her own. "In your dreams."

Another step towards her and she made herself hold her ground and not press back against the door. "I have to admit," he said, his voice dropping to a murmur, "I've thought about it. Who wouldn't?"

"That's all you'll ever do." Ava returned coldly.

She would not be intimidated by him. And yet... the courtyard was empty. Ava didn't think Ellie or Harriet were home, and who knew where Jace was? No one would hear her scream, and it had been a long time since she'd had to kick a bloke in the balls. At least she knew she was capable of it.

Simon glared at her for another endless moment, heat flaring in his eyes, his breath coming in near pants, disgusting her. Ava held his gaze, her fists clenched so hard she felt her nails digging into her palms. She bit her tongue hard enough to taste blood.

Simon let out a ragged breath and Ava had the blessed sense that the immediate danger had passed. "Where are they, Ava?"

"Where are what?"

"My mother's rings," he snapped, impatient now. "I was going through her jewelry and they're missing. It doesn't take a genius to realize where they went."

"Your mother's jewelry?" Ava stared at him in disbelief. "You think I took some of it?"

"As I said, I know you took two rings. Now I want them back." The smile he gave her was so sneering Ava's palm literally itched to slap it off his face. "Be a good girl and get them for me now and I *probably* won't press charges."

"Thanks for the reassurance, but I don't have any rings. I never even saw your mother's jewelry. As you probably are well aware, your father kept it all in a safe."

"I am aware and, while I don't know how you got your sticky hands on them, I know you did. So give them up before I call the police."

Ava let out a hollow laugh. "You sound like a caricature of yourself sometimes, Simon," she said tiredly. "I don't have any bloody rings." She held up her hand with the plain gold wedding band and single pearl engagement ring. "These are the only rings your father gave me."

"I don't believe you."

"I don't care."

His gaze narrowed. "I could search your house."

"Then I'll be the one calling the police."

For a split, stunned second, Ava thought Simon might strike her. He raised his hand and she braced herself, already anticipating the crack of a palm against her cheek, the ensuing sting that always came a few seconds later than she expected. Better to take a slap than anger him by dodging it or grabbing his hand. That was one lesson she'd learned, at least. By her feet, Zuzu whimpered. Then Simon released a slow breath and dropped his hand.

"Those rings were very special to my mother," he said quietly. "A plain sapphire ring my father gave her for her fortieth birthday, and a ruby one surrounded by diamonds that he gave her for their twentieth wedding anniversary." His gaze was level now, and Ava thought she saw a flash of pain in his eyes that amazingly made her feel a faint flicker of sympathy. "Please, Ava. They belong in my family."

Ava took a quick, sharp breath. She still felt shaky, not that she would show it. "I don't have…" she began, only to stop. She didn't have those rings, but she did have a sapphire pendant as well as a gold choker with a diamond-encrusted ruby. Both gifts from David for anniversaries or birthdays, and definitely the most valuable pieces of jewelry she'd received from him. Had they been Marian's?

"You do have them," Simon said, and he sounded furious again. He grabbed her arm, fingers biting into her flesh, and Ava felt too shocked to respond, her mind still numb and reeling from the realization she'd only just started to have.

And then Jace's truck pulled into the courtyard.

Simon didn't have time to let go of her before Jace was sliding out of the truck and striding across the courtyard. "What the hell," he asked pleasantly, "do you think you're doing?"

Simon threw Jace a startled and wary look before he dropped his hand and took a small step back. "This has nothing to do with you."

"I disagree." Jace's voice was still pleasant but he looked lethal, his fists lightly clenched as if he could let a punch fly at any second, as if he'd do so without a qualm or breaking a sweat, and Ava took strength from that.

"Simon just came over to retrieve something," she said, trying to sound normal and pretty sure she was failing. "I'll get it for him now."

"I'll wait," Jace said, smiling, and Ava almost wanted to kiss him.

She unlocked her front door with shaking hands, Zuzu shooting out between her feet as soon as she'd opened the door and scuttling for safety. Ava still felt trembly as she went upstairs and dug through her jewelry, not that there was that much of it.

She found the necklaces soon enough and she held them in her hands, the delicate chain of the pendant threaded through her fingers, the sapphire glinting in the sunlight. Tears gathered thickly in her throat and behind her eyes and resolutely Ava blinked them back.

So David had taken his dead wife's jewelry and had it fashioned into new stuff for his new wife. It didn't mean anything. She hadn't liked the ruby choker anyway. The night David had given it to her he hadn't wanted her to take it off while they'd made love, and Ava hadn't been able to shake the feeling that it looked—and felt—like a dog collar.

But they'd been gifts to her, and they'd meant something, and, to be brutally honest, she could have pawned them for a decent amount if she'd needed to. Never mind.

Ava took a deep breath and then rose, the two necklaces clutched in one fist. Back in the courtyard, Jace was lounging against a pillar as if he had all the time in the world and Simon was standing tense and angry by his car.

Ava lifted her chin and strode towards Simon. "Here." She thrust out her hand with the two necklaces, and Simon took them, his face full of suspicion.

"These aren't…"

"Your father remade them into necklaces for me. Make of that what you will."

Simon subjected her to another darkly suspicious look, but Ava didn't care anymore. The rush of adrenalin that had seen her through Simon's almost-assault had left, and now she felt as if she might collapse where she stood. She needed him to go. She needed him to go *now*.

"You got what you wanted?" Jace prompted in that easy voice of his and Simon slid the necklaces into his pocket with one last savage glance at Ava.

"You'd better not have taken anything else."

Ava let out a ragged laugh edged with hysteria. "Go away, Simon."

And then, thankfully, he was gone, climbing into his Beamer and then gunning it out of the courtyard so gravel sprayed up. Jace watched him go, shaking his head slowly, looking only amused.

Ava sagged and then swayed where she stood, and in the

space of a second Jace was next to her, one hand cupping her elbow.

"Are you all right?" he asked in a low voice.

His kindness made her want to cry. Again. Ava managed somehow to shake and nod her head at the same time. She let out another ragged-edged laugh. "I... I don't know."

"Let's get you inside." Still holding her arm, Jace guided her into number three. Ava let him, so glad someone was taking over, caring enough to see she was okay, that she couldn't even pretend to be strong.

Jace guided her over to the velveteen settee and she sank onto it, her legs feeling so weak she wasn't sure she would have been able to stand another second.

"Tea," Jace said decisively. "Strong, sweet tea."

"Is that what you prescribe for a situation like this?"

"Shock," Jace answered as he filled up the kettle at the sink, looking at ease, and just as masculine, at the kitchen as he did everywhere else. "Isn't this what everyone prescribes for it?"

"Maybe." Ava leaned her head back against the settee and closed her eyes. She heard the kettle click off and then what felt like only seconds later she heard him cross the room.

Ava opened her eyes to find Jace crouched in front of her, his face, and his body for that matter, disconcertingly close. He pressed the mug of tea into her hands and Ava took it with a murmured thanks.

She couldn't make herself look away from his face, the

stubble on his jaw, the look of sympathy in his usually amused eyes.

"Ava?" he prompted, his voice still sounding like chocolate over gravel and so, so gentle, and Ava, abandoning all common sense, blurted,

"I think I might be pregnant."

Chapter Eight

T O HIS CREDIT, Jace managed to look unfazed by her sudden confession. He rocked back on his heels and raised his eyebrows.

"What, by that knob?"

It took Ava a second to realize who he meant. *"Simon? No, thank God. Good heavens. No."* She started to laugh and Jace watched her, his expression calm and level, as if he could take anything she threw at him, whether it was hysteria, tears, or the simple, stark truth. Suddenly, surprisingly, Ava was glad she'd told him.

"No," she said when her laughter had subsided. "By his father, actually."

Jace cocked his head. "Your husband."

Surprised, she could only stare.

He nodded towards her hands cradled around the mug. "Wedding ring. Saw it on the first day."

"Ah. You're observant."

"I always check."

She laughed at that and then took a sip of tea, feeling

strangely lighter and happier than she had in quite a while.

"So." Jace stood up, sliding his hands into the pockets of his jeans. "You said you think you might be pregnant. You're not sure?"

"No, I'm not."

"There are tests, right? I know that much. They're pretty accurate, I think, or so the adverts say."

"You're the expert, are you?" Ava teased. This couldn't possibly be flirting, could it?

"Thankfully, no. I've managed to avoid that particular problem."

She sighed heavily. "Yes, because pregnancy is a problem, isn't it?"

"Not always." Jace gave her one of his considering looks. "Is it for you?"

Ava thought about that for a few seconds. "Yes and no," she said at last. "It's complicated."

"I guessed that much."

"How?"

He shrugged. "You're here, aren't you? And it seemed like you needed to move rather quickly."

"Right." Ava took another sip of her tea.

She could tell what Jace assumed. It was the obvious thing to think, that she'd had a quickie divorce, a sudden separation. And the weird thing was, she didn't even understand why she was reluctant to tell the truth. *My husband died. He's dead. I'm a widow.* All the words felt like marbles in her mouth, choking her, rendering her speechless. She couldn't say any of it.

"So, tests." Jace shifted where he stood, the only indication that he might find this conversation the teensiest bit uncomfortable. "Have you taken one?"

"No."

"Well, why don't you?"

"I don't know." She grimaced. "Because when I take one it becomes real."

"There are options, though." Jace cleared his throat.

Wow, he was actually uncomfortable. Ava was intrigued to see the faintest of blushes coloring those lean cheeks.

"I mean… better to know than to not know, right?" He persevered valiantly. Points for sensitivity, definitely.

"Maybe." Of course, she knew he was right, but she was still dragging her feet, dragging everything, because that was all she'd done since Brian had called and told her David had been rushed to the hospital. Over three weeks ago now and, yet, she still felt frozen. Paralyzed.

"Right, then." Jace took his hands out of his pockets and slapped his jean-clad thighs. "Why don't I go buy one of those tests?"

Ava stared at him in surprise. "Why," she asked slowly, "are you being so damned nice to me?"

Jace stilled, his expression turning thoughtful. "You make it sound as if you aren't used to people being nice to you."

Whoa, way too much perception for a bloke, and one she barely knew. "Not strangers."

Jace's mouth quirked upwards. "I'd rate myself slightly higher than a stranger."

"Still." Ava held his gaze, challenging him, daring him to say—what? Just what did she want him to admit?

Jace shrugged one massive shoulder. "Why not?"

"That's not a real answer."

"And you didn't ask a real question. I get what you're trying to do, Ava. You think I'm after something."

Her mouth went dry, her heart starting to thump. "Are you?"

"I'm just being nice." Jace looked annoyed now, and Ava was starting to feel seriously confused.

"But you know you're sexy, Jace. You work it. You flirt. You give those damnably knowing looks. Don't pretend you don't."

He shrugged, neither assent nor negation. And why had she just admitted all that?

Ava sighed and closed her eyes. "Perhaps you should just go get that test."

"Okay."

Without saying anything more, he walked out of the cottage, and Ava didn't realize he'd gone until she heard the click of the door shutting, and she opened her eyes to an empty room.

She took a few deep breaths to steady herself, and then

she rose from the sofa, dumped the rest of her tea in the sink, and then decided to put some proper makeup on. Not the full face in case Jace thought it was for his benefit, but a little eyeliner and lip gloss would make her feel better. Stronger.

As she carefully painted her mouth, her unblinking gaze on her reflection, Ava wondered why she'd told Jace everything she had, and whether she could backpedal a bit. Although it was hard to go back from *I think I might be pregnant*. Unless of course she wasn't. Still, she didn't need to let Jace in on every detail of her complicated life. He certainly didn't need a play by play. And she *definitely* wasn't going to start depending on him, because if there was one thing she'd learned time and time again, it was that trusting people led to nothing but disappointment, sometimes doable, sometimes crushing. Basically, trusting people sucked.

Had she trusted David?

The question hung there, practically shimmering in the air. She'd been married to him for five years. She'd loved him, mostly. Sort of. *Sort of?* How did she sort of love someone? And, had he loved her more than that, or even at all?

The questions threatened to do her head in. Asking them was bad enough, and answering would be far worse. So she wouldn't. And when Jace returned, she'd take the pregnancy test from him, give him her thanks, and then close the door in his face. Handle this whole thing on her own, the way she was used to, even if the thought of it made her wilt inside.

A knock sounded on the door, and not the incessant hammering she'd become used to. Jace, then, giving one light knock because he knew, of course, she was home and waiting.

Ava opened the door, the sight of Jace standing there looking sexy and slightly grizzled and just… *edible* made her insides clench. *Down, girl.* She held out her hand and he gave her a white paper bag; her fingers closed around an oblong-shaped box.

"Thank you. How much do I owe you?"

The tiniest pause, and then he said, "Eight quid."

Somehow she liked him better for not telling her not to worry about it, that he'd pay. "Just a sec." She left him standing on the doorstep as she went in search of her handbag. When she turned around, a crisp tenner in her hand, Jace was standing inside the cottage.

"You can keep the change," Ava said breezily, holding out the ten pound note. Jace took it slowly, sliding it into his back pocket.

"You want me to leave." It was a statement, but his gaze was searching her face, looking for something.

"I think it's probably best if you do." Her voice quavered slightly but she held his gaze.

"Okay." Jace didn't move. "You'll tell me if you need anything?"

"I won't need anything."

Something flashed across Jace's face, irritation perhaps, and he looked as if he might argue. Then he simply shrugged. "All right then," he said, and walked out of the cottage.

Ava stared down at the white paper bag clenched in her hand and wished she hadn't asked him to leave quite so abruptly. The truth was, she could have used a little hand-holding right about now, but never mind. It was better this way.

Slowly, she walked upstairs and into the bathroom. Opened the bag and stared at the box, the lurid pink, the over-large plus sign, the cheerful assurance that this test was ninety-nine point nine percent accurate and she could test five days before her period was due.

When *had* her period been due? With a queasy feeling Ava realized it had been about two weeks ago. She hadn't given it so much as a thought because of everything and, in any case, she'd stopped taking her birth control pills when David had died. What was the point?

Ava ripped open the box and took out the slim plastic stick. She hadn't seen one of these in quite a while. Hadn't had so much as a pregnancy scare in twenty years. Taking a deep breath, she tugged down her jeans and sat on the toilet. There was nothing remotely elegant about taking one of these tests. It felt awkward and messy and the wee always splashed on something. But it was done, and it wasn't until she'd capped the test and laid it carefully on top of the toilet tank so she couldn't see the little window that she realized why she was so anxious about taking this test.

Because part of her *wanted* to be pregnant. How crazy was that?

Ava washed her hands and then perched on the edge of the tub as she waited the requisite minute. Sixty seconds had never seemed so long and yet so short, because at the end of it she'd know. And she wasn't sure she wanted to know.

The minute passed and, with a hand that wasn't quite steady, Ava reached out and took the pregnancy test. Held it in her palm for another minute, waiting, postponing, feeling like her whole life—and maybe someone else's life—hung in the balance.

Then she turned the thing over and stared down at the little window. Blinked, and blinked again. Two lines. She really was pregnant.

Ava wasn't sure what she did then. Somehow she found herself downstairs, dizzy, dazed, the whole world seeming slightly out of focus. She tidied up the kitchen, washing her mug and the plate she'd used for breakfast that morning. She folded the cashmere throw and laid it over the back of the settee, all the while feeling as if she was outside of herself, as if the room was a stage and she was watching a play. What was going to happen next?

She stared around the still near-empty cottage and wondered how on earth a baby could live here. Could fit into her life. And what about work? Money? Too many questions.

Needing some air, Ava headed out to the garden. The grass was still overgrown, each blade beaded with dew. The sunshine of that morning had given way to clouds, the air now feeling damp and a bit chilly. Ava hugged her knees to her chest and tucked her chin on top and tried not to think.

That was more or less what she'd been doing for the last three weeks, but now she had a real reason to break out of her lethargy. She had someone else to think about. She had decisions to make. What on earth was she going to do?"

"Hello." A blond head popped over the stone wall, the girl who had been in the garden last night now smiling at her angelically. She was adorable and she knew it; Ava recognized the signs. Once upon a time, she'd been the same.

"Hello."

"Are you our new neighbor?"

"It would seem so."

The girl cocked her head, her expression turning sly. "Mummy says you're full of yourself."

Ava let out a surprised laugh. "Does she?" Ava thought of how she'd dismissed Harriet's dinner invitation. "I suppose I came across that way."

"What does that mean? Full of yourself?"

"It means you think you're more important than you are." Which was so far from the truth Ava almost laughed again.

"Oh." The girl considered that. "Do you?"

"Not really." What a surreal conversation.

"Why did Mummy say it then?"

"I don't know." Ava tried to keep her voice light as she added, "Perhaps you should ask her."

To her bemusement, the girl decided to do just that. "Mummy," she screeched, and Ava heard Harriet come running.

"Chloe." Harriet stood in the doorway, looking both hassled and relieved. "I thought you'd hurt yourself. Lost a finger at the very least."

"Why did you say our neighbor was full of herself?" Chloe asked, her piping voice carrying across all the gardens of Willoughby Close.

"What?" Startled, Harriet's gaze darted sideways and clashed with Ava's.

She flushed and Ava sat back, her hands looped loosely around her knees, and wondered how her yummy mummy neighbor was going to get out of this one.

"Chloe, I didn't..." She shot Ava an apologetic, and utterly mortified, look. "I didn't mean it quite... and anyway, you shouldn't go repeating things."

"Okay," Chloe said blithely, and skipped inside, leaving Harriet and Ava awkwardly alone, a lot more than a single stone wall separating them.

Ava decided to be kind and break the silence first. "Such refreshing honesty in one so young."

"I'm really sorry about that..."

"Sorry for Chloe telling me, or for saying it in the first

place?"

"Um… both, I suppose." Harriet's face was still red but she also looked the tiniest bit annoyed.

Ava supposed she couldn't rock the self-righteousness for too long. She had been a bit bitchy when Harriet had come to the door.

"I'm sorry I wasn't more welcoming when you came by the other day," she said abruptly, the admission so out of character she was half-amazed she was saying it.

"Oh." Harriet looked as surprised as Ava felt. "Well, that's… I mean… it's okay." She paused, clearly waiting for Ava to volunteer information, and with a sigh Ava did.

"Life's a bit complicated at the moment. I had to move here rather quickly."

"I understand." To her surprise Harriet's voice was full of not just sympathy, but warmth. "I did too."

"You did?" Now Ava was curious, the one waiting for more.

Harriet grimaced. "My life fell apart rather spectacularly. Although, it wasn't all that spectacular—more of a damp squib, if I'm honest. But it felt that way, you know. Like a bomb exploding."

"Mmm." Ava understood the sentiment, even if she was still waiting on the particulars.

Harriet hesitated, and Ava could tell she was deliberating whether to go into the specifics of her personal life deconstruction.

"My husband lost his job," she said at last. "Lost everything. Our house…" She trailed off, perhaps waiting for sympathy, but Ava just waited, sensing there was more. And she knew about losing everything and, if she was honest—and feeling a little mean—Harriet hadn't lost it.

"We were totally bankrupt," Harriet continued. "And so we had to move here."

Was that the whole story? It would explain some of the strain Ava had witnessed between Harriet and her husband, and yet… Ava felt there was something more her neighbor wasn't saying. Still, she could hardly demand answers, especially when she had no intention of giving any herself.

"I'm sorry," she said, aware that she'd come in a little too late with this paltry sentiment. She tried harder. "That must have been difficult."

"It was." Harriet looked as if she semi-regretted telling Ava all that. "What about you?" she asked.

Tit for tat, Ava supposed. Time to share. And why not?

"My husband died," she said, her voice a bit flat, and Harriet blinked. She'd just been one-upped in the tragedy stakes, although Ava hadn't meant it like that. Not exactly, anyway.

"Oh, no. I'm… I'm so sorry."

"It's okay." Ava waved a hand. "It's not quite…" How on earth could she finish that sentence? "Like I said, it's all a bit complicated." Harriet's eyes rounded and Ava mentally cringed, imagining the gossip and speculation that would fly the next time Ellie and Harriet had a coffee and a natter.

"Oh. Well." Harriet gazed at her for a moment and then said, "The dinner invitation is still open, if you'd like to come. We really would be happy to have you, no matter what I said." She had the grace to look abashed. "I really am sorry about that."

"No, it was my fault. And, yes, I'd love to come to dinner." Ava spoke firmly even though inwardly she quelled at the thought. Dinner? Small talk? Friends? *Danger.*

"Brilliant." Harriet's expression cleared. "How about tomorrow night?"

"All right—"

"Oh no, it's the fete."

"The what?"

"The fete, the village fete." Harriet looked at her expectantly, and Ava shook her head. Nope and nope. "Down on the green, it happens every time this year. Pony rides, bric-a-brac stall, coconut shy… you know."

No, she didn't, although she could sort of imagine. "If not tomorrow night, then maybe another time," she said. She was, to her own annoyance, disappointed to be let off the hook.

"Why don't you come with us to the fete, and then we can have dinner after?" Harriet suggested. "Since it seems you've never been to one before."

Ava opened her mouth to refuse, because that sounded like far too much time spent in someone else's company, but then she remembered the emptiness of her cottage, and the loneliness that rushed in, and she heard herself saying, "Sure, why not?"

Chapter Nine

TEN MINUTES INTO her foray with the Lang family, Ava was starting to regret her impulsiveness. There were so many children. Admittedly only three, but they felt like a lot. William, the boy she'd seen the other day, fired questions at her with machine-gun speed, most of them inexplicably involving geography.

"What's the capital of Tanzania?"

"Umm…"

"Dodoma." His voice was thick with disgust. "It used to be Dar es Salaam. What's the longest river in Asia?"

"Ah…"

"The Yangtze. What's the driest place on earth?"

Would he ever stop? "I don't know," Ava said.

"The Atacama Desert in Chile." William looked at her with a mixture of triumph and scorn. "Do you know anything?"

"*William.*" Harriet came out into the courtyard where they'd all been waiting, looking both harried and apologetic. "Sorry," she said to Ava. "He's been reading a book on geography facts and he tests everyone. No one knows any of the answers."

"You would," William told his mother, "if you were smart."

Harriet rolled her eyes good-naturedly and her husband Richard came out of their front door, smiling. It was going to be a party.

"Ellie and Abby are joining us, as well," Harriet said, catching Ava's eye, "and Jace."

Jace? Jace did not seem like the village fete type whatsoever. Ava did her best to school her expression into something pleasantly neutral. "What about Lady Stokeley?" she asked, only half-joking, and Harriet looked at her, surprised.

"What about her?"

"She's not coming as well?" Why not everyone from Willoughby Close and Manor, after all?

Harriet made a face. "I don't think she's up for it, and I'm not sure she'd appreciate the offerings of the fete."

"How is she doing?"

"She seems to be all right. She's had the week off treatment and the consultants are pleased with her results… but then you were there, weren't you?" Harriet gave her a curious look, and Ava shrugged.

"They didn't say anything to me, but she seemed happy enough."

"Yes, I think so. To respond to chemo treatment at age

eighty-six is no small thing."

Abby and Ellie came out of number one, Abby peeling off to walk next to Mallory, who had offered Ava a small smile by way of greeting, and Chloe danced ahead, looking, as Ava suspected she always did, overly angelic. William was now pestering Richard with geography questions, and Harriet was talking to Ellie about something to do with school, which left Ava alone just as Jace ambled up the drive. Perfect.

She hadn't seen him since yesterday afternoon, when she'd taken the pregnancy test and told him to go, and she had no wish to have a conversation now. Ava quickened her pace to match Ellie's and Harriet's and did her level best to insert herself into the conversation.

"School dinners," she said brightly, repeating the last thing she'd heard. "They can be dire, can't they?"

Harriet and Ellie exchanged a startled look. "I suppose they can," Ellie said. "But Harriet's just started as a dinner lady at the primary."

"Oh, really?" Cue an even brighter tone to compensate. Ava saw Jace out of the corner of her eye, walking easily behind them. "Wow," she said, because now that she thought about it, she was impressed. Harriet did not seem like the type to be a dinner lady. Perhaps when she'd said she'd lost everything, she'd meant it.

"It has its moments," Harriet said dryly, and then proceeded to regale them with horror stories from the school cafeteria while they walked down the lane towards Wych-wood-on-Lea's village green.

The green was abuzz with activity, and the four children surged forward, eager to try out the many amusements. Ava glanced at the various stalls, from bric-a-brac, houseplants, used books, and one more interesting one selling vintage clothing. Lady Stokeley could most likely supply that stall ten times over if she wanted. She wondered if the old lady would have liked to come. It seemed a shame for her to stay in that depressing old house while the sun was shining—mostly—and people were having fun.

"Ava," Ellie called. "We're going to have a look at the bric-a-brac stall. Do you want to come?"

Without meaning to Ava glanced around to see where Jace had gone, and saw he was heading towards the beer tent. Maybe he'd got the message, then.

"Sure," she said, and strolled over to join them.

The bric-a-brac stall was a treasure trove of junk, with the odd valuable or useful item. Beneath a battered Ludo box, Ava found a set of place mats and napkins that were still in their original packaging. The burgundy and dark green plaid wasn't her style, but she could hardly be choosy.

"What are you looking for?" Harriet asked when she saw Ava rooting through the piles of what was essentially other people's rubbish.

"Anything and everything. I moved in with very little." Ava shrugged. "So there's a lot I could use."

"Ooh, like what?" Ellie asked, abandoning her perusal of lurid romances from the 1980s. "Harriet and I could help."

"Well…" Ava hesitated.

She was so unused to this, the camaraderie, the kindness. She felt suspicious, the urge in her to back away still strong, but she'd been backing away her whole life. Maybe it was time to do something different. And Harriet and Ellie looked doggedly persistent. Ava didn't think they'd let her demur.

"I could do with some pots and pans," she said finally. "And a few pictures, perhaps. And salt and pepper shakers, actually…" She was starting to get on a roll. "Some decent knives, and a few more mugs, and wine glasses…"

Although if she was keeping this baby, she wouldn't be drinking much wine. Ava's stomach dipped as if she'd just plunged down a roller coaster. She'd managed not to think about her pregnancy for most of the day, although it lurked on the horizon of her mind, a dark cloud or a new dawn, depending on her mood of the minute.

"Got it," Harriet said, and starting digging through piles. Ellie joined her, and between the three of them they basically commandeered the bric-a-brac stall, ending up with an impressive pile of stuff at their feet.

"What is all this?" Mallory asked. She and Abby had returned to the 'rents to ask for money and, with a sigh, Harriet and Ellie handed them each a couple of pound coins.

"It's for Ava's cottage," Ellie said. "Just like we did, she needs some stuff."

"You needed stuff?" Ava asked. Had everyone moved to Willoughby Close in a hurry, with a story?

"I rather foolishly threw everything out when we moved," Ellie answered after Mallory and Abby had run off to try the mini Ferris wheel set up at one end of the green. "New start and all that."

"Right." She could use one of those.

"It took us awhile, but we got there. There are some brilliant charity shops in Witney."

"I've been to a few." They shared a smile of complicit understanding that made Ava feel weirdly light inside. Was this what friendship was?

"Is that everything?" the woman manning the stall asked when they lugged it all forward—the placemats and napkins, a pot big enough for a baby to bathe in, two framed prints of twee Cotswold scenes that Ava liked because they were kind of kitschy, salt and pepper shakers that were in the shape of hunting dogs, and a couple of throw pillows to help cover up the nubby velveteen of her one settee.

"Yes, I think so," Ava said. "I have no idea how I'm going to get this all back, though."

"There are a lot of hands between us all," Harriet said. "Besides, what are children for, besides slave labor?"

Ellie and Ava both laughed at that, and the volunteer rang up everything up. "That's eight pounds twenty."

"A steal," Ava murmured, and handed over a ten pound note.

The volunteer promised to keep all new purchases behind the stall until they were ready to leave, and so the three of them set off to explore the rest of the fete.

Harriet went to help Chloe at the hook-a-duck, and Ellie was called away by a friend, giving Ava an uncertain, apologetic glance, but Ava waved her away. She didn't mind being on her own. This friendship thing still felt new and strange.

She contemplated a few of the hanging baskets at the plant stall, wondering how many roots she'd put down at Willoughby Close. How many she could. Her hand started to creep towards her middle in that universal gesture of impending motherhood but, at the last second, Ava stayed it, which was a good thing because Jace appeared out of nowhere.

He stood close enough to her so she could smell his wood-and-leather aftershave and, for a second, she felt dizzy with simple, uncomplicated desire. It had been a long time since she'd felt that, the arrowing sensation low in her belly, and it alarmed and excited her at the same time. She edged away from him, pretending to give closer study of a clematis, but she didn't think Jace was fooled.

"You seem well," he remarked after a moment.

"Thank you. I am."

"Relieved?" he asked, and Ava leaned forward to inspect the clematis more closely. It really was a most fascinating plant.

"Not exactly," she hedged, hardly wanting to have such a

conversation here. And yet Jace deserved to know something, didn't he? He'd helped her. He cared, at least a little.

"Sorry, it's not my business," he said after a moment, his tone strangely formal. "I was just worried about you. That Simon bloke hasn't come back?"

"No, and I shouldn't think he will. I don't have anything more to give him."

"The jewelry…"

"Belonged to his mother. But…" She didn't know how much Jace had gleaned of her terse exchange of words with Simon. "They'd been given to me," she said. "But it doesn't matter. I don't need them."

Jace whistled between his teeth. "They were worth something, though."

"Yes, that's true. And I might have pawned them, if given half a chance, which is most likely just what Simon feared." She shook her head, and then added thoughtlessly, "I try to hate him, but I can't, not when his worst assumptions about me are so often true." She'd meant to sound wryly self-deprecating, but it didn't quite come across that way.

Jace frowned. "I don't think that's true."

"You don't know me," Ava reminded him.

"Even so."

She looked at him then, swallowing at the glimpse of concern in his whiskey-brown eyes, the softening of the strong lines of his face. Back to the clematis it was.

"Would you like to purchase anything?" the woman behind the stall asked rather pointedly, and Ava summoned a smile.

"I'll take one of the hanging baskets," she said firmly. By the time she'd got out her money, Jace had gone.

She reconnected with Ellie and Harriet by the coconut shy, watching William and Richard both give it their best shot. Richard was having a laugh, his balls wide off the mark, but William was starting to look grimly determined, *needing* to knock a coconut off its perch, and Ava thought she understood a little of what he was feeling, that desperate desire to prove himself even when no one else cared. She'd felt that, a long time ago, before she'd realized even if she did prove herself, it wouldn't change things. It wouldn't matter.

"Never mind, William," Harriet said, putting her hand on his shoulder. "Who wants a coconut, anyway?"

"Please, Mum." He turned to her, painfully earnest. "Let me give it one more go."

Harriet gazed down at her son in that mixture of exasperation and deep affection that Ava was already starting to recognize. "Oh, very well…" she began, and then rummaged through her bag for another pound coin. "Sorry, William, I don't have one."

Richard didn't either, and Ellie held up her empty hands with an apologetic smile. William looked gutted, and then Ava found herself reaching inside her own purse and holding out a pound.

"I've got one," she said.

William muttered his thanks before snatching it out of her hand. Ava held her breath, willing him to win it this time. She didn't know why it mattered so much to him, only that it did, and that was enough.

A pound paid for three tries and each time William lined up his shot carefully. The first nudged the coconut but didn't knock it off, and the second missed by a wide margin. Ava blocked out the cries of dismay and focused on William, whose gaze was narrowed, intent only on that blasted coconut.

He sent the ball flying, and it hit the coconut squarely, causing it to tumble on the ground. Cheers went up around him, but William was oblivious, so intent on receiving his hard-won coconut that cost about fifty pence from Tesco.

"Coconuts taste disgusting anyway," Mallory said loftily as William starting hurling it to the ground in an attempt to crack it. "Like milky water."

"Let him be, Mall," Richard said mildly, and everyone walked on.

They spent another couple of hours milling about stalls, watching Chloe take a plodding pony ride and Mallory and Abby enter a dance competition, before ending up lounging on the grass by the beer tent. Ava bought herself a lemonade and ignored Jace's inquiring glance. What business was her baby of his?

Her baby. The words caused both a shiver of trepidation

and a frisson of excitement to ripple through her.

It was early evening by the time they started walking back to Willoughby Close, the sun still high in the sky now that it was mid-June, when it didn't set until ten o'clock. Ava loved this time of year, the sunlit evenings, the rippling grass, the sense of time stretching enticingly onwards.

Last year around this time, she and David had gone to see an outdoor screening of the 1940s film *The Lost Weekend* up at Blenheim Palace. David hadn't seen the point of it besides the champagne and being able to lounge on a blanket under the stars, chatting with other well-to-do strangers.

Ava had been entranced by the film; she loved old movies, loved the casual glamor, the sultriness of women who knew how to be women and made no apologies. She'd got her inspiration from women like Joan Crawford and Bette Davis, women who were smart and ambitious but also sexy. She'd tried to be like them, at least a little, and sometimes she thought she'd almost succeeded. Sometimes she didn't.

"Ava? What do you think?" Harriet called back, and Ava was drawn out of her reverie.

"Sorry…?"

"We're thinking of ordering takeaway fish and chips and eating in the garden. I know it's not exactly what you expected when I invited you over to dinner…"

"It's fine," Ava said quickly. "Of course, it's fine."

They all ambled back to Willoughby Close, everyone carrying something of Ava's, which she dumped inside her cottage before heading over to the Langs'. It wasn't until she was out in their garden, with its proper garden furniture and fairy lights strung across the little terrace, that she realized the invitation had extended not only to her but also to Ellie, Abby, and Jace. Practically a street party.

Ava retired to a deep-seated wooden chair in the corner of the terrace, tucking her legs up under her as everyone sprawled around the garden, relaxed and happy. Ava let the conversation drift over her—Ellie talked about Oliver, who was at a conference, and how she was taking a marketing course and dreaming about opening her own shop on the high street, something that sold a little bit of everything.

Richard seemed to be starting a PGCE course in September. Harriet was doing some PR event for the tearoom on the high street, and Ava almost contributed then, wanting to say how she knew Olivia too. Sort of. But the moment passed and she relaxed back into silence, content to be part of the group without speaking.

This was what normal people did, wasn't it? Had dinner in each other gardens, brought out a bottle of wine, ate fish and chips on their laps, laughing and talking. It seemed so easy for everyone, and yet Ava couldn't remember what she'd done something like this before.

Oh, she and David had both gone to and hosted plenty of social occasions. She hadn't been a recluse, for heaven's sake. But it had felt different, because it had been David's friends, David's world, and now that he was gone and she was out of it, she was realizing more and more, feared more and more, than he'd never even tried to make her a part.

But maybe she could make her own world. Maybe, by some miracle, she could fit into this one here, at Willoughby Close, with neighbors who seemed surprisingly willing to accept her, and a pleasant little cottage to make a home. There was the not insignificant issue of finding a job and needing money, but… perhaps that would come in time? If she tried?

Ava glanced around the garden, the sky darkening to indigo and the first stars coming out. The fairy lights twinkled and Ellie's laughter floated on the breeze. Richard went inside with a sleepy Chloe on his shoulder, and Harriet poured out the last of the wine.

"Ava? Sure you don't want any?"

"I'm fine with water, thanks." Ava could feel Jace's considering gaze on her but she didn't look his way. She had been determinedly not looking at him all evening, which was a problem. Better to be indifferent than ignoring and so aware.

Still, it had been a lovely evening, a lovely day even, and one that made her hope. Hope was a dangerous thing, because it put cracks in her armor and her head over the parapet. Ava didn't think she could take more than a small dose of it.

But, oh, what just a little bit of hope could do. She imagined herself next door, in her own garden, a baby on a blanket and the sun shining high above. Happy. *Forgiven.* The word flitted through her mind and then thankfully vanished again. She was not going to think about all that.

No, best to focus on the future, fragile as it seemed, and contemplate the wondrous what-ifs that a single day in the sun had brought. What if all this could really *work?*

What if she could keep her baby and make a life for herself at Willoughby Close?

Chapter Ten

"I'M SURE YOU understand."

Ava was really starting to hate those four words. They never, ever boded anything good. She shifted on the hard plastic chair and smiled at Tracy, with her shellacked blond hair and too-white smile.

"Of course… but surely experience counts for something? I do have ten years of it."

Tracy's smile froze and she flicked her glance back at Ava's CV lying on her desk. "Yes…" She sounded dubious.

Ava hadn't expected this to be so hard. After her moment of epiphany in Harriet's garden, she'd decided, rather impulsively, to take some action. She'd gone to the library to print out her CV and then rung a recruitment agency in Witney and booked an appointment for Monday. She'd felt ebullient doing that much, except now it didn't seem like much at all. When she'd entered her office, Tracy had taken one all too brief look at her CV and frowned.

"You haven't worked for five years?"

"No…"

"Maternity leave?" She suggested and Ava gritted her teeth.

"No, just married."

"I see." Tracy had pursed her lips, and Ava was afraid she *did* see.

"The thing is," Tracy said, leaning forward as if to invite some wretched confidentiality, "business and technology change so quickly, don't they? Everything's moved on quite a bit in five years, and employers are really looking for people who are competent in all of the latest software."

"But surely you don't need to do that for every temporary assignment," Ava said, trying to sound reasonable and not desperate. "Answering phones, filing…" Things she didn't want to do, but she needed a job and that was what she knew.

"Oh, no." Tracy let out a little laugh, as if Ava had just said something utterly absurd. "Any assignment would be need several skill sets, at least. No one simply answers phones anymore, not with everything automated these days."

"Oh." It seemed things *had* moved on in five years.

And then Tracy had given her that awful line, *I'm sure you understand,* when the truth was Ava didn't want to.

Ava slid her hands under her thighs, to keep from clenching them into fists. She'd wanted this to work. She'd dragged her feet long enough, and now she wanted, *needed* a job. She'd expected temping to be her fallback, not her reach.

"The thing is," Tracy said slowly as she began to read Ava's CV more thoroughly, "you haven't stayed at any of these positions very long, have you?" The question hung in the air, unanswered. And why should Ava say anything? She could see that Tracy was already doing the arithmetic in her head. "You haven't stayed in a single office for more than a month."

"Well." Ava cleared her throat. "They were short-term assignments."

Tracy's gaze narrowed. "You never looked for a longer assignment or permanent employment?"

"I like variety." Ava did her best to meet the woman's assessing gaze. Why did this have to be so *hard?* Why couldn't Tracy see all her experience, say how fantastic it was, and set her up answering phones for a construction company outside Oxford? Seriously, this wasn't rocket science. She knew she could do it. At least, she *thought* she could.

"Hmm." Tracy tapped lacquered nails against the desk for a moment before seeming to come to a decision. "I'll tell you what, why don't you sit some tests, and then we'll take it from there."

"Tests? A typing test, you mean?" That was one thing she was decent at, at least. She'd taken a free online course at the library when she'd moved to London and realized she didn't to be a waitress for the rest of her life. Typing she could do.

"Among other things," Tracy said easily. "We like to assess candidates' abilities in a variety of skills—typing, spreadsheets, use of internet browsers and email…"

"That sounds fine." Ava was starting to sweat. The only thing she'd done technology-wise in the last five years was surf the web and a little bit of email, and she did both on the tablet David had given her. Besides printing out her CV at the library, she hadn't used a proper computer in years, and she feared it showed on her face. Tracy was acting all breezy but her eyes were narrowed, and Ava had a sick feeling this glossy woman would enjoy seeing her fail.

"There're a couple of other people taking the test now," Tracy said as she rose from the desk. "So please be quiet as we enter the room."

"What, right now?" Ava knew she sounded panicked, but *good grief.* She hadn't practiced. She didn't even know what Excel was, not really. "I could come back…"

"Oh no, I wouldn't want you to have to do that," Tracy said sweetly. "Much easier if you do it now, and we tick all the boxes, as it were."

"Right."

Miserable and starting to panic properly, Ava followed Tracy out of the office and into a small, boxy room with several large, old-fashioned computers lined up on tables. Two other women were in the room, a worried-looking woman in a dark dress and hijab who was mouthing the words silently, and a young woman with pale white-blonde hair who was staring at the screen as if she had no idea what to do. Ava was in good company, then.

"Just follow the instructions on the screen," Tracy said as she tapped a few keys and the screen blinked to blue life. "If you're having trouble, just press 'skip'." She spoke as if that was no problem at all, but Ava imagined that a single skip on this kind of test would tank any chance of being taken on.

"Right. Thanks." Tracy disappeared and Ava stared at the dialogue box that had appeared on the screen. Her mouth dry, she started to read the instructions about how to take this wretched test, but her brain felt as if it was buzzing and she couldn't concentrate.

She glanced at the woman in the hijab a few seats down and the woman, sensing her gaze, turned to her with a cautious smile.

"Is difficult, yes?" Her English was heavily accented and carefully spoken, and Ava felt a flash of both sympathy and admiration for her. She couldn't imagine taking this test in a foreign language.

"I haven't even started," she admitted, "and I'm already panicked."

"Is okay. Take your time. There is no…" She struggled to find the word, and Ava supplied,

"Rush?"

"Yes, that is it."

"Thanks." She smiled at the woman and turned back to her screen. Apparently, there was something of a rush, because the dialog box of instructions had changed to the start of the test, and a little stopwatch was ticking the seconds in the corner of the screen. She wondered if the other woman had noticed that, but as she was now busy doing something on her screen, Ava decided to let her be.

The first question seemed fairly easy—open a word document. She could do that, surely. She'd done it at the library, when she'd had to access her CV from email and open it in Word. She could absolutely do this.

Except everything on the screen looked unfamiliar, and when Ava accidentally clicked something a red box flashed up with a warning. And before she could correct it or try something else, the test had moved on to question two.

Damn.

She glanced at the woman on her right, who looked to be about eighteen. She was pecking at the keyboard with two fingers, and after a second Ava realized she was taking the typing test. Poor girl, she wasn't going to get far.

Farther than Ava, though, because the test had skipped on to question three without her even looking at question two. There damn well was a rush.

Somehow she bumbled through the next few questions, getting some things right and having the dreaded red warning message come up on others. When she finally came to the typing test, she could have wept with relief. This she could do, but she feared sixty-five words a minute wasn't going to be enough to land her a job.

The other two women had already left by the time Ava

finished the typing test, and when she went out to the reception area they were both sitting there, holding printouts of their results and looking dour. Tracy was nowhere to be seen.

"That was tough, huh?" Ava said, and the young woman looked up, managing a sad smile.

"I never knew computer skills could be so difficult. I'm supposed to be the generation that knows all this stuff." She let out a shaky laugh and then stuffed the test results into a battered batik bag. "Oh, well."

"You could still…" Ava began but the woman was already opened the door and disappeared through it. Tracy had already given her the bad news, it seemed. Ava had a feeling she'd be next.

By the time Ava had driven back to Wychwood-on-Lea she was thoroughly dispirited even as she tried to be pragmatic. So one interview hadn't gone well. It wasn't the end of the world. She'd find something else. Something better.

She was just about to pull into Willoughby Close when she glimpsed the Tudor gables and crenellated tower of Willoughby Manor, and on impulse she turned up the sweeping drive. She hadn't seen Lady Stokeley in over a week, since she'd driven her to the hospital, and she was curious how the old lady was doing. Harriet and Ellie both seemed so busy, Ava suspected they didn't visit her as much as they meant to.

She parked her Mini in front of the entrance, wondering

as she climbed out if she was just going to be adding insult to injury that day. She'd already suffered one crushing rejection. Did she need to court another one?

Still, some contrary impulse made her climb the steps and lift the big, brass lion knocker. Some part of her identified with Lady Stokeley—the isolation, the loneliness, the desperate attempt to keep her dignity. Ava didn't know whether that was cheering or pathetic.

It only took about a minute for the door to open, and Lady Stokeley stood there, dressed in her usual twinset, this one in mauve tweed. Ava wondered how many she possessed.

"Good afternoon," Lady Stokeley said after a brief, arctic pause. "May I help you?"

Ava was struck with a sudden, horrible thought. "Good afternoon, Lady Stokeley. Do you... do you remember me?"

"Of course I do," she answered with obvious affront. "I have cancer, not dementia. You're the blowsy bit of stuff who took me to the hospital last week." She sniffed. "I wonder, is that wedding ring on your finger real?"

Ava let out a startled laugh and put her hands on her hips. "My goodness, the cat has her claws out today, doesn't she? A blowsy bit of stuff." She shook her head slowly. "That's quite an assumption."

"Tell me I'm wrong, then," Lady Stokeley challenged, and Ava laughed again.

She didn't know why she enjoyed Lady Stokeley's sharp words and plain speaking so much, but she did. Her observations would have hurt coming from someone else but, for some reason, when Lady Stokeley delivered her stinging retorts in her unvarnished way they made Ava respond with just as much honesty, and more than a little mischief.

"You're not far wrong," Ava allowed. "But the wedding ring is real, thank you very much."

"Ah." Lady Stokeley nodded knowingly as she turned from the door. "Bagged a rich one, did you?"

Ouch. Ava blinked, determined not to let that one sting. "I thought I did," she said.

Lady Stokeley was moving to the back of the house and Ava wondered if she was just going to leave her there.

"Come on, then," Lady Stokeley called irritably. "You can make me some tea."

"All right, then." Cheered by the command—it could hardly be called an invitation—Ava followed Lady Stokeley inside, down a long, narrow, dark corridor, and then through a green baize door to the cavernous kitchen.

"The tea's by the cooker," Lady Stokeley said, and went to sit down at the table tucked into the corner. Ava glanced around the huge room, not knowing even where to begin. A huge, black dragon-like range took up a good part of one wall, and a small, modern cooker had been squeezed next to it. Ava supposed she meant that one.

"You could hire this place out," she remarked as she took a box of budget tea bags out of a near-empty cupboard. "For period dramas on the BBC and that."

Lady Stokeley made a snorting noise of disgust at the idea, and Ava lugged the big brass kettle—there didn't seem to be any other—to the sink to fill it. "You never fancied a refit?" she asked, squinting through the gloom towards Lady Stokeley. The kitchen windows were covered with creeping ivy, and so the little sunlight that filtered through was greenish, making the room even darker and more dismal. "Granite countertops?" she continued. "Proper Aga?"

"I believe I already made you aware of my financial situation," Lady Stokeley replied, but she sounded distracted.

"So you did." Back with the kettle to the cooker, where it perched precariously on the much smaller ring. Ava went looking for cups and saucers. "I'd give old Henry an earful, if I were you," she remarked, aware this was a one-sided conversation. "Tell him you need a bit more to keep you going." She opened the fridge to find the milk, and gaped at the barren depths within. "Lady Stokeley," she demanded, dropping the lightness, "where is your food?"

"Eh?" Lady Stokeley looked up, blinking. "I'm not hungry."

"Maybe not right now, but you need to eat." Ava gestured to the fridge, feeling the first stirrings of proper fury. Bloody Henry Trent had a lot to answer for. "There's nothing in here but some disgusting UHT milk and an opened tin of Spam, which I hope is for the cat you don't seem to have."

"There is nothing wrong with Spam."

"It's revolting." Ava shuddered. After her mum had gone, her father would open a tin of Spam and leave it on the kitchen counter, tea sorted. She absolutely hated the stuff. "Why do you live like this?" she demanded, her voice rising in her fury on Lady Stokeley's behalf. "Surely Henry Trent would give you more money. It's almost as if you want—"

"Enough." Lady Stokeley's voice was the crack of a whip, shocking her. She stood by the table, one hand resting on its top for support. "You are being melodramatic. I don't get out to the shops very often and so I need food that keeps. It's as simple as that. And if you are concerned about the state of my larder, rest assured that I have meals delivered by a very capable service several times a week. Now I am done discussing such matters with you. The kettle is boiling."

Ava yanked the kettle off the hob, feeling suitably chastened. Who was she, to tell Lady Stokeley about her life? Who was she, to waltz in to a woman's house and start giving her orders? She felt ashamed.

"Sorry," she said quietly as she made the tea and then handed Lady Stokeley a cup. "You were absolutely right when you said I was impertinent."

Lady Stokeley looked up with one of her old glimmers. "I know I was." She turned back to the paper she'd been holding, and Ava saw it was a letter.

"Good news?" she asked as she sipped her own tea.

"Of a sort." Lady Stokeley sighed and put the letter

down. "It is from an old acquaintance of mine, Violet. She wishes me to visit."

"That's good, isn't it?" Privately Ava thought it would do Lady Stokeley a world of good to get out and see someone socially.

"Perhaps." Lady Stokeley touched the letter lightly, her face creased with concern, or perhaps just memory. "I'm not sure."

Ava was intrigued, but she knew better than to press. She'd been nosy enough about Lady Stokeley's life. In any case, Lady Stokeley turned to her.

"So, if that wedding ring is authentic, where is your husband?"

She didn't pull her punches, and so Ava didn't either. "He died," she answered. "Almost a month ago now."

Lady Stokeley nodded, accepting, unfazed. "I'm sorry for your loss."

"Thank you."

"He was older than you, I presume?" she asked, and Ava knew she presumed a lot more than that.

"Yes, he was sixty-six. Died of a massive heart attack while on the golf course, which seems like a cliché, but there you are."

"Clichés exist for a reason," Lady Stokeley replied with a small sigh. "The where or how doesn't change the outcome."

"No, I suppose not."

"And you moved to Willoughby Close." She eyed Ava

shrewdly. "Why was that?"

Ava was pretty sure the old bird knew why. "Because my husband left me very little in his will," she said, feeling a familiar coldness settle inside her. *Why, David, why?* "Ten thousand pounds, to be exact, and my car and clothes. And dog." Which reminded her, she needed to get back to number three to let Zuzu out.

"Ah." Lady Stokeley nodded slowly, clearly unsurprised. "Money causes such a palaver, doesn't it?" she remarked after a moment. "Whether you have too much or too little or none at all. It's very tiresome, really."

Ava could think of other words to describe it, but she nodded. It *was* tiring to think of money all the time, to worry about it, to wonder if she'd be able to get a job. Her stomach cramped at the reminder of that morning's interview. After scanning her test results, Tracy had informed her rather grimly that she'd call her when something appropriate became available, which Ava suspected would be never.

But what did it matter anyway? If she was going to keep this baby, she'd need to take some kind of maternity leave in about seven months anyway. It wasn't as if she could bag a permanent job now. And yet… the money she could get from seven months of temping wasn't something to sneeze at.

With a sigh, Ava finished her tea and then cleared both her and Lady Stokeley's cups from the table.

"So are you going to visit your friend?" she asked as she

washed up in the enormous sink, but Lady Stokeley, gazing out the window, didn't seem to hear her. "Lady Stokeley?" Ava prompted, and finally she turned.

"Eh? Oh, I don't know. Violet lives out in a tiny village, miles from anywhere."

Ava cocked her head, trying to gauge Lady Stokeley's tone. Was she entirely dismissive, or was there a single note of yearning there? Or even of fear?

"I could drive you."

"Eh?" Lady Stokeley looked at her suspiciously. "Why would you do that?"

"Because I'm nice?" Ava suggested. Lady Stokeley looked unconvinced. "And I'm curious, and I'm also bored." Ava shrugged, smiling. "Why not?"

Chapter Eleven

A VA WAS JUST coming out of Willoughby Manor, having tidied up the tea things and left Lady Stokeley with her letter, when she saw Jace mowing the front lawn.

That was bad enough, because he looked far too sexy pushing a mower, his shirt sticking to his chest in patches, which should have been disgusting because, ew, sweat—but somehow wasn't.

What was worse was Jace saw her. He cut the mower and strode over, his gait easy yet purposeful, while Ava remained on the front steps, as frozen as a poor little bunny in those darned headlights.

"Hey." He nodded towards the house. "Madam all right?"

"As sassy as ever," Ava replied, deciding to be flippant. "She certainly has the measure of me."

Jace arched an eyebrow, clearly wondering how to take that. "I think she has the measure of everyone."

"Maybe so." She started towards her car. "Anyway," she said, apropos of nothing.

"What are you afraid of, exactly?" Jace asked, and Ava whirled around so fast she practically got whiplash.

"What?"

Jace shrugged. "Every time I see you you're giving me your school teacher impression or you're trying to get away as fast as you can. Makes me wonder."

"Then you can keep wondering," Ava snapped.

"Doesn't all that indignation get tiresome, after a while?"

Ava stared at him, bristling with, yes, indignation, and then suddenly she laughed and shook her head. "Yes, actually, it does get a bit tiresome." Because, just like with Lady Stokeley, why not? She felt a little reckless, and she wasn't sure if she liked it or not but, hey, she'd go with it. For now.

"Why?" Jace asked simply, peeling away all the layers to that simple seed of a question, and just what would it give root to? Did she want to find out? Did she want to let questions like that plant inside of her, *grow?*

Ava let out long, weary breath. "What am I scared of, is that what you asked?" She rested one hand on the door of her car, the metal warm beneath her palm, the moment spinning on under the sunlight, Jace waiting, steady and patient, a bee bumbling by, the smell of honeysuckle and cut grass in the air. "Everything," she said quietly, the word far more heartfelt than she liked or had meant. She made an attempt to rally. "But I think I do a good impression of not seeming it, and the fact that you somehow see through that is…" She hesitated, wondering why she was saying so much and yet *wanting* to somehow. "Tiresome *and* terrifying." She glanced up at him beneath her lashes, appalled and yet also relieved that she'd confessed to so much. What was it about this man? And why did he even want to know? Mere curiosity, or something more? "There's a lot you don't know about me," she said, and it came out as a warning.

"There's a lot you don't know about me," Jace replied, unconcerned.

What exactly was going on here? Ava hadn't moved but she felt as if she'd stumbled, as if her balance had gone right off, and the world around her was reeling. She took a deep breath and looked away. "I need to go."

"Where?"

"Home. Zuzu needs a walk." She wrenched open the door of the car and slid inside, grateful for the possibility of a quick and easy escape.

Jace moved towards the car, holding the door so she couldn't slam it shut. "Have dinner with me."

Ava eyed him in surprise. Of all the things she'd anticipated him asking, a simple date had not actually been one of them. "Jace," she said in exasperation, "I'm pregnant."

"I figured."

"How?"

Another shrug. "You didn't drink any alcohol the other night, and at the used book stall you picked up a copy of some pregnancy book."

KISS ME AT WILLOUGHBY CLOSE

He'd noticed that? She'd put it down almost instantly. Ava shook her head. "So, considering that I'm pregnant, you still want to go on a date?"

"Yep, pretty much." He smiled, revealing a dimple in one lean cheek, and that just made him sexier.

Ava thought about just telling him no point-blank, and then she thought about going out and enjoying herself, because she knew she would. "Ask me again later," she said, and Jace laughed.

"You want me to work for it?"

"I want to give myself time to think." Ava yanked the door from Jace's now unresisting grasp. "And, yes, I want you to work for it. What do you think I am?"

Jace was still smiling as she headed down the drive, and then Ava realized she was, as well.

Back at number three, Zuzu hurled herself frenziedly at Ava's legs, and even though she felt tired and slightly nauseous, Ava exchanged her heels for a pair of trainers and then clipped on Zuzu's lead and headed back outside. She felt the need to *move,* to keep active, because her brain was buzzing from that conversation with Jace and all its awkward, surprising honesty, and she needed to work that off somehow.

What are you afraid of?

How had he seen that? How could one man, one virtual stranger, see into her soul? She was being fanciful, of course, and melodramatic just like Lady Stokeley had accused her of being. Jace Tucker might be a bit more astute than the average bloke, but she'd handed him her inner thoughts on a silver plate! Everything, she'd said. *Why* had she said that? Why had she admitted so much, more than she even admitted to herself?

And why was it so scary, to admit to being scared?

Ava reflected on this question as she tramped through the woods, the leafy boughs overhead giving her a cool and welcome shade, Zuzu scurrying ahead, sniffing everything. Why not just say, *"Yes, I'm scared, so what?"* Everyone was scared of something. Most people were scared of lots of things.

There was nothing to fear but fear itself.

A small smile quirked Ava's mouth. She could wax philosophical about fear all she wanted, but the real question was, did she want to go on a date with Jace? No, she knew the answer to that one. The real question was, would she go?

Ava emerged on the other side of the wood, surprised to see a little house nestled there like something out of a fairy tale. It was tiny, with a little turret perfect for a mini Rapunzel, and a lot of latticed, scrolling stonework. Mullioned windows sparkled under the sunlight and the door had a diamond-paned stained glass window in it. The whole place was darling, and Ava half-expected to seem some elves frolicking in the garden, perhaps a fairy or two.

Then the front door opened and Jace stood there, shirtless.

What? Ava blinked, half-expecting him to disappear, or to turn into some shapeshifter. Or maybe she was hallucinating. Losing her mind, because…

"Hey." Jace, as usual, sounded unsurprised to see her anywhere and in any condition.

"What are you doing here?" Ava asked.

She would not check him out. She would definitely not check out his abs. Her gaze swooped down of its accord, a Pavlovian response to a Chippendale-like chest, and she noted the well-defined six-pack with a little fizz of excitement. Stupid, stupid, stupid. She should not be thinking like this. She was a *widow,* for heaven's sake. A pregnant widow.

"This is my house," Jace said, and Ava's gaze jerked back up.

"Wait—your house?" She took in the fairy-like house with its ornate stonework and little turret and couldn't keep a bubble of laughter from escaping. "You *live* here?"

"Yeah, yeah, go on and have a good laugh." Jace leaned against the doorframe, muscles rippling. Everywhere. "You're not the first to."

"It's just so…"

"Twee. Naff. Excruciatingly quaint?"

"All three."

"Thanks."

She shook her head slowly. "Where's your truck?"

"I park it at a nearby barn and walk. This used to be the gatehouse, back in the day, but everything got overgrown and now it's hidden."

"An enchanted cottage."

"Shut up." He spoke good-naturedly, his eyes glinting, and Ava found herself grinning. "Would now be a good time to ask you again?"

"Ask me what?"

"You know what."

This was definitely flirting and suddenly Ava's buoyant mood went flat and she felt sick with both apprehension and guilt. She shouldn't be doing this. David had died a mere month ago. She was carrying his *child*. The very last thing she should be doing was contemplating some kind of flirtation with a man she barely knew.

"Uh-oh." Jace scanned her face, clearly sensing her change in mood. "What happened?"

"A month ago I was married," Ava stated quietly.

"And now you're not, I hope?"

"No…" She took a deep breath and let it out slowly. "Because he died. My husband died."

The look on Jace's face was *almost* funny. He looked… horrified. There was no other way to put it. A flash, and then it was gone, and he was back to being his lazy, easygoing self. "That was not the complication I was expecting."

"No? Me neither." She sighed and he stepped aside.

"Maybe you should come in."

Ava hesitated, torn between getting more involved with Jace Tucker and wanting someone to talk to rather badly.

"Only if you put a shirt on."

Jace grinned. "Spoilsport," he said, and then disappeared inside, hopefully to put some more clothes on.

After an uncertain pause, Ava followed, Zuzu trotting at her heels. The inside of the house was not quite as quaint as the outside, the narrow hallway dark with faded flocked wallpaper. Ava poked her head into a small sitting room. It was neat enough, with two worn sofas facing each other in front of a little coal fireplace, and a scarred wooden coffee table between them. The furniture was heavy and dark, and Ava suspected it came from the same place hers did. Was Jace as much of a wanderer as she was?

"So." He came in the sitting room behind her, and Ava practically scurried out of the way. Thankfully he was wearing a shirt, a clean blue t-shirt that looked very good on him, but then Ava supposed everything would look good on him. The man was blessed. Jace sat down on one of the sofas, stretching his arms out along the back. "What happened?"

Gingerly, Ava sat down on the other sofa. "David, my husband, died of a heart attack on the golf course. Eighteenth hole, so at least he finished his game." *Ha-ha-ha.*

She could practically hear the polite titters of the funeral crowed, the perfunctory smiles. Poor David. She felt a pang of compassion for the man she'd married, the man she'd thought she'd loved, at least a little bit. Was that awful? To marry someone she only sort of liked? Ava closed her eyes, suddenly overcome by both shame and grief.

"Ava." The sofa creaked and then he was sitting next to her, his thigh pressed to hers, one strong, warm hand resting on her shoulder. The desire to curl into him, to seek comfort, was almost overwhelming. With what felt like superhuman strength, Ava stayed still.

"I'm sorry," Jace said quietly. "I'm an ass, to ask you out when you're obviously in no place to think that way. If it helps, I'm happy just to be your friend."

Ava's throat felt too tight to answer. Yes, she needed a friend. She had a feeling Jace knew that. Finally, after what felt like an age, when he simply sat there, his hand on her shoulder, his breathing slow and steady, she drew a quick breath and managed to speak.

"Sorry."

"What on earth are you sorry for?"

She opened her eyes and made herself shift a little bit away from him. Jace dropped his hand from her shoulder. "For nearly falling apart."

"You're recently bereaved and pregnant. I think you're entitled." He gazed at her seriously, an honest, friendly warmth in his eyes. "Have you thought about what you're going to do?"

"Yes." She took a quick, sharp breath. "I want to keep the baby."

Jace nodded slowly, his face thoughtful and yet giving nothing away. "That's understandable."

Because it would be a reminder of her husband? And yet,

Ava realized wretchedly, David had nearly nothing to do with it. She didn't want this baby because it was David's. She wanted it because it was hers.

"My marriage wasn't…" she began, and then had no idea how to finish that sentence.

"Wasn't perfect?" Jace suggested, and she let out a sad, tired laugh.

"You could say that."

"From what I gather, no one's is."

"You've never been married?" She estimated him to be in his mid to late thirties, so he could very well have had a marriage or two under his belt.

Jace shook his head, his expression turning a bit guarded. "No." Here was a man who didn't like to talk about himself.

"Well, mine was far from perfect," Ava said. "But after David died, I started to wonder if it was even less perfect than I'd thought it was."

"How come?"

"Because…" She blew out a breath. "He only left me ten thousand pounds in his will. And it's not even about the money," she said quickly, in case Jace assumed she was a money grubbing gold-digger just like Simon and Emma did. "At least, not entirely. I mean, ten thousand pounds is ten thousand pounds."

"True enough."

She didn't hear any censure in his voice, and so she continued, "But David is—was—a multimillionaire. Two houses, tons in savings… it felt like a slight. A slap in the face. He gave me the same amount he did the housekeeper, and she'd only been with us for eighteen months." Admitting this much felt like taking her finger out of the plughole, and the hurt and bitterness she'd tried to keep at bay came rushing out. "I mean, is that how he rated me? Someone he employed to service his needs? Because that's how it felt. And I know our marriage wasn't… well, I did like him. I *did,*" she said fiercely, and Jace simply nodded, accepting. She should stop this. She should stop this right now, because nothing she said was going to make Jace think better of her. "But it wasn't a big, grand love affair. He was sixty-six. Not that that has to make a difference, but… oh, I don't even know what I'm saying." She shook her head, thoroughly miserable, feeling guilty for all sorts of reasons.

"Tea," Jace said after a moment, rising from the sofa. Ava looked at him in surprise.

"For shock? Because I'm not feeling all that shocked, although you might be."

"No, for comfort." He gave her a quick smile as he headed out of the room. "I'd normally put a shot of whisky in it, but considering your condition, I won't."

Ava tried to recover her composure while Jace went to make the tea. Zuzu, sensing her mistress's disquiet, jumped up onto her lap, and Ava cuddled her, stroking her silky fur, taking comfort from the one creature in the world who wanted to make her feel better.

But no, amazingly, maybe now she had two. Jace was acting like a good friend, and the prospect of counting him as such amazed and humbled her. She didn't deserve his kindness. She was a stranger, and one who had a habit of blowing him off or falling apart, depending on her mood. Why he should persist on being friends with her she had no idea.

Unless he was playing a long game.

Ava forced that spiteful suspicion away as Jace came into the room with two mugs of milky, sweet tea. He handed one to Ava and then sat back down on the sofa opposite; she found she missed his steadying warmth next to her.

"So," Jace said after they'd both taken a sip of tea. "You wouldn't be the first woman to marry for money, not by a long shot."

Ava glanced away, strangely embarrassed by this state-ment. It sounded so *crass*. "I didn't marry him just for the money," she said quietly, gazing into the depths of her tea. "I wanted more than that."

Comfort, security, safety. They'd all been considerations. But, yes, the money had been important too, because she'd known what life was like without it for too long.

"I can't answer for your husband," Jace said. "Because I have no idea what was in his mind. But I imagine a sixty-six-year-old geezer is thanking his lucky stars to have a wife like you."

Her lip curled, his answer disappointing her even though

she knew it was the truth. "Because I'm young and sexy." Might as well call a spade a spade.

"And funny and smart and interesting," Jace returned without missing a beat. "But, yes, the young and sexy part is definitely a plus to any red-blooded male."

"I know. I *know.*" She shook her head. "It's so stupid to be bothered by what I knew all along. But five years we were together, and for the most part we got along." She wasn't going to think about the last year or so, when David had seemed to be losing interest. When sometimes she'd caught him looking at her like he wished he'd chosen differently.

"You cared about him," Jace stated quietly.

"Yes, of course I did." Ava spoke a little too quickly. "But now I wonder if I should have… or if he cared about me, even a little." She sighed and took another sip of tea. "I know you can't answer those questions. I'm not sure I can answer them, either."

"No," Jace agreed slowly, "but what you can do is think of the future for you and your baby. That's what's important now, isn't it?"

Chapter Twelve

AVA SAT ON a hard plastic chair and flipped through a year-old copy of *My Weekly*, trying to ignore the nerves jumping and writhing around in her middle like a bunch of grumpy snakes. After talking with Jace a few days ago, she'd decided to take some positive action and booked her first appointment with the community midwife at Lea Surgery. She'd spent the next few days tidying up the cottage, tweaking her CV, and trying to find a way forward.

And now she was here, waiting to be called in and feeling unaccountably nervous considering it was just a booking-in appointment.

Despite her nerves, it felt good to start taking charge of her own life, even in this seemingly small way. It also made Ava realize she hadn't been in charge of her life for a long time. She'd pretended that she had been, even to herself, but now as she flicked through the magazine, skimming an article on *Five Ways with Root Vegetables!*, she felt as if she was finally in control, even as her life was spinning out of it. It was an odd and uncomfortable feeling, to take charge when she was out of her depth, but it was much better than the numbness, boredom, or disguised unhappiness she'd been feeling for as long as she could remember.

"Ava Mitchell for the midwife." The sound of the receptionist on loud speaker jolted Ava out of her reverie—roasted parsnips drizzled with honey looked fairly tasty—and she glanced around to see if anyone she knew even vaguely was in the surgery and had heard that all-too-revealing announcement.

"Ava Mitchell," the receptionist repeated, an edge to her voice now, "for the midwife."

Just in case anyone had missed it the first time. Ava heaved herself to her feet, hurrying towards the desk before the woman decided to go for a third time.

"Ava Mitchell," she said. "That's me."

"Room three," the receptionist said and went back to her computer. Ava took a big breath and started walking down the hall.

There was no reason to feel quite so scared about this appointment. It was routine, totally normal, everything would be easy and fine. And yet… memories stirred, drifting through her mind like old leaves. Her sweaty hand in Jeff's. The hard beating of her heart, the cold, sticky vinyl of the examining table. The hope and the fear. At least then she'd had someone to hold onto. Now she walked alone.

It's just an appointment.

"Ava Mitchell?" The midwife, a neat, blonde woman in

her early thirties, looked up from her computer with a smile. "Laney Miller, the community midwife. Nice to meet you." She shook hands briskly before indicating Ava should take a seat, and she felt reassured by Laney's no-nonsense manner. "So." She gave Ava another quick smile before turning back to the computer and pressing a few keys. "This is your booking-in appointment for pregnancy, yes?"

"Yes."

"And when did you take a pregnancy test?" Laney swiveled in her chair to face her expectantly.

"Um, about a week ago."

"And the date of your last period?"

Ava was already starting to sweat. "I can't remember, but I know the, ah, date of conception."

"Well, that makes it simple." Laney raised her eyebrows, waiting.

Ava blurted, "Five weeks ago, give or take a few days." She couldn't remember the actual date, but she knew it had been early May, and raining. And it had been the first time she and David had had sex in months. Many months. The first and last time. Ava swallowed hard.

"In that case, you should be around seven weeks pregnant." Laney reached for a little colored wheel and started to spin it. Ava remembered the wheel from her last booking-in appointment, nearly twenty years ago. In a second, as if by magic, the midwife would come up with a due date.

"February seventeenth," Laney announced, and Ava

managed a queasy smile. With just two words it felt that much more real. In February she would have a baby. A child of her own, small and squalling. What was she *doing?*

"Now a few questions about your medical history," Laney said, and Ava nodded.

It all went swimmingly for a few minutes. No history of heart disease, high blood pressure, blood clots, cancer. Health-wise Ava had always been near-perfect.

And then—"This is your first pregnancy?" Laney looked up with a smile, pen poised to write the relevant information. The expected yes.

"No," Ava admitted. "It's my second."

Laney was unfazed. She was a midwife, after all. "And when was your last pregnancy?"

Quietly Ava gave the date. Nineteen years ago.

Laney didn't so much as blink, God bless her. "And you carried that pregnancy to term?"

"Yes."

"Any complications?"

Far too many to name. But physically? "No, it was pretty much a textbook pregnancy and delivery, as far as I could tell." Even if she'd only been sixteen.

"Great. Let's hope for the same again, shall we? But, since you are thirty-five, you are technically considered a geriatric pregnancy, which is a terrible term, I know, but there we are. We'll have to take a few extra precautions and screenings, and we'll book you in for a level two scan at twenty weeks." Laney rose from her seat and uncertainly Ava did the same. That was it?

"Schedule another visit in four weeks' time," Laney said cheerfully. "And by then we should be able to hear baby's heartbeat."

"Oh." Ava gave a tremulous smile as she imagined that galloping, whooshing noise. Goodness, but she was feeling fragile. "Brilliant."

Laney handed her a folder with a red plastic cover. "These are your notes. Bring them to each appointment, and also if you ever have to go to hospital. But in the meantime, try to relax, get some good sleep, and enjoy yourself." She smiled. "You haven't been feeling nauseous?"

"Not really." Occasional queasiness, but Ava had put that down to stress and bad eating habits. She'd have to do better for her baby's sake.

"Maybe you won't have morning sickness. Not everyone does. Did you last time?"

"Only a little."

"Lucky you, then!" Laney said and with a murmured thanks Ava left.

She still felt a bit dazed by it all as she started walking back to Willoughby Close, clutching the red folder to her chest. This was really happening. She was pregnant. She was keeping the baby. She'd been skirting the issue, toying with the idea, for days, alternating between hope and terrifying uncertainty, but with this appointment she'd made a choice.

She'd said yes. And in a little over seven months she'd have this baby. Have a *family,* for the first time since she was fourteen.

But what on earth was she going to do for a job? For *money?*

The question felt like slamming on the brakes of the vague happy families' fantasy that had been running through her head, of lullabies and sunshine and chubby toddlers running through grassy meadows.

Tracy from Temporary Solutions was not going to ring anytime soon. And the ten thousand pounds of a few weeks ago was now closer to seven thousand pounds, and dropping fast, especially with another month's rent due shortly. Seven thousand pounds, with rent and council tax and utilities and food, was going to be eaten up in a couple of months. Benefits, if she went that route, wouldn't cover her basic expenses. They never did. Ava pressed one hand against her still-flat stomach in the age-old gesture known to every woman. She was the only one who could provide for her baby. The only person to look out for her child. It was time to take control again.

Abruptly Ava turned and crossed the village green where she'd been heading towards the lane that led to Willoughby Manor and instead made a beeline for The Drowned Sailor. She felt a little reckless and a lot determined as she marched through the doors into the dim interior of the pub, breathing in the slightly stale, yeasty smell of beer.

It was three o'clock on a Monday afternoon and still there were a couple of workmen standing at the bar, pints halfway to their mouths as Ava entered.

One of them whistled softly, something she was well used to. She ignored the whistle as well as the appreciative looks and stated in a loud voice, "I'm looking for the owner or manager here."

"Are you now, love?" one of the men said with a laugh, and then a man appeared out of the gloom behind the bar, a damp tea towel thrown over own stocky shoulder.

"That would be me."

Ava eyed him for a moment, taking in the curly dark hair and ruddy face, a nose that had been broken once or twice and a cauliflower ear. When he'd spoken, he had a Welsh accent. Rugby player, she decided.

"Jace Tucker told me you were looking for bar staff."

The man's gaze traveled up and down her so quickly Ava almost missed it. He was good, this one. Quick.

"That's right, I'm looking for bar staff. Do you have any experience?"

"No, but I think I can learn pretty quickly." And a pretty woman behind the bar was always a plus.

Ava felt a surge of confidence, of determination. She could do this. She could damn well get herself a job.

The man laughed at that and stuck out his hand for her to shake. "Owen Jones." Definitely Welsh, then.

"Ava Mitchell."

"If you're free most evenings from six to eleven, you've got yourself a job."

Ava wilted a little inside at the thought of working on her feet for five hours a night, but here was a job and she needed the money. She was not going to balk at a bit of hard work. She nodded resolutely. "Thanks."

"Can you start tomorrow?"

She nodded again, even more resolute. "Of course."

"That's sorted, then." The man grinned. "Come a bit early and bring some ID with you, and we'll sort out the paperwork."

"Okay." She felt as if she'd been standing on the edge of an abyss and she'd just taken a massive step out into mid-air. "Thanks."

She felt both buoyant and worried as she left the pub, striding out into the sunshine. She'd just signed on to thirty hours of work a week, *hard* work, on her feet, at a wage of six-fifty an hour plus tips. She'd be likely to earn no more than three hundred pounds a week, which was not enough to keep her going long-term. As a temp she could make nearly twice that. And what about when the baby came?

With an impatient sigh, Ava brushed the worry aside. She had seven months to figure out a long-term plan, and in the meantime, at least she had some sort of income. She'd made a positive change to her life.

She was just strolling up the lane to Willoughby Close when she heard her name being called, and turned around to see Harriet walking up with her three children, all of them dragging school jumpers, backpacks, and various papers.

"Hi," she called back, smiling uncertainly at all of them.

She might be having a baby but children, in all their bluntness and hyperactivity, still scared her more than a little. She had no idea what might come out of Chloe's mouth, and William seemed capable of head butting her. Accidentally, but still.

"I've been meaning to stop by," Harriet said as they all drew closer. "How are you getting on in number three?"

"Oh, fine, I think."

"Settling in?"

"Getting there."

Harriet smiled, distracted momentarily by William trying to scare Chloe by acting like what Ava assumed was a zombie, and Chloe screeching loudly. That girl had some lungs.

"Actually," Harriet said, her tone turning a bit hesitant, "I wanted to ask you a favor."

"Oh?" First Ellie, now Harriet. Ava supposed it was a sign of friendship, something she wasn't used to, but she couldn't help feeling a bit wary. She put on her politely interested smile and waited.

"I've been driving Lady Stokeley to Oxford four times a week," Harriet explained, "but as I think I told you the other night I'm planning an event at the tearoom on the high street and the next few weeks are going to be fairly manic for me. I was wondering if you'd be able to do it? Drive, I mean? Lady S seems to have taken a liking to you."

"What?" Ava did a theatrical double take. She couldn't help it. "Actually, I have the feeling I irritate the hel—heck out of her," she said, with an apologetic grimace towards the children. William was still acting like a zombie, staggering around the lane with his arms held out in front of him and a comically zoned-out look on his face.

"I think everyone feels that way with her, but she told me yesterday that you have spirit, which I think must be high praise indeed." Harriet gave her a lopsided smile. "She certainly hasn't said anything like that about me."

"Wow." Ava shook her head, still finding it hard to believe. Lady Stokeley liked her? The best Ava had been hoping for was toleration.

"So do you think you might be able to drive her? For, say, the next two weeks? She pays, by the way. Seven pounds an hour. I know it's not much, but every bit counts, right?"

"Right." Ava brightened at the thought of another paying job. And she liked Lady Stokeley, even with, or perhaps especially because of, her plain speaking. "Sure," she said recklessly, and then added her mantra as of late, "why not?"

"Brilliant." Harriet looked relieved, and then, inexplicably, she froze. After a tense pause Ava saw that Harriet's gaze had dropped down to the red folder she still clutched to her chest.

Ava was scarcely able to believe that Harriet could guess

what that folder contained—but then, all the pregnant women got them, or so her midwife had said, and Harriet had been pregnant, plus she undoubtedly had that mummy spidey sense that could detect a pregnancy at ten paces.

"Brilliant," Harriet said again, with just a little too much jollity. "Really brilliant. If you could start Monday, that would be great." She was looking determinedly at Ava's face, as if the folder didn't exist and, despite the awkwardness, Ava appreciated the gesture. She was not ready to go public with her pregnancy, and she hoped Harriet could keep a secret as well as Ava could.

Although, Ava reflected as she opened the door to number three, greeting Zuzu's excited yips with a smile, it wasn't as if she had all that many people to tell.

Still, she'd accomplished something today. She had two jobs, and more importantly, she had hope. Briefly she wondered what Emma or Simon would think of having a half-brother or sister. Not that she'd ever tell them. And what about Jeff? She let her mind drift back to that once all-consuming relationship, when she'd been so sure the family life she'd lost was once again on the cards. She and Jeff had been going to create it, silly children that they were. And then her mind betrayed her and tripped down a dark and closed-off lane of her memory, and she thought of her mother.

For a second, Ava could feel soft hands pressing against her cheeks as she dropped a kiss on her forehead; she could breathe in the scent of her mother's cheap perfume from the chemist's, one step up from Impulse body spray. She felt the longing and the confusion, because then her mother was gone. The note had been stark and simple: *I couldn't stay. – Lara.*

Ava dropped the folder on the kitchen counter as she resolutely pushed that memory back down that dark, dark road, a place she never went to in her mind. No good ever came of it, remembering her mother's kindnesses, the kisses and the sadness, the inexplicable confusion that still seethed in the pit of Ava's stomach, an unholy ferment. One thing she was going to be damn sure of. She'd be a much better mother than her own had been to her.

Chapter Thirteen

I T WAS QUARTER to five on a Saturday evening and the pub was already starting to heave with people intent, it seemed, on getting drunk. Ava stepped in cautiously, smoothing down the white t-shirt and dark jeans she'd decided were appropriate barmaid attire for her first day of work at The Drowned Sailor.

The stale, yeasty smell of beer hit her again as she headed towards the bar, just as it had yesterday afternoon, and her stomach stirred queasily in response. That morning she'd pushed her coffee away in disgust and then nibbled a piece of barely-buttered toast, afraid she wouldn't be able to keep anything else down. It seemed morning sickness was going to hit her harder this time than it had when she'd been sixteen. She wondered what other lovely surprises were in store for her as a geriatric mother.

"Ava." Owen greeted her from behind the bar with a brisk nod. "Let's get your paperwork started and then I'll show you how to manage the drinks as well as the till. Steve is on cocktails, so all you have to do is pull pints and the odd glass of wine and take people's money, of course."

"All right." It sounded simple enough, but Ava felt surprisingly nervous.

It had been a long time since she'd been in a working environment, and her one experience of waitressing had been when she'd been seventeen and newly living in London. She'd lasted a week in a busy restaurant in Leicester Square, and then another two months in a cocktail lounge, the kind of tawdry place where she worried about getting STDs from the seats. Then she'd finally taken the typing course and turned to temping, in the hopes of snagging something—or someone—better.

But here she was again, starting over, right at the bottom. That was okay. She was determined that it would be. She handed her ID over to Owen, signed a few forms, and then he was showing her how to pull pints at the bar. They had several ales on draught, and more in bottles, all standard stuff, no microbrewery offerings with hints of wheat or subtle notes of blackberry here. The wine was bog standard too, a house red and white that were kept open and could be bought at any off license. Bowls of pretzels and nuts littered the scarred mahogany of the bar, and pork scratchings and "posh crisps" were sold from behind the bar.

The cash register was simple enough and since she didn't have to handle any food or cocktails, it all looked easy. Except somehow it wasn't, because the moment Owen finished the pub seemed to fill right up to the rafters with people demanding drinks, waving tenners in her face and ordering for entire tables of people, so Ava had to keep track of half a dozen drinks.

After giving her a quick, distracted smile, Owen had disappeared to the back, and Ava was left on her own, trying to pull pints as fast as she could, but not too fast, in order to let the head rise as Owen had instructed.

The trouble was, people really wanted their drinks. The bar was loud and raucous, as far from the restrained snobbery and elegance of The Three Pennies as was possible. Workmen stretched muscular forearms with crumpled ten pound notes across the bar, grabbing their foaming pints with the other, careless of the spill on to the bar, or even on to Ava herself.

And of course having a pretty new barmaid handing them their beers was noticed. From the moment she started working, Ava fended off a lot of thoughtless flirting and the occasional more concerted attempt, especially as the evening wore on. Fortunately, she knew how to handle such bumbling attempts, whether it was with a stern look, a pointed elbow, or simply ignoring some drunken bluster. She was well used to that kind of attention; she'd been getting it since she was thirteen.

An hour in and Ava's feet started to ache and her stomach growled. She'd forgotten to eat dinner, and now she was sincerely regretting that fact. Plus the smell of beer was *everywhere*—on the sticky bar in front of her, on her hands and clothes, in her hair. She was going to need to take about five showers. She started breathing through her mouth, wondering how she was going to survive an entire evening of this, never mind the next seven or so months.

And then Jace came into the pub. Somehow Ava wasn't even surprised, although she acknowledged the ripple of— yes, it was pleasure—that went through her at the sight of him standing in the doorway, hair rumpled, expression lazy, wearing his usual faded jeans, t-shirt, and beat-up work boots. Did the man possess any other clothes? Did it matter?

Ava yanked her gaze away, focusing on the pint of Doom Bar she was pulling for a surly man with a flat cap jammed low on his head. He'd slammed a couple of pound coins onto the bar with purpose, and Ava could tell he was here for the duration, and did not see the necessity of small talk or simple courtesy.

She slid the pint over and took the coins, discreetly keeping an eye on Jace all the while. He'd shouldered his way into the bar and was now chatting with a few guys Ava didn't recognize. She didn't recognize anyone here, of course; this was hardly her and David's kind of crowd, although it had been, funnily enough, her crowd once upon a long time ago, the rough and ready, people wanting to drink and have a good time and nothing more.

"Hey, beautiful." Even though it wasn't even eight o'clock, the man who now approached the bar was slurring. Ava merely raised her eyebrows, waiting. "You're new here, aren't you?" The man persisted, his gaze dropping predictably to her chest. Ava didn't reply, just waited him out. Easier than engaging by far. "Come on now, be nice," the man insisted, a hard edge entering his voice, and Ava recognized the kind of drunk who could get mean. Once upon a time she might have humored him. Not anymore.

"Would you like a drink?" she asked in as neutral a voice as she could manage.

The man leered. He was cringingly obvious, but that was what happened when someone was drunk. The only person who thought they were being subtle was them. "You know, love, what I'd really like is a piece of—"

"A pint of Guinness, please." Jace appeared at the bar, neatly shouldering the drunk out of the way. His gaze was steely as he looked at Ava, and she felt both annoyed and the tiniest bit pleased that he'd taken it upon himself to act like her knight in shining armor. Not that she needed one. She most definitely did not.

"Hey, she was seeing to me first," the man protested, squinting at Jace, and Jace turned to him with a cold stare.

"Was she? Or were you just annoying her?"

Exasperated, Ava pulled the pint and slid it across to Jace. "It's fine, Jace. And that will be four pounds fifty."

Jace handed her a five pound note while the drunk continued to bluster. Ava tuned him out, but Jace didn't seem to be able to.

"I think," he commented in a voice that Ava could tell

was trying to be pleasant and failing, "you should order your drink and then leave the bar."

"Who put you in charge?" the man demanded, and Jace simply stared him down.

Ava didn't know whether to laugh or groan. What on earth got into Jace? He was coming over all caveman, and that didn't seem his style at all. Admittedly, she'd shown him a side of her, an emotional, needy side, that nobody else had seen, but he didn't know that. And he didn't have to act as if he had rights to her now, as well as responsibilities.

"It's fine," she told him yet again, and then turned to the man. "Now what would you like?"

"A pint of bitter," he said sulkily, and Ava served him silently, pushing his pint over and then taking his money. When she looked up, Jace had retreated to a corner of the pub. He still looked grim.

An hour or so later, Ava managed to take a break, nipping to the back for the loo—her bladder wasn't what it once was, that was for sure. Her stomach growled and her head was starting to feel light. She'd only been at The Drowned Sailor for four hours but it felt like forever.

"Hey, beautiful." The familiar words had her tensing as she pried herself out of one of the tiniest loos ever and stood in the cramped and darkened hallway in the back of the pub.

The drunk man from the bar had followed her here and was now blocking her exit. Perfect.

"Hey, yourself," she replied in a neutral, non-encouraging tone and started to move past him, making sure she didn't so much as brush against his bulk.

He grabbed her arm just as Jace came around the corner.

"What the hell do you think—" Jace began, picking up his pace, and, with an instinct she'd forgotten she had, Ava twisted the man's wrist backwards until with a howl he was forced to loosen his grip.

He clutched his wrist, glaring at her. "You mad bi—"

"Don't," Jace advised, and with a muttered curse the man stalked back down the hall towards the pub, pushing past Jace and still cradling his wrist.

In the dim corridor, Ava could barely make out Jace's expression. She felt the once-familiar delayed icy rush of shock that always came after such an altercation, and she released a slow breath, determined to regain her composure, and quickly. "What is your problem, Jace?"

Jace's jaw dropped, which was satisfying since he always seemed so darn unfazed. "*My* problem?" he repeated in disbelief.

"Yes, you've been glowering at me all night, following me around, *interfering.*" She put her hands on her hips, the anger she'd felt at the random drunk bloke now directed, unfairly perhaps, at Jace. "I can take care of myself."

"What are you doing, working here?" Jace demanded, and now Ava's jaw was the one to drop.

"What does that have to do with the price of eggs?" she asked, using an expression of her dad's that hadn't passed her lips in decades.

The tiniest smile quirked Jace's mouth. "Nothing whatsoever, but it doesn't strike me as a suitable place of employment for a pregnant woman."

Ava rolled her eyes, still hardly able to believe Jace was pushing this. "Seriously? You don't think there are any pregnant women working in pubs?"

"Couldn't you have found something else?"

"Why should I? And you were the one who told me about this job in the first place."

"I know, but…" Jace raked a hand through his rumpled hair and then dropped it. "I don't like the thought of you on your feet all evening, having to fend off drunken men…"

Ava stared at him in disbelief. What was going on here? Jace wasn't her boyfriend. He was barely her friend. He had no say over what she did, and he didn't seem like the type to muscle in. And yet here he was, trying to get into a fistfight on her behalf, telling her didn't like her job, about to order her around.

A line had been crossed, and it was so surprising Ava didn't know what to make of it at first, or how to respond. It occurred to her that before David, before his death, before this *baby,* she most likely would have sashayed across that line, happy enough to have found a man to take care of her. Wasn't that what she'd always wanted? Someone to protect her honor—ha—and pay the bills. Give her an easy life, basically, but God knew before David there hadn't been much of that.

But, in any case, she didn't want to do that anymore, and she certainly didn't want Jace, a sexy near-stranger, doing it for her. She was trying to be different, and she wouldn't let Jace, kind as he could be, get in the way.

"Jace," she said quietly. "It doesn't matter what you like or don't like. You said you wanted to be my friend, and that's fine. But this?" She shook her head, a sudden flash of anger firing through her at his presumption. "Back off."

Jace stared at her, looking stunned—and, Ava realized, not by what she'd said, but by what he'd done. This wasn't the usual for him, not by a long shot, which made it even more alarming.

"Back off," she said again, more gently this time, and then slid past him and back into the pub.

She spent the next few hours in a numb fog, pulling pints and pouring glasses of wine and trying not to *think*. If she let herself dwell on Jace's behavior, her head would start to spin.

And, she realized as the night wore on, if she let herself dwell on Jace's behavior and what might have been motivating it, she'd be tempted to accept his high-handedness. To need it, because that had always been the way she operated— find a man and let him do the work. All she had to do was keep him happy.

But she didn't want to fall into that old trap again. She wanted to be different. Damn it, she was trying to be strong.

And Jace Tucker possessed the power and, yes, the sexiness, to completely mess that up.

She was going to have to set him straight, and it wasn't going to be easy, because the truth was she was tired and vulnerable and lonely, and the thought of having a kind, sexy man take care of everything was… rather wonderful. But she wasn't going to let it happen. She couldn't.

By eleven o'clock Ava's head and feet both throbbed, and her stomach felt both empty and queasy. She smelled like a brewery.

"You did good," Owen told her as he gave Ava her share of the tips. "Same time Monday?"

Ava stared at him wearily. In less than forty-eight hours she'd have to do this all again. At least she had all of Sunday off, thank goodness. "Monday it is," she said, and then she stepped outside, stifling a shriek of surprise when a dark shadow emerged to her right. A man.

"Ava, it's me, Jace."

"Jace." She shook her head, too weary to do battle with him now. "What are you doing here? No, let me guess." She held up one hand. "Walking me home in case I run into trouble between the high street and Willoughby Close."

"I will walk you home," Jace answered evenly, "but I'm really here to apologize."

She sighed and started walking. "Okay, let's hear it, then."

Jace let out a huff of laughter. "Sorry."

"That's it?" Ava slid him a smiling glance. This was *not* flirting. "That's all you've got? Okay. Thanks."

Jace did his signature move, raking a hand through that gorgeous, chocolate-brown hair, letting it flop onto his forehead. "I don't know what I was thinking," he admitted in a low voice. "I have no right to... all I can say is, I was worried."

"About what?"

"You." He didn't look at her as he said it, and Ava felt a swirl of—something—in her belly. This conversation was not going how it needed to.

"You don't need to worry about me."

"I know." Jace shoved his hands in the pockets of his jeans and quickened his stride. "I know," he said again. "The message has been received." He glanced back at her with something like a smile. "This is me, backing off."

They'd reached the narrow lane that led to Willoughby Manor and, as they navigated the twisting road shrouded in complete darkness, neither of them spoke. Ava tried to figure out her feelings, which were, as usual it seemed, complicated.

Because while part of her knew this was the right thing, the best thing, she couldn't help but feel disappointed. She was just starting to make friends here, build this fragile new life. She didn't want people backing off. But she didn't know how else she could stay strong.

They turned up the drive that led to Willoughby Manor, the great house barely visible under a moonless sky, a silvery, ghost-like mist rising over the rolling fields beyond. The air was damp and chilly even though it was mid-June, the warmth of the last few days having well and truly vanished.

Jace hesitated at the turning for Willoughby Close; the path to his house was through the wood on the other side. "Well," he said, and it sounded like the precursor to a semi-permanent goodbye.

"Jace, I still need friends," Ava blurted. "I really don't have that many." In the darkness, she couldn't see his face and she was glad. This was hard enough already. "In my… previous life I didn't have a lot of friends. Or any. It was David and me and that was it." And her life had, she was realizing more and more, been both lonely and dull and so very constrained. "I want things to be different now," she continued stiltedly. "I want to have friends, and I want to make a life for myself, and I want to be strong. So…" She shrugged, not sure what else to say. What else to feel.

"Okay," Jace said after a moment, his voice sounding gruff in the darkness. "I think I can manage that."

Relief poured through her, surprising in its strength. She had only known him a little while, but she didn't want to lose Jace. She didn't want to lose any of it—her cute cottage, her friendly neighbors, a man who seemed determined to stand by her.

"Good," she said.

Jace turned towards the wood and Ava started up the lane to Willoughby Close. The cottages around the courtyard were dark, curtains drawn against the damp night, everything and everyone tucked up for bed. She walked slowly to number three, greeting a sleepy Zuzu with a quick cuddle as Ava stepped inside. *Home.* The word reverberated through her with a deep, satisfying thrum. Maybe this was starting to become her home.

Chapter Fourteen

"**R**EADY?"

Ava smiled brightly at Lady Stokeley, who gave her usual gimlet stare back.

"As ready I shall ever be with this sort of thing," she said grimly, and walked past Ava out to the waiting red Mini. It was another beautiful day, the damp chill of Saturday and Sunday blown away on a summery breeze. After spending nearly all of Sunday lounging in bed, recovering from her first honest evening's work at The Drowned Sailor, Ava felt energized enough for a drive to Oxford and a couple hours' worth of Lady Stokeley's company.

Her morning sickness had unfortunately worsened, leaving her unable to drink coffee or tea, or eat anything but toast or jacket potatoes, which she'd inexplicably developed a craving for. It was tiresome, all this nausea and craving, and yet there was something kind of wonderfully miraculous about it at the same time. Her baby was *growing*.

Ava slid into the driver's seat and glanced at Lady Stokeley in both sympathy and apprehension. She seemed more stoic than usual today, staring straight ahead, her arms folded.

"Everything all right?" Ava asked as she drove away from Willoughby Manor.

"Why do you ask?" Lady Stokeley turned to her, one thin, white eyebrow arched. "Do I seem less than my usually bubbly self?"

Ava burst out laughing, and was rewarded with the tiniest smile. "Lady Stokeley," she said after a moment when she'd caught her breath, "there are many wonderful words I would use to describe you, but bubbly is not one of them."

"No," she agreed musingly. "I never was bubbly, even as a young woman. That was more Violet."

"Violet?" The name rang a bell. "Your friend, the one who wrote?"

"I wrote her first, actually, but yes."

"Are you going to visit her, then?"

Lady Stokeley settled more deeply into the seat. "I don't know."

"I am happy to drive you."

"Yes, I recall your kind offer. Thank you." She looked out the window as if to end the conversation, but Ava wasn't going to be so quickly deterred.

"How long has it been since you've seen her?"

Lady Stokeley pressed her lips together, and Ava didn't think she'd answer. "Sixty years," she finally said, and Ava's jaw dropped.

"Sixty…"

"I never said we were close."

Ava pondered that as she turned on to the A40. "But you wrote her first," she said slowly, "after all this time." Lady Stokeley didn't reply and Ava continued silently ruminating. "Is there something," she finally asked, "that you wanted to say to her?"

Lady Stokeley shifted in her seat, her face still stubbornly aimed at the window. Ava sighed and kept driving.

They stayed in silence all the way to Oxford; Ava let Lady Stokeley out at the front and then went to park. By the time she'd caught up with her in the oncology ward, Lady Stokeley had already gone in to the examining room, leaving Ava in the reception area, flipping through *Countryfile* and glancing surreptitiously at the various patients sitting around the room. A woman without any hair had a three-year-old on her lap and was reading her a story. Clearly, Ava was hormonal, because the sight nearly brought her to tears.

Who was she, to complain about anything, when a woman had to bring her daughter to her chemo treatment?

"I'm done." Lady Stokeley stood before her, her expression set in resigned lines.

"Everything okay?" Ava asked lightly as they headed back downstairs. "Did they do any more tests?"

"No, just gave me the wretched pill, and now I get to feel sick for the next three days." Lady Stokeley shook her head, and Ava felt a pang of sympathy. Cancer was awful. Being eighty-six didn't make it any better at all.

It wasn't until they were back in the car, heading towards Wychwood-on-Lea, that Lady Stokeley spoke again, her tone abrupt.

"I'll go," she said, "if you're still willing to drive me."

Fighting her own brand of nausea and tiredness, it took Ava a moment to realize what she was saying. "You'll go? To Violet's, you mean?"

"Yes, she invited me on Friday, if you're free."

"Of course I'm free." Ava grinned. She was pleased Lady Stokeley was going out. "What are you going to wear?"

Lady Stokeley gave her a disdainful look. "What on earth does that matter?"

"Hey, it's a social occasion, and pardon me for saying so, but I think you want to look your best."

"My best?" Lady Stokeley pursed her lips. "Young lady, I have cancer. I'm hardly going to look my best."

"The best you can," Ava persisted. "Why not splash out? Go for a makeover?"

Lady Stokeley looked incredulous. "A *makeover?*"

"Why not?" Ava continued blithely, determined now. If Lady Stokeley couldn't splurge on something, take a chance, then who could? "I could do your hair, if you like. Get the curlers out."

For the first time Lady Stokeley looked tempted. "I did have such nice curls once," she mused. "This wretched chemotherapy has made my hair wispy and flat, but at least it hasn't all fallen out. That's a mercy, I suppose."

"Let's do it," Ava said. "I'll come a couple of hours early to help you get ready. It'll be fun." She waited, seeing the indecision on Lady Stokeley's face, and then she shrugged and nodded.

"Oh, very well. Violet will no doubt make an effort, so I should do the same." Her lips twitched. "I can't have her looking nicer than me, not after all these years."

"That's the spirit," Ava said as she wondered what the history between the two women was.

By Friday, Ava was seriously dragging, having spent every night at the pub, every morning retching into the toilet, and then driving Lady Stokeley to and fro. She looked terrible too, her hair long and limp instead of the usual bouncing waves and curls she spent considerable time and energy on looking effortless.

Now she really did look effortless, she acknowledged wryly as she slapped on some concealer over the purple circles under her eyes and called it a day makeup-wise. Her stomach was starting to rebel against the dry toast she'd made herself eat that morning.

She was eight weeks pregnant and she looked, Ava was forced to acknowledge, fat. Well, not fat precisely, but the tight clothes David had insisted on buying her did her no favors. She was going to need some new things, proper maternity clothes, which of course would cost money.

With a sigh, Ava pushed that worry out of her mind, for

another day. Today she wanted to focus on Lady Stokeley. She'd packed up all her makeup, all her sprays and gels and mousses, as well as her set of curlers. She lugged it all to the car and then drove up to Willoughby Manor, intent on giving Lady Stokeley some star treatment.

Lady Stokeley answered the door in her dressing gown, one Ava hadn't seen before. Gone was the neck-to-ankles quilted chenille and in place was a dressing gown reminiscent of a 1930s film star, all wispy ivory silk, edged in delicate lace.

"Wow," Ava said in appreciation, and Lady Stokeley raised pencil-thin eyebrows.

"I haven't dressed yet."

"I love the robe, though," Ava said. "Seriously vintage."

"I am seriously vintage," Lady Stokeley answered tartly, and turned to the stairs.

Ava just smiled. Lady Stokeley seemed pricklier than usual, and Ava suspected that was because she was nervous about meeting her old friend—or was it an old enemy? Something had gone down a long time ago.

"Right," she announced once they were up in Lady Stokeley's bedroom, "let's get to work. Have you chosen an outfit?"

"I am deciding between several," Lady Stokeley answered haughtily. "Perhaps you could offer your opinion?"

"I'd love to." Ava set down all her makeup and hairstyling kit and crossed to the window, now covered by fusty drapes of crimson velvet. "First, though, we need some sunlight."

"Argh!" Lady Stokeley threw an arm over her face as Ava pulled the drapes open with a screech of the curtain rings and a cloud of dust.

"What are you, a vampire? It's so gloomy up here." Ava put her hands on her hips. "And I can't do makeup in the dark. Natural light is crucial."

"Very well." Lady Stokeley lowered her arm. "It's just so *bright.*"

The sunlight flooding the bedroom highlighted all its threadbare shabbiness, the patina of dust on every surface. Ava pursed her lips. She wasn't much of one for housework, but even she yearned to give the room a thorough scrub and polish. She'd settle for giving Lady Stokeley one instead.

"Right, where are these outfits?"

"Hanging on the dressing room door."

Ava peered into the dressing room and could not keep from letting out a squeal of pure pleasure. "Lady Stokeley, these clothes. I'm in heaven."

Lady Stokeley came over to join her in the dressing room, which was bigger than Ava's bedroom. "I did have some nice things, didn't I?"

"You still do." Reverently Ava reached for a shift dress in orange waffle weave. "Is this Chanel?"

Lady Stokeley nodded. "From, oh, I'd say, 1965. I wore it to Olivia and Clive's wedding in Southampton. Dreadfully dull affair."

"It's amazing." Ava stroked the nubby material.

"Most people would turn their nose up at all this," Lady Stokeley remarked. "Say it's not in style any longer."

"Then they'd be crazy. Haute couture never goes out of style." Ava replaced the Chanel dress and glanced at another dress of rust-colored velvet, with a floppy bow and a shapeless bodice. Even that could be made to look fashionable. It was still quality.

"So the outfits you're thinking about," she said briskly. She turned to the three outfits Lady Stokeley had hung on the door. The first was a lavender skirt with a deeper mauve sweater, the kind of thing Ava saw her in every day. "No," she said decisively, and put it aside.

Lady Stokeley looked disgruntled. "That's cashmere, you know."

"And it's boring. This is a special occasion, isn't it? Don't you want to look like you made an effort?" Unlike Ava herself. She was still feeling queasy and she had a feeling she hadn't rubbed in the concealer under her eyes, just left it in beige streaks.

"Yes," Lady Stokeley answered after a moment. "But not too much of an effort."

"Of course." Ava nodded knowingly. "I get you. Trust me, you will not look you've been trying too hard. But we're losing the twin sets." She rifled through the closet until she found the kind of thing she was looking for—a bright red sheath dress that looked to be about fifty years old but was still classic, simple linen cut in starkly beautiful lines. "This is what I'm talking about."

A funny look came over Lady Stokeley's face. "I never actually wore that dress."

"You didn't?" Ava looked up in surprise, sensing a story. "Why not?"

"Gerald didn't like me in red. He thought it was too bold for a woman of my station."

"Ah." Ava suppressed the urge to say something cutting about Lady Stokeley's dead husband. "Men are funny that way."

"Irritating," Lady Stokeley replied after a moment. "I was always quite bold."

Ava laughed and then dared to hold out the dress. "Well?" Lady Stokeley stared at it for a moment, and in her wrinkled face Ava saw a host of conflicting emotions— sadness and longing and realization that all those dresses, all those years, were a thing of the past. Even more reason to make today count.

"Oh, very well," Lady Stokeley said on a sigh, as if everything had become rather tedious, and she reached for the dress.

"Did you have a happy marriage?" Ava asked impulsively as Lady Stokeley went into the dressing room to change and she began to set up all her products and potions.

"Why do you young women always ask that?" Lady

Stokeley demanded from the depths of the dressing room. "As if a thing is happy or it isn't. Marriage, at least in my day, was far more complex than that."

"Mine too," Ava said after a pause.

If someone asked her the same question about her own marriage, she didn't know how she'd answer.

"Exactly." Lady Stokeley emerged from the dressing room, brilliant in red.

"That looks fantastic," Ava said firmly.

"It's too big and you know it." Lady Stokeley plucked at the fabric. "I'm swimming in it."

"We'll use a belt," Ava answered. "Make it even more stylish. You must have some belts?"

Lady Stokeley nodded to a drawer and Ava opened it to find at least two dozen belts of varying widths and materials, from thin patent leather to gold chain links that would have been high fashion in the 1970s.

"Oh, Lady Stokeley." She sighed. "You make me very happy."

Lady Stokeley let out a dry rustle of laughter at that, and Ava selected a wide black leather belt with a crocodile-skin pattern.

"So why do you like vintage clothing so much?" she asked when Ava had gently steered her to the powder puff stool.

"With a figure like mine? I'm more Marilyn Monroe than Kate Moss, you know? Vintage suits me better."

"I've only heard of the first, but I gather what you mean." Lady Stokeley answered dryly. "I was the opposite. Twiggy had nothing on me."

"I bet you looked amazing, and you still will." Ava angled the mirror away from her. "No peeking until I'm done."

"If you make me look like some painted woman, I will be quite put out." Lady Stokeley warned her. "My father always said makeup was a shallow girl's sport."

"And I say there are no ugly women, only lazy ones," Ava quoted right back at her. "Why not make the most of what you have? We're not talking liposuction and chin lifts here."

Lady Stokeley pursed her lips, and Ava suspected she was hiding her smile. Good. She wanted Lady Stokeley to enjoy today. Ava knew she was.

"So we'll start with some primer," she said, and using the tips of her fingers, she gently worked the clear gel into Lady Stokeley's skin. It felt like creased tissue paper, and yet was surprisingly soft.

Lady Stokeley tensed underneath Ava's hands, but after a few careful strokes she started to relax, and then she let out a little sigh.

"Do you know, it has been so very long since I've been touched."

Ava had to blink back tears at that. She missed being touched, and it had been less than two months. She decided to take her time and let Lady Stokeley enjoy the experience. A makeover didn't have to be something to be endured.

"And now some foundation, nothing too heavy," she murmured.

Lady Stokeley's pale skin was a far cry from her own golden complexion, and so she'd splurged on some appropriately toned foundation from Debenhams in Witney, and she was gratified now to see she'd got the shade right.

She brushed it in slowly, taking time with each stroke, while Lady Stokeley waited, her eyes closed, her face tilted up like a baby bird's accepting nourishment from its winged mama.

"So," she said after a moment, when Ava had finished with the foundation and was now moving on to her more exciting bag of tricks, "was your marriage happy, by your own definition?"

Ava paused. This was the first time Lady Stokeley had asked her a genuine question and seemed interested in the answer, and she wanted to take her time with it, just like with the makeup.

"I don't know," she said slowly. "I thought we were happy enough at the time. I don't remember feeling actively unhappy. But…" Carefully, she arranged the tubes of lipsticks and cases of eye shadow. "Since he's died, I've started to wonder. Things that seemed straightforward at the time suddenly feel complicated."

"Ah, yes." Lady Stokeley nodded, her eyes still closed. "And he's not around for you to demand answers. Clarification isn't possible, so you're left with endless wondering."

And didn't that sound grim. What did Lady Stokeley wonder about? What did Ava? If David were here, what would she ask him? The obvious question was, why the hell did you only leave me ten thousand pounds, the same amount as the housekeeper? The second was, did you really love me at all?

Suddenly Ava had a lump in her throat. Damn these hormones.

"What," she asked a bit thickly, trying to desperately to dissolve that lump, "would you ask Gerald?"

Lady Stokeley was silent for a long moment. Ava picked out an eye shadow and lipstick.

"I'd ask him," she finally said, "why he really didn't like me in red." She paused, her lips pursed. "And then I might ask him, you knew what I was like when you married me. Why did you want me to change?"

"That," Ava said quietly, "is a very good question."

Lady Stokeley sighed. "Is it? I think we all want the people we love to change. We want them to become better versions of themselves even while we stagnate. It's really most vexing."

"Yes, especially when they don't want to change at all." The trouble was, she didn't think David had wanted her to change. Quite the opposite. She suspected he'd wanted to put her in a box and keep her there. And that box was pretty darn small.

But, like Lady Stokeley said, Ava couldn't ask for clarification and she didn't want to become stuck in the cobwebs of the past, not when she had so much to hope for. To try for.

"Pucker up," she told Lady Stokeley, deciding they'd both had enough emoting. "I'm going to do your lipstick."

Chapter Fifteen

"THIS WAS A mistake."

Lady Stokeley peered in the rearview mirror of Ava's Mini as she dabbed at her very tastefully done lips. A Touch of Lilac, the color had been called, and Ava thought it suited Lady Stokeley perfectly.

"Don't you dare." She admonished as she got in the driver's seat. She'd spent well over an hour getting Lady Stokeley ready, and Ava had no desire to see her ruin all of Ava's hard work before they'd even set off. "Do you think I'd actually do you up like a tart?"

Lady Stokeley gave her a narrowed look and Ava laughed. "I may be many things," she said, "but one of them is classy." Although her type of classy wasn't necessarily Lady Stokeley's. Ava's brand of classy had always come with a healthy dose of sex appeal, because she couldn't escape her looks or bra size for that matter, and that was what men wanted. And since she was fourteen that was all she'd cared about, which was a rather depressing thought.

"The lipstick looks nice," she persisted, because Lady

Stokeley was still looking doubtful. "And the curls."

With a small smile, Lady Stokeley patted the loose curls Ava had spent a tense hour on. "I do like my hair." She tucked her handkerchief back in her sleeve with a little sigh. "But I wonder if this entire venture is a mistake."

"Don't you want to see old Violet?" Ava asked as she started down the drive. "See what she's been up to? Whether she looks as good as you?"

"She won't, unless she's had her teeth fixed."

Ava laughed again. "Then what do you have to worry about?" She paused. "Unless that's not what you want?" After all these years, what *did* Lady Stokeley want from a woman she hadn't seen in sixty years? Somehow Ava doubted it was something as petty as making sure she still looked better, although admittedly that never hurt.

"I want to ask her to forgive me," Lady Stokeley said quietly, and then broke the serious moment by letting out a dry laugh. "That's what happens when you get old and think about death. You want to make things right, as best as you can. It's all very melodramatic, especially considering how small and petty things can be."

"What do you mean?"

Lady Stokeley gazed out at the rolling green of Wychwood-on-Lea, her expression faraway. "I stole Violet's beau, as they said in my day," she said. "Her fellow, her fiancé, what have you." She frowned, her gaze distant. "My husband."

"You mean Gerald?" Ava jerked round in surprise before turning back to face the road. She'd seen Lady Stokeley's wedding photograph in her bedroom, a black and white of two stiff, unsmiling figures, Gerald in some kind of military uniform, not quite looking at the camera.

"Yes, Gerald. Lord Stokeley to you."

"Sorry," Ava murmured.

Lady Stokeley sighed. "He'd asked Violet to marry him at a house party one summer. It was an impetuous decision, but then that's the sort of man he was. Always being taken with some idea or another, and he hated being told he was wrong, but then what man likes it?"

"None I know."

"Quite. In any case, Violet knew I'd fancied him a bit, and that was the reason she went after him. We were best friends once, but it wasn't a very nice kind of friendship. Always trying to outdo one another." She shook her head, lost in reminiscence. "What sad little girls we were."

"And so what happened? Gerald—Lord Stokeley— proposed to Violet, and then…?"

"She gloated all weekend how she'd snagged him. Because," Lady Stokeley explained, "he was rather a good catch."

"I'm sure."

"She was so smug about it! Parading around, putting her head on his shoulder…"

"Scandalous," Ava murmured.

"It was, actually. I can only imagine what goes on today, but Violet was… well, she was a silly little girl. And so was I. I determined I'd get Gerald for myself, whether I really wanted him or not."

Intrigued, Ava asked, "But did you want him?"

"That is neither here nor there," Lady Stokeley said frostily. "We married, and I respected my vows. But for the rest of that weekend I did everything I could to ensnare him. It might seem incredible now, but I could be quite charming when I chose."

"I don't find that incredible at all," Ava said sincerely.

There was no denying Lady Stokeley had a certain charismatic presence, even when she was trying to be her most off-putting. One couldn't help but listen and admire.

"And so you got your man," Ava stated.

"Violet's man." Lady Stokeley sighed. "After that first flush of victory, I really felt quite badly about it."

And how, Ava wondered, had she felt about Gerald? She wasn't brave enough to ask.

"But in any case, Violet and Gerald would have been disaster," Lady Stokeley said. "He needed a firm hand without realizing that's what he had and she was a flibbertigibbet if there ever was one. Still. I wish… I wish I'd behaved differently, I suppose."

"That's understandable."

All the conversation seemed to have exhausted Lady Stokeley and she lay her head back against the seat and closed her eyes.

Ava glanced at the sat nav; she needed to follow narrow lane after narrow lane lined with hedgerows to their destination, the village of Little Waring. It was only thirty miles away but on these roads, it would take well over an hour. And her stomach was feeling queasy and she hadn't brought snacks.

"So do you know what happened to Violet?" she asked after a few moments. "Did she ever marry?"

"Oh, yes. I don't know how *happy* she was." Lady Stokeley gave Ava a look filled with irony. "He died a few years ago. I wasn't able to go to the funeral."

"And so now you're going to tell Violet you're sorry about stealing Gerald all those years ago?"

"I admit the gesture might seem pointless and trite after so many years." Lady Stokeley was silent for a moment. "But it still needs to be made, regardless," she continued. "For my sake as much as Violet's. These old hurts, petty as they might have been, still have the power to wound. And then to fester." She sighed. "And now that is quite enough melodrama for now."

"If Violet is the only person who needs your forgiveness," Ava said, "I think you're in pretty good shape."

"Well, I didn't say that." Lady Stokeley's mouth turned as wrinkled as a prune. "But it shall suffice for now."

They drove in silence until they reached Little Waring, and Ava trawled the hamlet's high street until she found

Hawthorn Cottage, a sprawling, comfortable house of golden Cotswold stone that looked as if it had seen better days, but was no less pleasant for it.

"Well." Ava parked in the drive and glanced uncertainly at the front door with the weed-choked planters on either side. "Do you want me to come in with you?"

"No, thank you," Lady Stokeley said with dignity, and got out of the car.

Ava watched covertly as she knocked on the front door, standing there looking, Ava didn't mind admitting, pretty amazing in her bright red dress.

What would this reconciliation hold for her and her friend? Would they fall into each other's arms, laughing and crying? Would they be all stiff upper lip, typical English aristocracy, even after all this time?

The door opened and a woman stood there, hunched over, wearing what looked like the prerequisite tweed and twinset for any woman of a certain age and class. They spoke, and then the woman moved aside and Lady Stokeley went into the house. The door closed, and that was that.

In the stillness of a summer's afternoon, Ava felt assailed by a sudden pang of loneliness and regret. If she could make up with anyone the way Lady Stokeley was trying to do, who would it be? Dreadful Simon and Emma? Her mother? Her father? She swallowed hard and pushed such thoughts away. She had too many people, far more than Lady Stokeley seemed to have, to forgive.

Ava sighed and slid out her phone. No service. Wonderful. She gazed outside at the tangled garden and the fields beyond, hazy and touched with gold under a summer sky. It was a beautiful, pastoral scene, with nothing, not even the distant sound of a car, to mar its sleepy perfection.

Sitting there with the sun shining down she started to doze a little. Vague thoughts drifted through her mind, worries about money and work and the baby nestled inside her that she couldn't seem to mind so much when the sun was shining and she felt so sleepy.

And then, somehow, she'd fallen asleep and right into a dream about Jace. The details were vague—were they in that barn where the furniture had been kept, or the little sitting room of his house? It didn't matter, because the dream was about him. She could smell the wood-and-leather scent of his; she could feel the hard wall of his chest. It was a vague dream, and embarrassingly erotic, no more than hazy images and feelings, hands and lips, sliding skin, swirls of pleasure deep down, a montage of sensation and yet through it all she knew, even in the dream, that it was Jace. *Jace.*

She woke up with a start, Lady Stokeley tapping on the window, Ava's heart racing, her blood still high, memories rushing through her, making her feel boneless and fuzzy-headed. Plus the car was boiling hot.

"Hello?" Lady Stokeley demanded, and Ava realized the passenger door was locked. Still feeling confused she reached over and unlocked it and then sat back against the seat, her heart thudding, her whole body flushed. How was she ever going to look Jace in the eye again?

"How was it?" she asked as Lady Stokeley got rather grumpily in the car. Had she been waiting long? Ava had a horrible image of her passed out in the front seat, very clearly in the throes of a sexy dream. Damn these pregnancy hormones.

"It wasn't what I expected," Lady Stokeley said after a moment. Ava glanced back at the door of the cottage, now closed, and then started the car.

They drove in silence for a while, Lady Stokeley lost in thought and Ava concentrating on the narrow road as well as trying to forget that dream forever. The trouble was, it was rather hard to forget. Dream Jace had been a very good kisser. Slow, thorough, knowing. Just the memory of it, imagined as it had been, made her shift in her seat.

"She didn't remember," Lady Stokeley said abruptly.

Ava glanced at her in surprise before hurriedly turning back to look at the road. "She didn't remember? You mean…"

"I mean, she didn't *remember*. She doesn't remember much of anything. Dementia." Lady Stokeley pressed trembling lips together. "At times she forgot who I was."

"Oh, Lady Stokeley…"

Lady Stokeley harrumphed, moving past that one split second of vulnerability. "You might as well call me Dorothy at this point."

"How about Dot?" Ava teased gently.

"No, thank you. Dorothy will suffice." Lady Stokeley straightened, seeming to gather her composure around her the way she would a cloak or a shawl. "It's to be expected, I suppose. Violet was always absent-minded."

Ava didn't think that necessarily had anything to do with the genetics of dementia, but now was not the time to debate the point. "That must have been difficult," she said after a pause. "But at least you did what you needed to do. To apologize. You did say it was for your sake as much as hers."

Lady Stokeley—Dorothy—shook her head. "I should have done it before, when there was *time*. When she was well in her mind. Years or even decades before." She let out a choked sound, and then closed her eyes briefly, looking so old and sad Ava's heart ached. "When you're young, even when you're middle-aged, you think you have so much time. You can put things off, you can wait. And you think such petty little problems are so very important. Pride!" She made a sound of disgust. "You cling to it, because it feels like the only thing you have. But then… to lose it…" She opened her eyes, her face drawn into stark, sad lines. "Even now, when I know how little I have left to lose, I can't bear that."

Ava was silent, moved by Lady Stokeley's lament. She sensed they weren't just talking about Violet anymore. But what—or who—was Lady Stokeley talking about? What others regrets did she have? And did she dare press?

"I can understand wanting to hold onto your pride," she

said after a moment. "It's like your dignity, isn't it? Without it..." she shrugged. "Sometimes it feels like the only thing that can't be taken away from you."

Lady Stokeley nodded slowly. "And what," she asked after a moment, "was taken away from you, Ava?"

It was the first time she'd said Ava's name, and it made her reply honestly. "A lot of things, at different times and in different ways." And here came the tears again, thickening in her throat, stinging her lids. She needed to get a grip. "It doesn't matter. We were talking about you."

"I've had quite enough of talking about me."

"Likewise."

Lady Stokeley let out one of her raspy laughs. "Poor Violet," she said after a sigh. "She has a full-time carer with her now. At least I've been spared that so far."

Ava knew Lady Stokeley had someone who came in a few times a week to help, but she still managed to retain most of her independence. And yet for how long? The prospect of Lady Stokeley losing what independence she had made Ava feel despondent. Was life nothing more than a slow march to death, the gradual but inevitable loss of everything, including dignity and pride? Was this what she was bringing her baby into?

"Never mind," Lady Stokeley said after a moment. "There's no point being grim about it. And at least I looked good." She made a harrumphing noise and added, "For my age, anyway."

"You look amazing," Ava said, and then some impish but necessary impulse made her ask, "Why don't we put the top down?"

Lady Stokeley gave her one of her regal looks. "Is that some sort of euphemism?"

Ava laughed. "It could be, I suppose, but I meant it literally. It's a beautiful day. Why don't we put the top down of the car and enjoy the sunshine?" Enjoy life, while they both had it. It suddenly felt important, to take this moment, this sunny afternoon of blue sky and butterflies, and enjoy it. Squeeze every drop of pleasure out of it if they could.

Lady Stokeley glanced askance at the roof, and Ava braced herself for one of her stunning setdowns. *Young lady, why would I engage in something so undignified? You may think such behavior appropriate but, I assure you, I do not.*

Then Lady Stokeley gave a little shrug of her bony shoulders. "It will ruin my curls, but why not?"

Ava laughed again and pulled the car over to a passing point. "That's why you have this," she said, and fished one of her vintage silk scarves out of her bag. "I carry them for just such emergencies."

"What about your hair?"

"I didn't go to the beauty parlor today," Ava quipped. "I'll manage."

"Very well."

Lady Stokeley tied the scarf under her chin, arranging it carefully over her curls, while Ava got out of the car and took the top down. Moments later she was revving the engine, eyebrows raised in Lady Stokeley's direction.

"Ready to do a Thelma and Louise?" she asked, although perhaps that wasn't the best analogy. She had no intention of driving off a cliff, not that there was one in the Cotswolds.

"Now that is a euphemism I do not appreciate," Lady Stokeley said.

"Good thing," Ava murmured, and pulled back onto the road.

The breeze ruffled their hair and the sun kissed their faces as Ava drove down the narrow lanes, birds twittering in the hedgerows, butterflies flitting among the blossoms, and the sky high and hazy-blue above. It was a perfect English summer's afternoon, and Ava took a deep breath of sweet, warm air, letting it buoy her lungs and fill her with hope. Fill them both with hope.

Lady Stokeley tilted her face to the sky, smiling faintly, her eyes closed. "This is lovely," she murmured.

It *was* lovely, with the sun and sky and the rippling breeze, peaceful and perfect, and then Ava crested a hill a little too fast and her stomach did one of those roller coaster free falls, and she nearly lost what little breakfast she'd eaten.

Lady Stokeley's eyes flew open and she let out a gasp of shock, clutching at her chest.

"Sorry," Ava said, hoping she hadn't given her charge a heart attack. "That was a bit fast."

She slowed down and Lady Stokeley turned to her with

her eyebrows raised. "If we're going to do the thing properly..." she said and it took Ava a moment to realize what she
meant.

"You want to go fast?"

Lady Stokeley gave a regal nod and, with a laugh that
carried away on the breeze, Ava revved the engine once more.

Chapter Sixteen

THE NEXT TWO weeks passed in a blur of exhaustion, nausea, and work. Six hours every night at the pub was taking its toll, with Ava's aching feet, endless fatigue, and also the unpleasant side effect of always smelling like beer.

She also felt as if she were out of sync with everyone around her, coming home late and then sleeping in. After letting Zuzu out, she'd stumble back to bed and sleep until she had to take Lady Stokeley to chemo, and then often she'd have a nap afterwards, until she'd crawl out of bed to eat something and go to work.

The result was she barely saw anyone besides Lady Stokeley, which she supposed was a semi-good thing, since she was avoiding telling Ellie or Harriet about her pregnancy, and as for Jace… That dream still possessed the power to scorch her cheeks, especially because she'd had a few more, and these had been even more vivid. She had a horrible feeling Jace was the kind of man who would be able to tell she'd had sexy dreams about him from just looking at her face.

Still, it felt lonely, sleeping, working, and driving to the hospital. After that sunny afternoon, driving with the top down, Lady Stokeley had retreated into her usually chilly self, and Ava's attempts to brighten her life a little bit, whether it was buying some proper high quality tea or dusting her bedroom, seemed unappreciated if not downright resented.

Early one Wednesday evening, as Ava contemplated what to choke down for dinner, a knock sounded at her front door. Persistent, which meant probably Ellie. But when she opened it, she saw it was Harriet, smiling brightly. Ava had noticed that Richard had moved permanently into number two, and both he and Harriet, when she glimpsed them from afar, seemed pretty loved up. And she was not going to feel envious about that at all.

"Hey."

"You look terrible."

Ava let out a wry laugh. "Thanks for the honesty."

"Sorry, it's just you're usually so glamorous." Harriet frowned. "Are you okay?"

Ava stepped aside to let her inside. She could bumble her way through some lame excuse about having a summer cold, but Harriet had seen that red folder, after all.

"I think you know why I look like this," she said on a sigh, and Harriet, bless her, didn't pretend to misunderstand.

"I didn't want to say anything…"

"Well. I'll say it first. I'm up the duff." She went back to the fridge, which she'd left open in contemplation of its unappealing contents, and closed the door. "Due February seventeenth."

Harriet regarded her cautiously. "This is a good thing…"

"Yes," Ava said, a little surprised by how firm she sounded. How certain. Because, in the fearful quiet of her own mind, she didn't feel certain at all. "Yes, it is. But I'm feeling rather wretched at the moment, which is surprising because…" She stopped, appalled at what she'd been about to say. *Because I wasn't the last time I was pregnant.* No way was she going into all that.

"Because…" Harriet prompted, and Ava just shook her head.

"I don't know, I just didn't expect it."

"Is it morning sickness?" Harriet asked after a moment, when Ava clearly wasn't going to offer any more information. "Because ginger tea can help. Or eating protein first thing, and snacking often…"

Ava nodded. She'd read the same tips online, and if she had the energy, she'd probably try one of them. "Thanks."

"This is probably the last thing you feel like doing, but the Summer Strawberry Tea is this Saturday afternoon at Olivia's tearoom."

"Oh, right, of course." Back on the day of the fete, Harriet had told her about the grand reopening of the tearoom that she was coordinating. It was why Ava had taken over chemo duty with Lady Stokeley.

"Anyway, if you want to go…"

Belatedly, Ava noticed how uncertain Harriet looked, and she realized this tearoom thing had to be a big deal. She'd been working as a dinner lady for the last few months, and doing event planning was a big step up. "I'd love to go," Ava said as warmly as she could. This whole having friends thing still felt new and awkward, but at least she was trying. "Thanks."

"Okay. Fab. And let me know if you need anything... or I can help? I've got bins of baby clothes still..."

"Those would be helpful," Ava answered. "Eventually." She couldn't quite imagine needing baby clothes yet, or nappies, or a cot, or any of that paraphernalia. Could not imagine that in less than seven months she would actually have a baby in her arms. A *child.* A ripple of emotion went through her, and she didn't know whether it was excitement or terror.

"Actually," she said impulsively, "I could really use some maternity clothes. I'm only ten weeks along but these clothes were tight already." She plucked at the t-shirt that she feared made her look like a pole dancer.

Harriet smiled and nodded. "I'm sure I have some in storage." She paused. "They might not be your style..."

Ava suppressed a grimace. "I think I'm ready to reinvent my style," she said. "At least a little."

She'd always liked dressing sexily but, after five years of David buying her clothes, she thought she might branch out a little, especially considering she'd soon be sporting a baby bump.

After Harriet had gone—she and Richard were taking the children out for a midweek pizza in Chipping Norton—Ava decided to be sensible for once and make herself a proper meal. She plonked a pot of water on the stovetop for pasta and then went to switch on the gas. A click and then nothing. No blue spark, no whoosh of flame under the pot. Nothing but the soft hiss of gas, and the ensuing odor.

Ava frowned and tried again, and then turned the burner off. She switched the stove off at the outlet and then on again, and tried it all over again, but nothing. She tried every burner and when none of them worked she kicked the stove for good measure, only hurting her toe and not, of course, the inanimate object of her annoyance.

And she still smelled gas.

A flare of alarm went through her. She'd read stories of people dying in their beds thanks to a dodgy stove and the soft, malevolent hiss of gas. Hurriedly she went over to the French windows and threw them open to the damp and gray early evening.

But what if she turned on a light and the spark caused an explosion? She thought she'd read about that somewhere. There was an emergency helpline for this sort of thing, wasn't there?

Ava did a hurried internet search on her tablet and then went to call the number… but she had no reception on her mobile. Swearing under her breath, she called for Zuzu and then went outside, holding her phone up in desperate search of a signal.

She glanced around the courtyard and saw that both numbers one and two looked empty. Ellie and Abby were in Oxford with Oliver, and Harriet had been about to go out for pizza with her family. The lonely stillness of the close felt like a sucker punch to the gut, and left her with one unwelcome alternative. She was going to have to ask for Jace's help.

Clipping on Zuzu's lead, Ava headed grimly towards the path in the wood that led to the old gatekeeper's cottage. The ground squelched under her feet and the air in the wood smelled fetid with wet undergrowth. The sky was dank and gray, and even though sunset was still hours off it felt dark and unwelcoming in the wood.

She came into the clearing with a breath of relief, even though she wasn't looking forward to seeing Jace. No, that was a lie. She *was* looking forward to seeing him and that was the problem. After those crazy dreams she'd had, it was going to be even harder to stay just friends.

Not, she reminded herself, that Jace wanted anything else from her anymore. He might have asked her out on a date and come over all protective at the pub that first night, but he'd been keeping his distance these last few weeks, something Ava realized now actually hurt a little.

Well, she'd keep it businesslike. She had a problem with her rental and he was the caretaker that had to sort it out. With that thought foremost in her mind, she rapped smartly on the door.

Jace opened it after a few seconds, looking rumpled and sexy and, yes, shirtless.

Ava glared at him. "Do you ever wear a shirt?"

"I just got back from work," he answered, laughter in his voice. "Sweaty work. Do you always come to the door when I'm changing?"

"It would seem I do."

He arched an eyebrow, waiting, and Ava's brain chose that unfortunate moment to remind her of the dream she'd had just a few nights ago. A dream that had involved his impressively muscled chest. She forced her gaze not to stray downwards, and gave him a hard stare instead. At his face.

"Who's going to blink first?" Jace asked softly. He knew exactly what was going on.

"I can't turn my cooker on," Ava said abruptly. "And there's a smell of gas."

Jace dropped the flirt instantly. "Did you ring the emergency service?"

"I couldn't get any reception." Ava held up her phone which still was registering no bars.

"Okay, I'll ring, and then I'll check it out. Come inside."

Ava stepped into the narrow hallway while Jace dialed the emergency number on his phone and put a shirt on at the same time. Skills.

"They'll be out in about half an hour," he said after he'd explained the situation to whoever had answered the phone.

"I'll go have a look."

"What if it's dangerous?" Ava asked, and then wished she didn't sound quite so much like a wilting female.

"I'm not stupid," Jace answered with a smile. "I won't go in if it seems dangerous."

Which was such a man thing to say, but whatever. Ava stood in the doorway of the cottage, Zuzu clutched to her chest, and watched Jace stride through the woods and then she turned back into the house.

She was alone in Jace's home. It occurred to her she could do some rather serious snooping, and she was more than a little tempted. Okay, she was incredibly tempted. Jace was, with his laughing looks and slow smile, quite the enigma. A delicious enigma, as her dreams testified, but still… a man of mystery and someone Ava was curious about.

She contented herself with having a quick prowl around the downstairs, which didn't offer up all that much information. The small kitchen in the back of the cottage was neat, with a single mug and bowl drying in the drainer next to the sink. A furtive glance in the cupboards and fridge revealed the expected—cereal, packets of pasta, milk, beer.

The small sitting room she'd been in the last time she'd been here looked the same, two worn sofas on either side of a small fireplace. There was a decided lack of personal mementoes—no books, no photos, no post, even. The only thing of interest was a battered-looking acoustic guitar propped in the corner. Jace probably played soulful ballads when he was sitting here on his own. Just another reason to fall in love with him.

Whoa. She had not just thought that.

Restless, Ava left the sitting room and poked her head in the small room on the other side of the front hallway. It looked to have once been a dining room, judging from the built-in glass cabinets, but was now filled with cardboard boxes. Here were the personal mementoes. Why hadn't Jace unpacked? How long had he been living here for?

None the wiser, she went back to the sitting room and sat on the sofa, annoyed with herself. What had she been looking for, anyway? A dead body crammed in a cupboard? Some photo or knickknack that would completely explain who Jace was and tell her what he was hiding?

Because he *was* hiding something. She knew it, because she was hiding something too. She recognized the signs—the light tone, the deliberate evasiveness. But what was it?

She waited for another half hour, Zuzu sprawled on her lap, for Jace to return. Her stomach growled and surged with nausea and she felt a little lightheaded. She still hadn't eaten anything. At least she didn't have to work tonight. The thought brought a little comfort as she tucked her feet up under her and wondered if she should walk back to her cottage, all the while knowing she wouldn't.

Then the door opened and Zuzu jumped off her lap with a frenzy of excited barking. A few seconds later, Jace appeared in the doorway of the sitting room.

"It's sorted," he said. "The cooker's faulty, apparently, and the gas valve doesn't shut off properly. I'm surprised it hasn't been an issue for you sooner."

That might have been because she hadn't actually used the cooker all that much, or even at all. She'd always been a microwave kind of girl. Jace, typically, saw all that in her face and he grinned.

"First time you used the cooker?"

"Maybe."

"Well, it needs to be replaced now, so you'll have to wait awhile to have another go."

"Okay." She paused, unsure how to navigate this moment.

Jace wasn't being particularly chatty, and there seemed no real reason to stay, except... she was lonely. And the thought of spending the rest of the evening alone in her cottage with nothing but Netflix for company made her die a little inside.

Still Jace said nothing, made no offer, and so slowly Ava uncurled herself from the sofa. "I suppose I should get going."

No protest, no suggestion of staying awhile. Disappointment curdled like sour milk in her stomach, and speaking of sour, a sudden surge of bile rose in Ava's throat as she struggled up from the sofa, fighting both nausea and dizziness.

"Ava…"

She sank back onto the sofa with a groan, and then rested her head on her knees as the world swam around her and her stomach continued to rebel. "Sorry," she managed through lips that suddenly felt numb. "I think… I think I'm going to be sick."

To his credit, Jace didn't swear or exclaim or, it seemed, so much as draw a breath. He simply left the room, returning moments later with a metal mixing bowl that he placed on the floor beneath her.

Ava tried to mutter a thank you, but she didn't get that far because her stomach surged again and then she was heaving into the bowl, although there was nothing to heave, because she hadn't eaten anything for hours. Still she retched as her stomach continued to contract.

Stupidly, tears came to her eyes even though she didn't want to cry. She didn't even feel sad, not really. It was just so… so *horrible,* sitting here doubled over, her head hanging down, making the most awful noises while she wished she could have a break from her body. It was so humiliating.

Eventually she stopped and Jace crouched down to press a glass of water into her hands.

"Thank you," Ava whispered.

"You didn't bring up much." He observed kindly.

"I didn't have much to bring up," she said, and took a sip of water. No matter that there had been nothing in her stomach, the taste in her mouth was still vile. "Sorry. That was rather disgusting."

"It didn't bother me."

Ava wondered how he could be so nice. It wasn't fair. It made her like him too much.

And just what was the problem with that?

"Do you want something to eat?" Jace asked. "Since your seemingly empty stomach is even emptier?" Ava let out an uncertain laugh and he continued, "Plus I have this notion that pregnant women need to eat."

"It's hard to eat when you feel like hurling half the time."

Concern roughened his voice as he asked, "Have you been feeling this bad for a while?"

"A few weeks. I haven't seen you," she added, and realized it sounded like an accusation.

Well, perhaps it was.

Jace didn't answer for a moment and Ava steeled herself to lift her head and look at something other than the bowl she'd just retched into.

"I thought I'd give you some space," he said, shifting where he stood. "You did tell me to back off, remember."

"I also told you I needed a friend," Ava reminded him, aware she sounded needy and possibly, *probably* pathetic. But darn it, she'd missed him. Against all her efforts and resolutions, she'd started to depend on him a little bit.

"You did," Jace agreed. He raked a hand through his hair and then dropped it, which for Jace was as close to fidgeting as he probably ever got, and Ava had the feeling he wanted to say something but was choosing not to. "Let me make you something to eat. I've got a fairly limited repertoire, I'm afraid. Scrambled eggs or plain pasta."

The mention of food usually made Ava grimace, but scrambled eggs miraculously hit some culinary sweet spot. "Eggs, please," she said, and she realized she was kind of starving.

"Great." He reached down for the bowl, and Ava let out a squeak of protest because even though there hadn't been anything in her stomach the bowl was no longer clean.

"Trust me, I've seen worse," Jace said, and on weak legs Ava followed him into the little kitchen. "Here." Jace yanked a chair from under the small, rickety table and pushed it towards her. "Stay awhile."

"Okay." She sank into the chair.

Even though she'd just been sitting she still felt tired. Overwhelmingly exhausted, really.

"So you've been poorly," he said, a statement, and Ava nodded.

"Yeah, the constant nausea pretty much sucks. I didn't have that last time."

It was a testament to her weakened state that she didn't even realize what she'd said until she saw Jace had gone still, a couple of eggs held in one hand, as he looked at her without expression, his face so darn neutral and yet somehow saying so much. The penny dropped with an almighty thud. Ava could think of no way to backtrack.

"Umm…" she said, uselessly, and Jace cracked the eggs one-handed into a bowl.

"You don't have to tell me," he said, his voice as neutral as his expression. "You don't have to tell me anything."

And yet, amazingly, strangely, Ava wanted to tell him at least some of it. Tell someone and, yes, tell *Jace*.

She took a deep breath. "I was sixteen," she said quietly, and Jace turned back to look at her, a flash of sympathy in those whiskey eyes.

"Go on," he said.

Chapter Seventeen

WHAT NOW? AVA sat in silence, trying to figure out a way forward, if there even was one. Thankfully, Jace didn't seem to be in any hurry for her to spill her guts; he turned back to the counter and started whisking the eggs in the bowl.

"My mother left when I was fourteen," Ava blurted, and then gulped.

She'd been going to talk just about her pregnancy. Not her mother. Not the gaping grief that still, after all these years, felt like a bullet hole in her chest when she let herself think about it, which was almost never.

Why couldn't she get over it? Why couldn't she bloody well move on? She wanted to. She'd been trying for years. Yet here she was, thirty-five years old, and still trying not to cry because her mummy hadn't loved her enough to stay.

"Left," Jace said, stirring the eggs. It was both a statement and a question, and spoken in a typically neutral voice.

"Yes, left." Ava stopped, struggling to figure out how to clamber of the hole she'd just plunged herself into.

She didn't want to talk about her mother, or her father, for that matter. She'd just been going to say *I had a baby when I was a teenager* and leave it at that.

Wasn't she?

Jace slid her a quietly speculative—and far too under-standing—glance as he poured the eggs into the frying pan. "Why did she leave? Do you know?"

"Sort of." It was a question that had looped endlessly through her mind, trying to find answers, reasons, excuses. Something that made it make sense, other than that her mother hadn't cared anymore. "She said she was tired."

Jace's eyebrows rose at that. "Tired?"

"She left a note while I was at school and my dad was at work. All it said was 'I'm tired'. Dad thought she might be thinking of killing herself, and so we rang the police and for a few days it was a big drama." Those days felt like a blur, her father grim and white-faced, policemen pawing through their house and then trawling through Smestow Brook looking for a body.

"But she hadn't?"

"No, she'd gone off to Stockport and kipped with a friend." Ava shook her head, remembering with a rush of guilt the unexpected feeling of disappointment she'd had when they'd found out where her mother was—almost as if she would have preferred her mother to have died than deserted. "She phoned us after a few days to say she wasn't coming back anytime soon."

Jace nodded slowly, as unfazed as ever. The tightness in Ava's chest was easing, like a fist inside her unclenching. Maybe, after all these years, she could talk about this normally. She could not betray herself, her old fears and hurts that had scabbed over without ever being healed. What had Lady Stokeley said? *These old hurts, petty as they might have been, still have the power to wound. And then to fester.* Yes, that much was certainly, and unfortunately, true. Sometimes, Ava felt like nothing more than a walking scar, with a good layer of slap on top, her pathetic attempt to hide her wounds.

"And did she?" Jace asked, and just like that the composure she'd been trying to reassemble cracked right open.

"No, she never did." Ava drew a quick, steadying breath, trying desperately to keep her voice from wobbling. "I visited her in Stockport a couple of times in those first few months, but then she moved to Norfolk, and it was too far and she didn't seem interested, so…" Shrug.

Shrug like none of it really mattered. Like she hadn't been fourteen and in desperate need of a mother to guide her through the confusion of her teens, boys who were far too persistent, a bust that defied normal bra sizes, the feeling that she inhabited a body that made people assume things about her. Eventually, she'd realized it was easier to let those assumptions be right.

Would she have made different choices, better ones, if her mum had been around? The answer, which made a crack right down Ava's heart was, *maybe.*

But she wasn't ready to tell Jace any of that. Not when she already felt so exposed, with so much of her emotional baggage on display. She felt as if she'd just waved her dirty knickers in front of his face, only worse. Far worse.

"Well," Jace said after a moment, as he pushed the scrambling eggs around with a spatula, "that all sucks. Sorry."

She gave him a small smile, relieved the pressure in her chest was easing again. Sort of. It was as if she'd edged towards an emotional precipice and was now thankfully inching away towards safety. And maybe Jace understood some of that.

"Yeah, pretty much," she said.

"And the pregnancy?" He kept his eyes on the eggs. "Looking for love in all the wrong places?"

"Basically. My father more or less checked out after my mother left. Buried himself in work—he was a building contractor—and ignored me as much as he could." Which was something else that still hurt.

Before her mother had left, they'd been a *family*. They might not have been worthy of the golden glow of some television sitcoms; her father had drunk too much and her mother had severe mood swings, but *still*.

They'd been a unit, the three of them. There had been presents under the Christmas tree; hell, there had been a Christmas tree. There had been hot meals several times a week, and occasional evenings out at the cinema, and the feeling, so important in retrospect, that they were normal, muddling along like everyone else. All of that had changed after her mum had gone.

"And the boyfriend?" Jace slid the eggs from the pan onto a plate and handed it to Ava. "Dig in."

Ava picked up her fork with murmured thanks. The boyfriend. When had she last thought seriously about Jeff? She found she could barely picture his round-cheeked, pimply, teenaged face.

"He wasn't a bad guy," she said after she'd nibbled at some eggs. They were just as she liked them—cooked dry, with a little bit of salt. It was almost as if Jace had known.

"No?" Jace braced one hip against the counter, giving her a level look that said as clearly as if he'd spoken the words out loud that he had his doubts about that.

"We were going to stay together," Ava said.

Strangely this didn't hurt as much as talking about her parents. Maybe because she'd never really loved Jeff. She'd just loved the dream—a family again, mum, dad, child, that precious unit.

"We even talked about getting married." Naïve notions of setting up house, playing happy families, but the reality would have been different—grim poverty, benefit scrounging, and despair.

Her father had made it clear he wasn't going to support her, not financially, and certainly not emotionally.

"But you didn't?" Jace prompted. He was leaning against

the kitchen counter, booted feet crossed, arms folded, his expression alert and yet also bland, giving nothing away.

"We didn't get that far. When I was six months pregnant Jeff scarpered. We'd just taken our GCSEs—I'd scraped several—and he took off for a mate in Liverpool and some job on the docks. His parents wouldn't tell me where he was. They were glad he was shot of me, I'm sure. He wasn't uni material, but they'd had better hopes for their son than knocking up his tarty girlfriend at sixteen."

Jace arched an eyebrow. "Tarty girlfriend?"

Ava shrugged. "Like you said, I was looking for love in all the wrong places."

"So what did you do then?"

"I left home. Things had got rather dire by that point, between my dad and me. They'd been bad for a while, and we survived by ignoring each other, but after Jeff left..." Ava shrugged. "I couldn't take it anymore. He'd basically written me off as a slut and, in some respects, I suppose he wasn't—"

"Don't." The single word was surprisingly lethal, quiet and heartfelt.

Ava blinked. "Don't what?"

"Don't run yourself down. There are enough people to do it for you. You were a teenager who'd been given a very raw deal."

Oh, these pregnancy hormones. She was going to cry and, while she generally hated the prospect of tears, this was a nice sort of crying, a healing, because Jace was more understanding towards her than anyone she'd ever encountered before.

Ava let out a shaky laugh and carefully dabbed at the tear that was forming in the corner of her eye, the one that threatened to trickle down her cheek. "You're too nice to me."

"How can anyone be too nice?"

"Because it makes me like you."

Jace leaned back, looking both amused and affronted. "You don't want to like me? You told me you thought we were friends."

Ava dabbed at another tear. Damn it, they just wouldn't stop. "I don't mean like that," she said quietly.

"Ah." Jace rocked back on his heels. "Why," he asked eventually, "do you think I stayed away for two weeks?"

Nonplussed, she simply stared at him. And dabbed some more. "Umm…"

"It's hard just to be your friend, Ava. Even when you were sitting there looking like death while you were puking your guts out, I still wanted you." He shook his head, rueful now. "Sorry, but there it is."

"Oh." She felt a silly smile form on her face.

She'd been wanted before, of course. Desire was nothing new. But to want her when she was sick and sad and *puking?* When she looked terrible and she'd told him all the truths she'd crammed down deep inside? That was something entirely new. Something scary and kind of wonderful too.

Jace was looking at her closely. "You don't mind?"

"Not… not exactly."

He folded his arms, biceps rippling, reminding her suddenly and quite inconveniently of the dreams she'd had about him recently.

"I thought you didn't want that kind of interest," Jace said.

Ava started to blush. Images were unreeling in her mind, ones she should not be thinking about right then. "I'm not sure I know what I want."

Jace's eyes narrowed. "Why are you blushing?"

"Because I had a dream about you," Ava admitted.

If she put it out there maybe they could both move beyond it.

"A dream?" He raised his eyebrows, waiting.

"You know what kind of dream." Ava shook her head, embarrassed now. "And I'm not giving you the porno details, so nice try."

Jace's slow smile, the way one corner of his mouth quirked up first, sent a sizzle through her body, right down to her toes. "Okay, fine. I'll just have to imagine them on my own."

The very air seemed to crackle. How had they got here? And why had she mentioned that silly, sexy dream? The answer was suddenly obvious—because she'd wanted to. Because she hadn't felt this heart-stopping kind of excitement in forever.

"If you keep looking me at that," Jace said in a low voice, "I won't be imagining anymore."

And, for a second or two, Ava thought about it. Pictured it. She remembered Lady Stokeley saying how good it felt to be touched, and that had just been the stroke of fingers on her face. How amazing would it be to be touched by *Jace?* To find both comfort and craving in his hands, his mouth…?

And yet… she couldn't. She was pregnant and David had only been dead for two months. And besides that, she was *raw.* Sex was not a good idea when she felt so intensely vulnerable, so very fragile.

"Sorry," she muttered. "I shouldn't… that is… I'm not… I'm not trying to be a tease."

"I know." Jace let out a rather ragged sigh. "So now you see why I've kept my distance. Do you want more eggs?"

Ava looked down at her empty place in surprise. Somehow she'd eaten them all without even realizing. "No thanks. They were delicious."

"Coffee? Tea?"

She grimaced. "I'm off both."

He nodded. "So the boyfriend left," he stated. "And you left home. Where did you go?"

She'd thought they were done raking up the past. Her past. She still didn't have the first clue about Jace. "I stayed with a friend for a few months." Sleeping on a bedroom floor when she was in her third trimester of pregnancy was not recommended.

"Until you had the baby?" Ava nodded. "And then?" Jace asked.

"I gave it—her—up for adoption." Ava had held her daughter for all of ten minutes, ten of the most agonizing minutes of her life. Her baby had been pink and perfect, with a scrunched-up face and rosebud lips, tiny fists waving. Sometimes, Ava still dreamed about the warm weight of her against her chest. "I didn't have the resources to do anything else."

"You don't have to justify your actions to me, Ava."

"I'm just trying to explain." And yes, justify.

Because twenty years she still struggling with guilt, that she could just hand her daughter over to strangers. But what else could she have done? Sixteen years old, penniless, homeless, emotionally empty?

"And after that?" Jace asked. "What did you do?"

Ava grimaced. "I stole a hundred pounds from my friend's parents—not something I'm proud of—and bought a bus ticket to London. Worked in cafés and cocktail bars for a few years."

Jace nodded, and Ava knew he was reading into that all she hadn't said, and he could undoubtedly imagine the grimness of those years. The poverty and pain, the dead-end relationships—if she could even call them that—with tossers who only wanted one thing. And she'd given it, because what else could she have done?

"Anyway," she continued after a beat, her voice coming

out high and bright, "I realized that sort of life wasn't going anywhere good and so I did a typing course at the library and started temping in offices. And eventually I met my husband, David." And became the best she'd felt she could hope for—a trophy wife. The not-so-happy ending to her story.

Jace didn't say anything, just kept looking at her in a slow, speculative way. No judgment in his gaze, but it still unnerved her. She needed to make a move.

"I should probably head back to Willoughby Close…"

Jace shook his head. "The cottage still smells like gas. The emergency service guys thought you should sleep somewhere else tonight if you could."

"What?" She stared at him, shocked even though it made sense. Because, of course, she knew what Jace was going to suggest next.

"You can sleep here," he said, and then added, with a glinting grin, "in my bed. But don't worry, I'll sleep on the sofa."

"You don't…"

"I'm not going to let a pregnant woman sleep on a sofa while I sleep on a bed," Jace informed her in a tone that brooked no arguments. "But first, let me put some clean sheets on it."

After everything she'd just shared—including the dreams—the thought of sleeping in Jace's bed was… exciting. But it also made sense, and she was determined to treat this like a normal event. They were friends, after all. Just friends.

"Okay. Thank you."

"You can help me with the duvet," he said as he pushed off from the counter and headed for the bedroom and, after an uncertain pause, Ava followed him up the narrow stairs, around the tiny landing with its stained glass window, to the bedroom with a mattress in an enormous, ornate frame that looked like it might have belonged to a king a few centuries ago.

"This place looks like it's furnished with the same stuff as mine," Ava remarked as Jace began bundling some navy sheets off the bed and tossing them into the hallway.

"Yep. I didn't come here with much."

"Where did you come from?" Now that she'd spilled most of her story she wanted to hear his.

Jace looked up with a wary look. "Newcastle," he said after a moment.

Ava waited for more, and then she realized that was all he was going to say.

"How long have you been working for Lady Stokeley?"

"Since December." He moved around her to retrieve some clean sheets from a laundry basket in the hall.

"And before that? What did you do?" Ava asked.

Jace's monosyllabic answers felt repressive, but she was curious.

Jace sighed. "Construction," he said, and he handed her two corners of a fitted sheet. "Help me put this on."

"In Newcastle?" she pressed. "How did you end coming here, then?"

It seemed an odd move for a man like Jace. And he had said Lady Stokeley had done him a great kindness. What was that about?

Jace sighed and didn't answer, just shook out a sheet. So she was right, and he did have some secrets.

"You know," she said conversationally, "anything I imagine will be worse than what you tell me."

"You have no way of knowing that," Jace pointed out as he fitted the sheet on his side of the bed. "But nice try."

A frisson of—something—went through her. Jace had spoken lightly enough, yet what *had* he been doing?

They worked in silence for a few minutes, putting on pillow cases and then wrestling with the duvet cover. When the bed was made Jace gave each of the pillows a good whack to plump them and then turned to Ava with a direct and strangely resigned look.

"You're not the only one with a past, Ava, as well as regrets. You want the truth? I'll give it to you, because I think I can trust you to keep it to yourself. Before I was here…" He paused, seeming to weigh his words, the import of them, before he finished flatly, "I was in prison."

Ava blinked, realizing she wasn't all that shocked. She'd expected something like this, something he was doing his best to keep hidden. And yet he'd told her.

"Where?" she asked, because the question seemed fairly

innocuous and she needed a moment to gather her scattered thoughts.

"HMP Wakefield." He folded his arms, waiting for the next, inevitable question, and so Ava asked it.

"What were you in prison for?"

Jace stared her straight in the eye as he answered. "Murder."

Chapter Eighteen

H E'D BEEN TRYING to shock her. Ava could tell by the way Jace held her gaze, a sense of challenge to the lift of his chin. And, the truth, she did feel shocked. Shocked and horrified. *Murder.* That was no small thing. No small thing at all.

And yet this was *Jace,* who had been kinder to her than anyone in her memory, who had bought her a pregnancy test and taken away her puke bowl, and a dozen other things, but... murder? Was there any way around that? Any way to explain it?

"The door downstairs is unlocked," Jace said as he whacked the pillows again for good measure. "In case you feel like doing a runner. But don't sleep in your place tonight. It really does smell like gas still." He took a step back, hands on his hips, waiting for her to do what? Run away?

"I'm not going anywhere, Jace." She recognized his tactics.

Drive people away. Act like you don't care. She wouldn't

be so easily fobbed off or fooled, even if she still felt blind-sided by the murder charge. She'd known Jace had been hiding something, but *that...?*

"Fine." He shrugged as if it didn't matter very much, and then turned and headed downstairs.

After an uneasy pause Ava followed.

She found Jace in the kitchen, letting Zuzu out the back door. "I brought some dog food from your place," he said. "I figured she needed her dinner."

Zuzu did need her dinner and Ava suppressed a guilty pang she hadn't thought of it earlier. Her poor little puppy, brought hither and thither.

"Thanks," she murmured and took the bowl Jace proffered, along with the sack of dog food.

Neither of them spoke as she dealt with Zuzu's dinner, the clatter of kibble into her bowl sounding loud in the tense silence of the kitchen. Ava set the bowl on the floor and then opened the back door which led into a tangled garden overrun with nettles and brambles. Jace kept the grounds of Willoughby Manor looking pristine but clearly he didn't do much for his own patch. The lack of furniture, the lack of care, suggested a man who hadn't been there very long... and perhaps wasn't going to stay.

"I was guilty," Jace said from behind her, "in case you're wondering."

Ava turned around as Zuzu scampered inside and rushed her bowl. Actually, she hadn't been wondering. She'd already known. What that said about her or Jace, she had no idea.

"Do you want to tell me about it?" she asked quietly.

Jace shrugged, hands jammed in the pockets of his jeans, his expression remote, his gaze on a spot somewhere to the right of Ava. This was as hard for him as her soul-baring had been for her.

"I probably shouldn't have said anything," he said. "I just thought, since you'd said so much, you had a right to know."

"Thank you." She was silent, unsure how to navigate this new and unfamiliar territory. "Let's go sit down," she said finally. "Before I collapse. Eight p.m. and I turn into a pumpkin these days."

"All right."

They both went into the sitting room, followed by a contented Zuzu. Ava sat on one sofa, Zuzu springing up into her lap, and Jace sprawled on the other, arms outstretched along the back, a deliberate pose of careless ease even though Ava could see or at least sense how tense he was.

Neither of them said anything for a little while. Ava stroked Zuzu and wondered how long to let the silence go on. What questions to ask. In the end, Jace spoke first.

"It was an accident," he said. "If that makes it any better, which I suppose it doesn't. Dead is dead."

"What happened?"

Jace was silent for a long time, his gaze still distant and shuttered. Even grim-faced, he was sexy, with the stubble on his jaw and those pouty lips, the broad shoulders, the perfect abs. Even now, Ava couldn't help but notice—and respond—even as her heart both ached and trembled. Did she really want to hear what he was going to say? What if it changed everything between them, fragile and uncertain as it already was?

"I was in the pub," Jace finally said, his voice low, "having a drink with my mates. We'd all been working on a construction site together, and the foreman had laid a bunch of us off that afternoon. The investor ran out of money or something, I don't remember what, but it was a blow. It wasn't easy to find work, and we'd been counting on the job lasting for a few more months." He paused, shaking his head, and then resumed. "So this tosser comes in, a real toffee-nosed bloke from the uni in Durham, slumming it with his friends, looking down on all of us, insulting everything in a loud voice. You know the kind of guy I mean?"

Yes, unfortunately she did, all too well. She'd encountered enough of them in her life, and used some to her own advantage. "And what happened then?" Ava asked quietly.

"We were at the bar, both of us waiting to be served, when this guy cuts in front of me, elbowing me out of the way, says I need to let my betters go before me. He was spoiling for a fight, I could tell. I fired something back at him, I don't know what, and then he took a swing."

Ava let out a breath that she hadn't realized she'd been holding. "And you punched him back?"

"Yes." Jace was silent for a moment. "But I wasn't a one

punch killer, if that's what you're thinking. Nothing that simple."

"Oh." Because that was what she'd been thinking. Hoping for. People heard it all the time, didn't they, the sad stories of someone tragically killed by a single punch, and the unfortunate bloke who threw it and had his life ruined as a result? Wasn't that what was going on here?

"He barely hit me. He could hardly make a fist. He wasn't a fighter, not really." Jace paused, seeming to weigh up what to say next. How much to admit. "And the truth is, I kept hitting him," he stated flatly. "Even after he was on the ground. I was drunk, I don't even remember it all that well, but the witnesses nearby said I punched him two or three times at least." He drew a quick, shuddering breath. "And the coroner said he wasn't dead by that first punch. It was the second or third that killed him. Cerebral hemorrhage."

"Oh, Jace." Ava didn't know what else to say.

It was so terrible, and so sad, and she saw the regret etched in every line of Jace's bleak face. Her mind raced to find excuses, justifications, but the stark reality remained. He'd killed someone. There was no way around that, no way to make it understandable or acceptable or better. It simply was.

He shoved his hands deeper into his pockets, his expression so very grim. "I've thought about those punches so many times. What was I thinking? Why did I keep punching him when he was down? I don't even remember, that's the sad truth. My blood was up, I suppose, and I was angry about being laid off. I'd drunk too much, but… is that an excuse? No. Nothing is."

"You served your time," Ava said softly. "Didn't you?"

Jace let out a huff of humorless laughter. "Yes, I suppose I did. Seven years at Wakefield. I was paroled in early December."

Shock blazed through at that admission. Seven *years*. And he'd only been out of prison for a handful of months. The enormity of what Jace had told her, what he'd experienced and endured, hit her afresh, and she was left speechless and reeling. He was still Jace, sexy, kind Jace, and yet… he was a convicted felon. An ex-con. She hated those words, despised labels, and yet… they remained in her mind like a poisonous whisper.

Something flashed across Jace's face in light of her silence, and he let another huff of that hard laughter. "Well, now you know."

"I'm sorry." She wasn't even sure what she was apologizing for, only that she *was* sorry, for all of it. "I can't even imagine, and if I'm staying quiet, it's because I don't know what to say." She was trying to picture Jace drunk and aggressive, punching some bloke while he was down. She couldn't imagine it and yet at the same time she *could,* blurry and out of focus, but there. She wanted to unsee it; she more than half wished Jace hadn't told her. That she didn't know.

"Yeah." Jace rubbed the back of his neck. "God knows, I'm sorry too. I've had seven years to be sorry."

"It seems like a harsh sentence," Ava ventured cautiously, although she didn't really know. "Considering you didn't mean to kill him." How much did a man get for manslaughter? For taking a man's life?

"Yeah, well." Jace shrugged. "He had friends in high places, didn't he? His brother made sure I got the maximum that I could. He wanted me to get life but the judge gave me ten years and, fortunately, like I said, I was paroled after seven." That didn't seem all that fortunate to Ava, yet Jace spoke matter-of-factly, without bitterness, accepting it as his due.

"And how does Lady Stokeley fit into this?" Ava asked slowly. "You said she did you a great kindness once."

"She got me this job. I came out of prison with nothing, no home, no money, no friends, even, and she arranged for me to work as groundskeeper here."

It was an extraordinarily gracious thing for her to do, considering Jace surely hadn't owed her anything and was a convicted killer. "Don't take this the wrong way," she said. "But why?"

Jace gave a small, rueful smile. "I know, it seems mad, doesn't it? She did it because the bloke I punched—the man I killed—was her nephew, Archie Trent."

Ava's jaw dropped. Okay, *that* was unexpected. "Her nephew? You mean, Henry Trent's—"

"Younger brother. Yes."

"So it was Henry who threw the book at you?" Jace nodded. "But why…" Ava's mind was spinning.

"Why would Lady Stokeley do me a favor when I killed her nephew?" Jace filled in. "It makes you wonder, doesn't it? There's no love lost there, it seems, but I think she felt Henry treated me unfairly. If he hadn't put on the pressure, I might have only got a couple of years, been out in eighteen months." He paused. "And not been sent to Wakefield."

"What's wrong with Wakefield? For a prison, I mean?"

Jace hesitated, seeming reluctant to explain, and then he shrugged. "It's a Category A prison, which means it's high security, for men convicted of murder and worse. But Wakefield, for whatever reasons, holds some of the most unpleasant and dangerous blokes to be convicted." He grimaced. "A real monster mansion. Sex offenders, men who committed crimes against women and children, all that kind. People you never want to know, that's where they end up."

And he'd been there for seven years? Ava stared at him in horror.

"It wasn't a fun time," Jace said shortly. "Obviously. But I'm out now and I'm never going to get into that kind of situation again. When I go to the pub, I stick to one pint. Always. And I've never raised my hand to anyone since that night."

"Oh, Jace." Tears started in her eyes, and Jace shook his head, the movement vehement.

"Don't feel sorry for me. I didn't pity you and, trust me, Ava, the last thing I want is your pity. I deserved what I got. I've accepted it and I've moved on. Now it's getting late and you're obviously exhausted. I think we should both go to bed."

Ava thought about saying she didn't pity him, but she doubted Jace wanted to hear it right then. He looked like he was seriously regretting telling her everything that he had, and she could understand why. It wasn't comfortable, stripping away his security, telling his secrets. It wasn't comfortable at all.

"Thank you for telling me all that," she said quietly. "I'll let Zuzu out and then I'll go upstairs."

Ava stood at the kitchen door, breathing in the cool night air, fragrant with damp earth and rain. The sky had deepened from indigo to black and, when she tilted her head up, she saw a few, faint stars glimmering through the shreds of cloud. The sight of those stars stirred something in her soul, reminded her that even when the world was dark and damp and chilly, when clouds covered the sky and all she could see was gray, rolling fog, the stars were still there. Still shining.

Did Jace believe that? Did he see those stars?

Zuzu snuffled around in the weeds and Ava leaned against the doorframe as a wave of exhaustion crashed over her, threatening to drag her under. It was as if she'd experienced several lifetimes in the last few hours and, on top of her natural pregnancy fatigue, she felt as if she could barely crawl upstairs to bed. She certainly couldn't begin to process all, or even any, of what Jace had told her, or what it meant for him, for her, for *them…* if there even was a them, of any description.

But one thing, at least, she knew deep in her bones. She wasn't afraid of him. He was the same man who had been so kind to her, who had treated her with more sensitivity and compassion than anyone else in memory, and that was what mattered, not a terrible tragedy from seven years ago. She had some hard history and so did Jace. That didn't have to make a difference to anything.

To *what?* Were they friends? Something more? After everything that had happened and been said tonight, Ava had no idea what the answer to that question was, or even what she wanted it to be.

"Will Zuzu be all right in the kitchen?" Jace asked. He was holding an old fleece blanket that he folded into a makeshift bed. That small, thoughtful gesture made Ava's heart twist painfully. This was a good man.

"Yes," she said, and her voice came out in a scratchy whisper. "She'll be fine."

Jace gave her a questioning look, and Ava knew she must look emotional. She felt emotional. And she wanted to say something of what she felt, all she felt, but she had no idea how to begin. And that was probably a good thing, because she'd certainly regret turning this moment into something more, emotionally or otherwise, by morning.

"Goodnight, Jace," she said quietly, and turned to go upstairs.

Chapter Nineteen

"HEY, AVA, I have those clothes for you."

Feeling muzzy-headed, Ava stopped where she was and looked across to Harriet, who was locking her front door. It was ten o'clock on a Saturday morning and Ava had just been letting Zuzu out before figuring out breakfast, or lack of it.

"Clothes?"

"Yes, you know." Harriet lowered her voice, not that anyone else was listening. "Maternity."

"Oh, right." She definitely needed some maternity clothes. Last night when she'd been getting undressed for bed, she'd looked down at herself and seen the small baby bump that seemed to have sprung out of nowhere. She was almost eleven weeks pregnant, but second time around the muscles, despite years of Pilates, were clearly slack. She'd had to stop zipping up her skirts and trousers a week ago, and now she had a gentle rounding in the belly area. Not so gentle by the end of the day, if she were brutally honest with herself.

"That's wonderful," she said. "I'm busting out of all of my outfits."

Harriet nodded, her gaze dropping down to Ava's admittedly super-tight t-shirt. Her clothes had already been tight. Now they verged on the obscene, and that was not a good look when she was serving pints to hard-working but fairly drunk blokes most evenings.

"Do you want to come by and pick them up sometime? I've got the summer tea at Olivia's this afternoon…"

"Of course." Ava gave herself a mental slap upside the head. With everything that had happened recently with Jace, she'd completely forgotten about Harriet's tea thing. "I'm looking forward to it," she said.

"Oh, brilliant." Harriet grinned, clearly relieved and pleased that Ava had remembered. "See you there, then? And I can bring the clothes by afterwards, if you like."

"That would be lovely."

"Clothes?" Ellie, unseen by either of them, was locking her own door. "What clothes?"

Harriet looked momentarily stricken and Ava did a mental eye roll. There was no getting around it, and it was becoming kind of late for hiding, anyway. She had her next prenatal appointment on Monday. "Maternity clothes," she told Ellie. "I'm pregnant."

Ellie's jaw dropped and then she beamed. "Oh, fantastic." Her expression wavered for a second. "I mean, it is fantastic, isn't it?"

"Yes, it's fantastic." Why did people have to ask her if it was? The lack of a life partner might have something to do with it, but still.

"Wonderful. Congratulations." Ellie looked so pleased for her Ava regretted her less than charitable thoughts. Her new friends were lovely and they always meant well. "So, you need maternity clothes?" Ellie said, brightening even more. "Because I have some stashed away, I think."

"Do you? You're not going to need them anytime soon?" Ellie was pretty serious with her professor boyfriend, Oliver.

"Oh, not... that is..." Ellie blushed, and Ava quickly backtracked.

"I'll be finished with them in about six months, anyway."

"Don't forget the fourth trimester," Harriet chimed in. "That baby weight doesn't just melt off."

"Right." Had it last time?

Ava couldn't remember. The months after her daughter's birth were a blur thankfully—running away to London and losing herself in a bunch of dead-end jobs and men... better not to revisit that time in any sense, for any reason.

"Oh, this will be fun," Ellie exclaimed. "We can both bring our maternity clothes over and you can have a fashion show! I'll bring the wine." She wagged an admonishing finger. "Only sparkling apple juice for you, though."

"French women drink all through their pregnancies, don't they?" Harriet protested. "She can have a small glass."

"I'm off wine and coffee and pretty much anything delicious," Ava informed them. She wasn't quite sure how she felt about parading maternity clothes in front of Harriet and Ellie, but she could tell she wasn't going to get out of this one. "But thank you."

"I'd better get a move on," Harriet said as she headed for her car. "This event isn't going to run itself."

"Is Lady Stokeley going?" Ava asked suddenly. Lady Stokeley had had the week off her treatment and so Ava hadn't seen her for a few days. Harriet and Ellie exchanged uncertain glances.

"I wasn't sure she'd want to…" Harriet began.

"I'll ask her," Ava said firmly. "She should get out more while she can."

"You're absolutely right," Ellie said suddenly. "I should have thought of that. We both should have. I don't think about her leaving the house because she hardly ever does, but she might like getting out a bit more."

"I'm sure she would," Ava said with more conviction than she possessed.

She had no idea what Lady Stokeley wanted on any given day. Still, after feeding Zuzu and throwing on some clothes, Ava started up to Willoughby Manor with determination. It was high summer now, which could mean anything in Britain but in this case meant blue skies and warm breezes, drowsy bumblebees, and the smell of cut grass. It was a perfect day to get out somewhere.

"You again," Lady Stokeley said when she opened the

door to Ava's knock, not sounding entirely displeased. "I don't have to go to Oxford. It's a Saturday."

"I know, but I thought you might like to go to the party Harriet's been planning," Ava said cheerfully. "A cream tea at the little tearoom in town, a grand reopening of sorts."

Lady Stokeley frowned. "Why would I want to attend such an event? I've never been to that tearoom before."

"Because it's a sunny day and Harriet's your friend and also, free scones?" Ava suggested. "You don't have to stay in this—" She almost said *mausoleum* but kept herself from it at the last second. "Place all the time, do you?"

"And how do you suppose I am to get out and about?" Lady Stokeley demanded. "I don't drive and it's too far to walk."

"On this occasion, I can drive you. We can even take the top down again." Lady Stokeley looked unconvinced. "You might like it, you know," Ava said. "You might enjoy yourself, even."

Annoyance flashed across her wrinkled features. "Why is it," she said in quelling tones, "that young people insist on treating the elderly as if they are stubborn and slightly stupid children? I am not a little girl, to be chivvied out to the garden to play. I am perfectly capable of managing my own time and affairs."

"Oh." Ava flushed, feeling very suitably chastened. "I'm sorry, Lady Stokeley. I didn't mean it like that, honestly—"

"If I recall," the older lady said, "I asked you to call me

by my Christian name."

"Of course... Dorothy." The name tripped awkwardly off her tongue.

"And I know you didn't mean it like that," Lady Stokeley added on a sigh. "You never do. That is the trouble with you young people. You don't ever think you will grow old. You can't imagine ever becoming like me one day."

"If I become like you one day, Dorothy," Ava said honestly, "I'll be honored."

Lady Stokeley stiffened in surprise, and then a tremulous smile bloomed across her face like a fragile flower. "Why," she said, "I think that is quite possibly the nicest thing anyone has ever said to me."

"I mean it. You have more class, dignity, and strength in your little pinkie than I could ever hope to have in my whole body, in my whole life."

"It seems flattery will get you everywhere, then," Lady Stokeley answered, her smile widening. "Or at least to this little tearoom on the high street."

A couple of hours later Ava was driving down the high street, looking for a parking space, with Lady Stokeley in the front seat. She looked rather lovely, in a tea dress of lavender silk with a chiffon overlay that looked straight from the 1950s and that Ava wanted for herself quite desperately. Lady Stokeley had paired the outfit with a hat of white straw with a wide brim and a cluster of purple silk flowers, white kid gloves, and a matching hand bag. She looked like she'd stepped out of an Audrey Hepburn film.

"I love it all," Ava had exclaimed when she'd seen her.

Lady Stokeley had smiled while looking down her nose—a feat Ava suspected only she was capable of—and said, "If you're going to do a thing, you might as well do it properly." Which of course was true.

Ava found she was looking forward to the tea now that she was in the car on the way to it. Besides that one rather intense evening three nights ago with Jace, she'd hardly interacted with anyone outside of work. And she hadn't seen Jace since then, something that made her feel uneasy and a little bit sad.

She had no idea what he was thinking about what she'd told him or what he'd told her. They both had a lot to process, and Ava hadn't yet given herself the time to think through what Jace had said, or what it meant. Whether it even needed to mean anything, since she wasn't sure whether they were acquaintances, friends, or something on the verge of being deeper. Was she ready for that? Did she want it?

"Here we are." She pulled into a space by the primary school and then came around to help Lady Stokeley out of the low-slung car.

The tearoom was full of people when they entered, and Ava glanced around the shop, suitably impressed. Colorful gingham bunting adorned the walls and, on top of the counter, a magnificent cream tea was laid out—fresh straw-berries and cream, scones and jam, and porcelain pots of several different types of tea.

"I only drink Earl Grey," Lady Stokeley informed Olivia with a sniff, although Ava knew for a fact she kept budget builder's brew back at Willoughby Manor.

"I'm sure Olivia has some."

Lady Stokeley sniffed again.

"This looks fab," Ava told Harriet when she'd settled Lady Stokeley with a scone and a cup of the prerequisite Earl Grey. "Really amazing." The whole shop looked as if it had been smartened up—fresh paint and plenty of polish, plus a new, more diverse menu, the usual jacket potatoes and baguettes spiced up with more exotic fillings than cheese or tuna mayo. "You've worked hard."

"So has Olivia," Harriet answered. "She's been working overtime trying to get everything looking brand new again, and to diversify a bit."

"Well, it's worked." Ava smiled at Olivia, who bustled over, looking both harried and happy. "Well done, Olivia."

"Thanks." She beamed. "Perhaps now more of the village will take notice of this place. Mum kept it going for as long as she could, but people want something a bit smarter now, don't they?"

"I suppose they do." And... small talk done.

It hadn't been so bad. Maybe she was getting better at it, with more experience.

"Do you know If Jace is coming to this?" Ava asked Harriet, and then wished she hadn't. Harriet looked surprised and instantly suspicious.

"Jace? I'm not sure if tea parties are his thing, to be honest."

"Right." Of course they weren't. "I just wondered if he'd been invited."

Harriet's eyes had narrowed alarmingly. "I did mention it to him, yes."

"I've got an issue with my cooker," Ava explained, which felt like a pretty thin excuse even if it was true. "It needs to be replaced. I was wondering if he had a delivery date, that's all."

"Ah, right." Harriet, naturally, did not look convinced.

Ava decided not to overegg the pudding by saying anything more about it.

"Anyway," she said brightly, and started to move off. "I'll let you two mingle."

She checked on Lady Stokeley and saw that she was sipping her tea happily enough, and then she noticed a familiar face in the back of the shop, looking down at a jam-covered scone as if it was her last meal before execution. It took Ava a few seconds to place the white-blonde hair, the pale, heart-shaped face and luminous blue-gray eyes, but then she remembered. It was the young woman who had sat next to her at Temporary Solutions, for the computer skills test. She'd pecked her way through a typing test while Ava had fumbled her spreadsheet questions.

The determined yet forlorn look on her face tugged at

Ava, and before she even knew what she was about, she pulled out the chair opposite her and sat down.

"Not to be stalkerish," she said, "but I think I know you. You took your computer skills test at the same time I did, didn't you?"

"What?" The girl's eyes widened and she dusted crumbs off her hands as she scrambled for some semblance of composure. "Oh, um, yes? I suppose so. I took a test there a few weeks ago, not that it did me any good." She grimaced.

"Me neither." Ava gave her a conspiratorial smile. "It was a don't-call-us-we'll-call-you type situation, am I right?"

The girl nodded, looking both surprised and relieved. "Right. And they have not called me."

"Me, neither." Ava paused, eyeing her speculatively. She was dressed in a too-big t-shirt and faded capris, both items looking worn and near threadbare. But beyond the cheap, old clothes, there was an air of quiet desperation about her that Ava remembered all too well. A feeling that she was staring straight down a dead-end with nowhere to go.

"So, what are you doing in Wychwood-on-Lea?" she asked conversationally. "Do you live here?"

"Oh, uh, not exactly." Something about the hesitant way she spoke, the shadows in her eyes, sounded a warning in Ava. Recalled a memory.

"You live nearby?" she prompted. "Witney?"

"Um, yes, I was living in Witney, but..." She shrugged. "I got kicked out of my housing. That is, they shut the place down. So." She tried for a smile, but her lips wobbled.

Housing, Ava noted, not house. Was this young woman part of the crappy social welfare system, caught in its ever-turning cogs? "Had some tough luck, eh?" she said, lowering her voice so no one else could hear.

"Yeah, I suppose so." The girl blinked rapidly as she stared down at her plate, one slender finger dabbing at the crumbs. "I've been looking for work, but it's not easy. All the jobs I've found don't pay enough to cover even the most basic rent."

"That's hard." Ava could relate, but her situation seemed a million miles better than this poor young woman's. She had a house, and a car, and a fair amount of savings still. She had a feeling the woman sitting opposite her had none of those things. "What's your name?"

"Alice. Alice James." She looked up with a shy smile.

"I'm Ava Mitchell." Ava stuck out a hand and they shook awkwardly. "So you're looking for work?"

Alice shrugged. "I couldn't find anything in Witney, so I thought maybe one of the villages might have something. It was a stupid idea, though, because I only had bus fare to come here, and there are so few shops." She sighed and stared down at her scone. "I should have tried Oxford or something, but the rent is so expensive there and I've never been good in cities. Stupid." She shook her head, her eyes still downcast. "I came into this tearoom to ask for work but the lady here said she didn't have anything. She said the scones were free, so I took one. But…" Her voice dropped. "That other lady," she nodded towards Harriet, "was asking for donations and I don't have anything. I'm not even sure how I'm going to get back to Witney."

"I can give you the bus fare."

"Oh." Alice's head jerked up, her eyes rounding in horrified realization. "Oh no, I didn't mean… I wasn't trying to scrounge off you, honestly. I was just explaining…" She looked wretched now, and whether it was pregnancy hormones, a deep-seated sympathy, or both, Ava's gooey heart melted a little more.

"It's okay," she said. "I know you weren't. I just want to help." She paused. "Where are you staying in Witney?" Alice's hesitation told her all she needed to know. "Because if you don't have a decent and safe place to stay, I have a spare bedroom." The invitation surprised her even as it felt satisfyingly right. She'd been in Alice's position once, and she wouldn't wish it on anyone, especially not a lovely young woman with her heart in her eyes and an air of being permanently, hopelessly lost.

"Oh… well." Alice swallowed, lowering her head so her white-blonde hair fell forward and covered her face. "That's… um. That's so kind."

"I know you don't know me, and I could be some crazy cat lady or serial stalker, but I'm offering because I've been where you are now, down to my last penny, with nowhere to go." Alice looked startled and Ava realized she might have assumed a lot. "That is, if you're…" She trailed off uncertainly, and Alice gave Ava a wobbly kind of smile.

"I am."

She'd known it. She remembered that half-starved feeling of not knowing how on earth she was going to make it to her next meal. It was such a crappy place to be. "Then you're welcome to come back to mine," Ava said firmly. "I live in a cottage in Willoughby Close here in the village, with Harriet"—she nodded towards Harriet—"and Ellie. And you can use my spare room for as long as you want. Until you find a job or whatever." It was a rather open-ended invitation, but so what? *Why not?*

"But you don't even know me."

"I like the look of you. I trust you." And even though it didn't exactly make sense, it was true.

Alice shook her head. "People don't do that," she protested. "Not anymore."

"You're right," Ava agreed. "I know that, because like I said, I've been where you are now. Which is why I'm doing it. But if it freaks you out, it's fine. No pressure." She didn't want Alice to feel beholden, and yet Ava wanted Alice to come, for her own sake as much as Alice's. She wanted to help someone. She'd done it so little in the past; she'd been so concerned and caught up with helping herself.

"Wow." Alice shook her head slowly. "That's so… I mean, that's really, really nice of you."

"But too creepy." Ava could tell she was going to say no,

and she was surprised by how disappointed she felt. Yet if she'd been in Alice's position all those years ago, she probably would have done the same thing. "It's okay, I understand. I just wanted to offer." She plucked one of the tearoom's little business cards from between the salt and pepper shakers and, taking a pen from her bag, scribbled her mobile number on the back. "Call me if you change your mind, okay? Or if you need anything."

Alice took the card with a little nod. "Okay. Thank you."

Ava stared at her helplessly for a moment, overwhelmed by a rush of something that felt suspiciously maternal. This young woman couldn't be much older than her own daughter. What if her daughter was drifting around coffee shops, lost and uncertain, needing a mother?

Reasonably, Ava knew the prospect was unlikely. Her daughter had been adopted into a solid, middle-class family, two parents, a detached house in a Birmingham suburb. They'd been trying to have a baby for ten years, and they'd been thrilled when Ava, at eight months pregnant, had chosen them. She'd met with them once, and while the visit remained somewhat of a blur, she remembered liking them. She remembered wishing she'd had a mum like the one that woman had promised to be.

No, her daughter, wherever she was, was most likely fine. But Alice James, sitting in front of Ava, wasn't, and there was nothing Ava could do about it.

"Call me," she urged. "If you need to. I mean it."

"Okay," Alice said with a little smile, and Ava rose from the table. Lady Stokeley was looking rather tired, and it seemed like it was time to go.

Chapter Twenty

"LET THE FASHION show begin!"

Ava glanced dubiously at the pile of tent-like maternity clothes before her with open skepticism. She was standing in the middle of Harriet's sitting room, with both Ellie and Harriet watching her expectantly, Harriet's three terrors safely in bed, and Richard safely at the pub. There was nothing to keep Ava from parading her pregnancy outfits in front of her two new friends except, of course, her own common sense and sanity.

Ellie and Harriet were both curled up on the sofa, cradling large glasses of wine, making Ava feel envious. Her morning sickness was starting to abate, at least, and she could manage three small meals a day but she stuck to sparkling water.

"I'm not sure about this," she said with an attempt at a laugh to disguise her decided lack of enthusiasm. "I mean… I feel fat." And some of those clothes looked horrendous.

"Well, you look gorgeous." Harriet shot back. Ava suspected she'd already had a few glasses. "As always. Like a sophisticated sex kitten." Yep, she'd definitely had had a glass or two.

"Thank you," Ava answered with a little laugh. "I think."

"It was a compliment," Ellie chimed in earnestly. "You have so much style—Harriet and I are just envious, that's all." Her face softened in sympathy as she added, "your husband must have adored you."

Something spasmed across Ava's face—she wasn't sure what—and Ellie's face crumpled a little. "Sorry, I shouldn't have said anything. It's just…" She paused, and Ava filled in what she knew Ellie was trying to say, the lumbering elephant in every room she walked into.

"It's just I never talk about him."

"It's painful," Harriet said quickly. "Of course we understand that."

"Yes." Ava hesitated, unsure how much she wanted to share. She was a tight-lipped kind of person, always kept her cards glued to her substantial chest. Depending on people, letting them in… it was far too risky. It hadn't really worked out for her in the past. And yet… Harriet and Ellie had shown her nothing but kindness. And they were her friends, even if she was still figuring out how friendship worked. "It's all a bit complicated," she said, "as I said before."

"All our lives are complicated," Ellie said with a sympathetic smile. "There's me, knocked up at seventeen with a deadbeat ex and Harriet…" She glanced over at Harriet who shrugged and knocked back more wine.

"Richard had a sort-of affair," she explained. "When he lost his job. With his slutty secretary, which is such a cliché, except they didn't actually have sex. Not even close. It was more… emotional. Long phone calls in the middle of the night." She sighed and leaned her head back against the sofa. "I'm over it now, and we're stronger than we've ever been, but it threw me for a loop, let me tell you."

"Right." Ava smiled at them uncertainly. They seemed to be waiting for her to say more. "My husband David was a lot older than I am," she ventured cautiously. "I met him when I was temping. He was the CEO and I was… well, the temp. We married after knowing each other just four days."

"Sounds romantic," Ellie commented, but her eyes were watchful.

Ava sank onto a chair, the pile of maternity clothes momentarily forgotten. "So I thought at the time. Or at least, I made myself think it. But the truth is…" She paused, finding her way through the words, through the truth that still eluded her. "I think he saw me as less than. Quite a bit less than. A trophy wife, and not worthy of…" She paused and then finished flatly, "Much."

"How so?" Harriet asked, alert now, and Ava shrugged.

"Lots of little things. I wasn't allowed to change anything in the house, and when his adult children came over, I had to leave."

"What?" Ellie looked outraged. "That's crazy."

"It was always phrased so nicely. 'If you wouldn't mind',

'you're so thoughtful', that kind of thing." A hard, jagged lump was forming in Ava's throat, making it difficult to swallow. To speak. And yet she kept on. "It was never anything I could put my finger on, and I always explained it away somehow. I wanted to be happy. I told myself I was."

"But now that it's all gone," Harriet asked slowly, "you realize you weren't?"

"Something like that." Ava reached for her glass of sparkling water, taking a sip in an effort to loosen that lump. It didn't work. "I question a lot of things, in light of…" She paused.

She didn't want to go into specifics, memories of David eyeing her appraisingly, the slight twist to his lips that she'd never liked, the comments that had seemed innocuous but now possessed a darker cast.

She couldn't even remember if any of it was real or not. Perhaps she was seeing everything though a cynical lens, in light of David's will and that awful letter.

"In light of?" Ellie prompted. They were both clearly curious, but trying to be sensitive. Ava thought curiosity would win, and she couldn't blame them.

"In light of David's will," Ava finished, and then explained its terms.

"Ten thousand pounds?" Harriet looked indignant on her behalf. "When he had millions? That's an insult. A crime." Ava shrugged.

"If you're married, you're married," Ellie agreed. "You're

not some second-class citizen. He should have left you properly provided for."

"I can't exactly confront him about it now," Ava pointed out.

She realized she was tired of being angry and outraged. She didn't want to remember David as the sugar daddy who seemed to have secretly thought she was a gold-digging tramp. There might have been a grain of truth to those assertions, but she'd genuinely liked him, and she thought he'd liked her.

Despite the tensions with Simon and Emma, despite the limitations he'd placed on her life, always wanting her at his disposal, putting her in her place in the most subtle and sly of ways, they'd still had some fun times.

They'd been able to laugh together and she thought they'd got along, at least until the last few months, when he'd seemed a bit more distant and disapproving. Almost as if he was getting tired of her… and perhaps he had been. But he was dead, their marriage was over, and she wanted to move on with her life without being weighed down by bitterness and hurt. She wanted to change and grow, not let herself be mired in the past and who she'd been, who David had wanted her to be.

"So how about this fashion show?" she said, eyebrows raised.

She was willing to parade tent-like clothing if it meant they'd drop the subject of her marriage.

"Let's do it," Harriet said decisively, and before Ava could protest she found herself in the bathroom, changing into a black jersey wrap dress, the tie fitting over her small bump. When she came downstairs Harriet had put some techno music on and they both started clapping.

It was all fairly ridiculous but Ava decided to drop her inhibitions—she was used to that, wasn't she—and go with it. She strutted down the makeshift catwalk between the sofas while Harriet and Ellie howled and catcalled.

"Work it, sister!"

"Own it!"

Ava started laughing, because she'd certainly worked and owned her sexiness before. She'd used it to her advantage, because at times it had felt the only weapon in her arsenal. But this... this was different. This was owning it in a whole new way, a wonderful way, when she was pregnant and feeling fat, with women friends, wanting to be sexy on her own terms, not because she needed something from a man.

She tried on every outfit, even the awful ones—a button-down smock complete with floppy bow, which she showed off as if it were a sexy cocktail dress. The three of them started adding commentary, as if it were a real fashion show, and by the end they were all nearly crying with laughter, Ellie and Harriet having finished off the bottle of wine.

"I can't believe I ever wore that," Ellie said, nodding towards the smock with its awful bow. "I bought it secondhand, but really... what was I thinking?"

"It's got a certain retro style," Ava said diplomatically. It wasn't classic enough to be vintage, at least the kind of vintage she normally wore. "Thank you for all this, though," she said, nodding towards the pile of clothes. "I don't know what I would have done without you."

Ellie and Harriet both smiled, pleased, and Ava smiled back, a little foolishly. It felt good to have friends.

On Monday, she drove Lady Stokeley to her next round of chemo treatment, noting with a pang of alarm that the older lady looked right worn out, her face pale, her eyes shadowed.

"Are you all right?" she asked, and Lady Stokeley sighed.

"I'm tired," she admitted. "Tired of treatment as well. This will be my third round, and I'm meant to have six before the consultant reassesses."

"But the last time they did your numbers, they were looking good? You were responding?"

"So it seems." Lady Stokeley didn't sound particularly enthused about that fact. "It's not my numbers that are noteworthy, however," she continued, a bit of color coming into her cheeks. "But yours."

"Mine?" Ava gave her a blank look before turning back to the road. "Sorry?"

"My dear, I may be old and riddled with cancer, but I am not blind. It is clear you are, as they say, eating for two."

"Oh." And now Ava was the one who was blushing. "Yes." She was wearing one of Harriet's maternity outfits, a stretchy top with an empire waist that made the most of her small bump. If she wore it to work that night at The Drowned Sailor, Owen and the rest would be sure to notice, but perhaps that would be no bad thing.

Lady Stokeley arched an eyebrow. "Your husband's, I presume?"

"Lady Stokeley!" Ava did her best to look scandalized. "How could you suggest anything else?"

Lady Stokeley shrugged, seeming both unrepentant and unfazed. "It's been known to happen. A widow needs comfort, after all."

"Did you need comfort of that kind?" Ava shot back, and Lady Stokeley pursed her lips.

"Truth be told, I just wanted to be on my own for a bit."

Ava smiled a little that. It might have seemed heartless, but she understood the sentiment. She certainly didn't want to jump into a relationship, no matter what was happening with Jace, and she liked having a double bed to herself, with no one snoring beside her. A small perk in what otherwise still felt like a tragedy.

"You were quite young when you were widowed, weren't you?" she mused out loud.

"Fifty-two. Hardly a girl." Lady Stokeley sighed. "I could have married again, if I'd wanted to, but I really didn't see the point. I was too old to have children, in any case."

Ava glanced at her sideways, sensing a world of pain underneath that matter-of-fact statement. It shamed her to realize there were great swathes of Lady Stokeley's life that she hadn't considered, such as her childlessness.

"Did you want children?" she asked, and Lady Stokeley gave her a look of scathing disdain.

"Of course I did. My husband was an earl, with a title and an estate to pass down. I wanted a son." Her voice choked a little, and she looked away.

Ava's heart twisted. She had, she realized, asked a very stupid question. "I'm sorry," she said quietly. "It must have been very difficult."

"Yes, it was. Especially…" She paused, her face turned to the window, before continuing softly, "I had a child, a little girl. Stillborn when I was six months gone. But it was a long time ago now, of course."

"Oh, Dorothy." The name slipped out naturally and Ava reached over to briefly touch Lady Stokeley's hand. "I'm so sorry. I… I know how hard it is to lose a child."

"Do you?" Lady Stokeley turned to her, all brittle composure now. "This isn't your first pregnancy, then?"

"No." Ava was silent for a moment. "I got pregnant when I was sixteen," she said, wondering whether Lady Stokeley would be shocked or disapproving. "I gave the baby up for adoption."

"A wise idea." There was no judgment in the older lady's voice, only weary sadness. "But heart wrenching, nonetheless. In my day, you wouldn't have had a choice."

"No." Ava considered that for a few seconds. "I don't

suppose I felt I had much of a choice, to be honest, but I guess I did. I could have kept her, but it wouldn't have been much of a life for either of us."

"No."

They didn't talk much after that, but Ava felt as if something had shifted and solidified between them, bound by shared grief and sadness.

"Everything okay?" she asked when, a short while later, Lady Stokeley emerged from the consulting room. She gave a quick nod and gathered her coat and purse.

"Fine. Back on Wednesday." And she strode quickly, for her anyway, out of the ward, making Ava wonder. She decided not to ask.

After dropping Lady Stokeley back home at Willoughby Manor, Ava drove to her appointment with Laney, the midwife at Lea Surgery. Last time Laney had suggested she might be able to hear the heartbeat, and the prospect filled Ava with hope as well as trepidation.

Sure enough, after checking her blood pressure and urine, Laney smiled and reached for the Doppler. "Ready to hear a lovely sound?"

Ava clambered onto the examining table, feeling only a little self-conscious as Laney lifted her top to reveal the soft roundness of her belly. "I might have to press a bit hard," she warned, "but it won't hurt the baby."

"Okay."

Moments later a whooshing sound filled the room; it

sounded like a galloping horse.

"There it is," Laney said with satisfaction. "Easy to find, and strong and fast too."

Ava listened to the sound with wonder as Laney timed the beats on the watch pinned to her uniform. "One hundred and forty-five beats per minute," she said after a moment. "Very good."

Ava nodded, gulping a little. The sound had made her a bit teary, but then everything was making her teary these days. Still, it had sounded so *real*. She wasn't just getting fat; she really had a baby inside her. She pressed one hand against her middle.

"So you're twelve weeks now," Laney said, "and you should be getting a notice through the post about your scan in Oxford. It could be anywhere from sixteen to twenty weeks."

"Okay."

"Any questions?"

Tons of questions, but not necessarily for a midwife. "No, I'm good, thanks."

Ava walked slowly back to Willoughby Close, the day drowsy and warm, her hand still cradling her tiny bump. Her baby. She thought about telling Harriet and Ellie, but while they'd be pleased, she knew they'd chip in with all their experiences of pregnancy and babies, and that wasn't quite what she wanted right now.

No, what she wanted was Jace, because he'd listen and be

pleased for her... and, well, she just wanted to see him. It had been almost a week since she'd spent the night at his place, and she'd hadn't even seen him from a distance, in his truck or mowing the manor's lawn. It was as if he'd gone into hiding, and perhaps he had.

Those thoughts disappeared like wind-chased clouds when she rounded the bend in the rutted lane that led to Willoughby Close and she saw Jace standing in front of her doorway, scribbling something on a piece of paper.

"Jace...?"

He looked up, a cautious smile quirking his lovely mouth. "I was just leaving you a note."

"I've been at the midwife's." She gave a self-conscious laugh. "I heard the heartbeat. It's the most amazing sound."

"I bet it is." Jace's gaze moved over her in an assessing way. "Is everything okay there? With the baby, I mean?"

"Yes. I have a scan in four weeks or so, at Oxford. A proper one, to check everything." She almost thought about asking Jace to go with her, but he might be appalled by such a suggestion. She had no idea where they stood... in any regard.

"So what was the note for?" she asked. "The cooker?"

"Oh, uh, no." Jace, for once, looked slightly embarrassed. "That's still on order, I'm afraid. I was just wondering if you wanted to go to a concert with me this weekend. It's a music and food festival, nothing like Glastonbury or anything, just a small, local event held in a farmer's field, but people say it's good fun." He shrugged. "I thought it might be nice to get out."

Was it a date? Ava decided not to ask. Not to worry or wonder.

"That sounds fun," she said, smiling. "I'd love to go."

Chapter Twenty-One

THANKFULLY THE WEATHER held for the concert on Saturday night, staying sunny and warm. Ava had asked Owen for the night off, which he wasn't happy about but was willing to give, because Ava had been such a good worker. The thought of an evening free of the pub filled her with relief, never mind that she was going on a date.

Because, yes, she'd decided to consider this concert with Jace as a date. Why not? David was dead. They were attracted to one another. She wasn't going to be stupid, and she doubted they'd so much as kiss, but she was going to dress up and enjoy herself and have fun, because heaven knew she hadn't had all that much of it lately.

Ava hadn't told Ellie or Harriet what she was doing or who she was doing it with, which felt slightly disloyal, but they'd add two and two together and get about forty-seven, and she wasn't ready for that quite yet.

She did take plenty of time with her appearance though, splurging on a brand new maternity top from a shop in Witney, something floaty and made of chiffon that didn't make her feel fat. She paired it with a pair of maternity cut-off jean shorts that looked decent, and wore her hair down, in loose curls and waves about her face. She kept the makeup discreet but detailed, taking time with the smoky eyes, the pouty lips. Nothing too obvious, but now that she was starting to feel less nauseous, she wanted to look good as well as feel good.

And the result, when Jace picked her late on Saturday afternoon, was worth it. He whistled softly under his breath as his admiring gaze traveled from the top of her head down to her toes.

"Wow," he said softly, and Ava thrilled to that single word.

"It's just shorts and a maternity top," she said dismissively, but she was smiling, her insides feeling like golden syrup had been poured over everything, sticky and sweet.

They drove to the festival in Jace's battered truck, the inside smelling of coffee and leather, and bearing signs of an attempt to make it tidy. Jace was wearing his usual uniform of faded jeans and a t-shirt, but the t-shirt looked new and the boots had been cleaned. He was freshly shaven and smelled of soap, and Ava could have eaten him up with a spoon.

She kept a lid on her raging hormones, though, and they made desultory chitchat on the twenty-minute drive, both seeming a bit nervous. It was funny to see Jace looking ill at ease, if only a little. He tapped his fingers on the steering wheel and shot her occasional, questioning glances, and this tiny bit of insecurity made Ava smile inside, because she felt the same, and the truth was, she liked Jace not feeling like she was a sure thing. Like she was worth a little nervousness.

The festival was in full swing when Jace pulled into a field used for parking and bumped over the tufty grass until he found a space. Ava slid out of the passenger side of the truck, squinting to catch sight of the festival itself—it looked like a few food and craft stalls, and a makeshift stage that was featuring some folk music involving Celtic pipes.

"I don't know how good the music will be," Jace said, grimacing, as he took a blanket and a proper, old-fashioned picnic basket, out of the truck bed.

"I don't mind," Ava assured him. She pointed to the basket. "That looks like something you might have found in Willoughby Manor's attics."

"Barns, actually, and I thought I ought to make good use of it, since no one else will. The food's pretty basic, though."

They walked across uneven fields, Jace taking her arm, to the meadow where the music was, and Jace spread out his blanket a little bit away from others, so they could both sit down.

Ava sat down, bracing herself on her hands behind her as she tilted her face to the afternoon sunlight, and felt almost perfectly content. Strains of music drifted by as Jace sat next to her, resting his forearms on his knees.

"Sorry, it's a bit down-market, isn't it?" he remarked,

and Ava opened her eyes and looked at him in surprise.

"Down-market?"

He shrugged. "Muddy field, mediocre music, and the smell of sausages frying. Plus, everyone's probably going to get very drunk in a few hours."

"It's perfect," she said, meaning it. "I've had enough of upmarket. Two-hundred-pound bottles of champagne and classical music—who needs it?"

"Was your husband very cultured, then?"

Ava paused, considering. She didn't want to talk about David right now, but not ever talking about him didn't feel right, either. "Not really," she said finally. "He liked to act as if he was—but so much of everything he did, everything everyone around him did, was an act."

"Including you?" Jace asked quietly.

"Yes, in part. He wanted me to be a certain way and so I was. That was the trade-off." She shrugged, trying not to let it hurt, knowing Jace of all people wouldn't judge her for the choices she'd made. He never had.

"You know," he said conversationally, staring up at the sky, "I think you judge your marriage, and yourself, far more harshly than anyone else does."

"What about Simon?" She dared to tease.

Jace turned to her, frowning. "That's the wanker who wanted your jewelry?"

"Yes."

"Him aside, then."

"And his sister, Emma."

"Jeez, there are two of them? Poor you." He shook his head, and Ava laughed.

"I do feel a bit badly about it all, though," she said after a moment, when her laughter had died, even if Jace's answering smile still felt like a glowing ember, keeping her warm inside. "I must have been their worst nightmare."

"But they got what they wanted, didn't they? Their inheritance."

"Yes, but they still begrudge my existence, I think. Not that I ever have to see them again."

"Good."

"But it does make me think," Ava said slowly, leaning back so she was lying down, propped on one elbow. She knew her pose could come across a little provocative, but her back had started to ache. "About people in my past. Whether I should try to reconcile."

Jace eased back so he was lying down too, braced on one arm, their faces rather close. Rather excitingly close. "I have a feeling you're not talking about Simon and Emma anymore."

"No." She was silent for a moment, feeling for the words. "My parents," she said finally. "I don't know where either of them are, or if they're even alive." Oh, stupid lump in her throat, go away. She didn't want to cry in front of Jace, not now, when the air was warm and the sun was shining and a butterfly hovered above his head. He'd seen enough of her tears, among other things. How many times had she fallen to pieces in front of him? And yet he was here, listening, caring. The thought just made the stupid lump get bigger.

"Is there a way you could find out?" Jace asked.

"Maybe. I don't know."

"When were you last in touch with them?"

"My father when I was sixteen. My mother, a year or two before that."

"There is the Internet. Have you searched for their names?"

"No." Ava shook her head. "I haven't wanted to find them, or be found. But now... well, Lady Stokeley said some things that made me think."

"Is she trying to reconcile with somebody?" Jace asked, his voice sharpening a little, and Ava glanced over at him.

"You mean with Henry Trent, don't you?" she asked slowly. "No, I don't think so. She's never talked about him with me, but you were right, I think, when you said there might be no love lost between them. Would that make trouble for you, though, if she did reconcile?"

Jace shrugged. "Maybe. Trent doesn't know I'm here, as far as I can tell. He hasn't been back since I started in December, except for Christmas, and I made myself scarce at Lady Stokeley's suggestion. But I don't think he could fire me, at least not while she's alive."

"But when she..." Ava didn't even want to put it into words.

Jace grimaced. "I imagine he'd give me the push right quick, but there's nothing I can do about that."

"No."

Still it made his life situation precarious, and Ava had no idea how hard it might be for an ex-con to get another job.

"It must be a worry, though."

"No point worrying when I can't do anything about it," Jace replied with a shrug.

"You were in construction, before?"

"I was in anything that paid. I left school after year ten and worked at whatever I could. I was a lad, I admit it—all I cared about was having enough money for beer and impressing the girls." He shook his head. "If I met my eighteen-year-old self, I'd box my ears."

Ava laughed. "If I met my eighteen-year-old self, I'd box her ears and give her a hug. I'm not sure which I'd do first, though."

Jace nodded. "Neither of us have had it all that easy."

"I can hardly compare my situation to yours." Ava was silent, working up her courage. "Was it terrible?" she asked softly, studying Jace's face, the strong lines, the golden-brown eyes. "Prison?"

Jace flicked his gaze away, and she wondered if she'd annoyed him. Why had she brought that up? She didn't want to talk about David; he didn't want to talk about prison. *Duh.*

"It was awful," he said quietly, his gaze still distant. "The worst thing I'd ever had to endure. For so *long.*"

"Oh, Jace." Ava blinked back tears, those hormones at it again. And yet this was worth her tears, because it was terrible. "I'm sorry."

"It made me question the point of humanity," Jace continued. "If that doesn't sound too melodramatic. The things those men did... and some of them, a lot of them even, would do it again if given the chance. I went in there thinking I was different, that I'd just been given a bad break, but after a while I started to wonder. To question whether anything kept me from being different from them. To wonder what I was capable of, in the right—or wrong—circumstances."

"And what did you decide?" Ava asked after a moment, her voice thick with the tears gathering in her throat.

"I realized that I didn't *want* to be like them, and that, at least, was a start. I'd been on a meandering path to destruction before I went to Wakefield—those were the chaplain's words, not mine, but I realized they were true. Working odd jobs, getting drunk as often as I could, flaring up whenever I felt like it. It was an empty life, and I told myself when I got out I'd go looking for more."

"And," Ava asked, her voice nearly a whisper, "have you found it?"

Jace studied her for a moment and Ava's heart bumped in her chest. She had no idea what he was going to say, but it felt important. Then he looked away, and the moment, its intensity, started to slip away, like a loose thread unraveling.

"Not quite. It's all been harder than I thought—getting a job, finding my feet, reporting to the system." At her questioning look, he clarified, "I have to see my parole officer every month for the next year and a half, and I can't leave Oxfordshire without permission. Plus, most jobs ask if you have a criminal record. It's not easy to start over, no matter how much you want to." He let out a sigh. "Not to whinge about any of it, of course."

"I can't imagine you whinging about anything. But it sounds hard." Incredibly hard.

And Ava thought she'd had a tough time, starting over. She'd had it easy in comparison to Jace. In comparison to a lot of people.

"Well." He shrugged her words aside, clearly uncomfortable with too much sympathy. "How about we eat?"

The food he'd packed in the enormous basket was as basic as he'd warned but also delicious—a baguette and some nice cheddar, a few sliced tomatoes and a container of strawberries.

"This is perfect." Ava assured him when he looked as if he might apologize again, since it wasn't caviar and champagne or some such.

They ate in companionable silence for a little while, and Ava was happy simply to be; the sun was still high in the sky and the music set switched to something a little more like smoky jazz.

"So what are you going to do when the baby comes?" Jace asked after a while, leaning back again.

Ava swallowed her strawberry before replying. "I haven't got that far."

"Working at the pub will be hard." He glanced at her, eyebrows raised, and she nodded.

"I know, but I haven't got much else going on, do I? And the truth is I can't stay in number three with what I earn from the pub." Ava frowned, the future crowding in on the wonderfully pleasant present. "I need a proper job, I suppose. I should take some online courses on spreadsheets and stuff and go back to that terrible temp agency."

"What was so terrible about it?"

"Oh, I don't know. It just felt like nothing you could do would be good enough, and for what? A temp job?" She thought of Alice sitting in Olivia's tearoom, trying not to look as woebegone as she so obviously felt. "I wish there was a temp agency for people who really need jobs, but don't necessarily have the qualifications. A place that was determined to find work for people rather than you having to prove something to them." She gave a little laugh. "But that sounds more like charity, I suppose."

"Not necessarily. There are a lot of people who would work hard and do well if given the chance, it's just they don't look so good on paper."

"Exactly." Ava nodded, heartened that he understood so easily. "People like that need a chance." Herself included.

She sighed and flopped back on the blanket. "The Temp Agency of Terrible Rejects."

"You could start an agency like that," Jace suggested. "I'd change the name, though."

"Me, start an agency?" Ava laughed with genuine humor. "You must be joking."

"Actually, I'm not. Why shouldn't you? You've had lots of experience in the temp world, you have a good head on your shoulders, and you're kind."

"Kind?" No one had ever called her kind before. "How do you know that?"

"Because I can tell. You're driving Lady Stokeley to Oxford, aren't you?"

"She's paying me."

"Did she pay you to do her hair and makeup for that visit a few weeks ago? Or take her to the tearoom?"

Ava shook her head, determined not to give into tears again. "That's not all that much."

"Why do you give yourself such a hard time, Ava?" Jace asked gently. "You judge yourself worse even than Simon or Emma do, I think. Why can't you believe you're a nice person? A good person?"

Ava looked down at the blanket, blinking back tears. Real tears, tears that threatened into great, noisy, ugly sobs. There were so many answers to Jace's question. *Because my mother left me. Because my father kicked me out. Because my boyfriend didn't stick around.* Nobody in her life had felt she was worth staying for, much less fighting for, even David. *That* was what hurt about her marriage—that he'd put her in a box and kept her there, not wanting her to get out. Not wanting her to be someone who could or would.

"That's a question with a complicated answer," she managed, still staring at the blanket, trying not to blink because if she did the tears would fall and then she had no idea how much she'd lose it.

"Maybe it doesn't have to be complicated," Jace said quietly. "Maybe there's a simple answer, which is that you are a good person, and you just need someone to tell you so."

Oh, help. He was going to make her fall in love with him. Ava felt it in her bones—terrifying and yet also unbearably right. She'd fall in love with him, she already was, and she hadn't fallen in love with anyone. Not like this, not with someone who'd seen her at her worst, who knew her secrets and weaknesses and fears, and yet miraculously was still there. Still seemed to care.

"Jace..." she whispered, but she didn't know what she wanted to say. To admit.

Gently he touched his finger to the tip of her chin and tilted her head upwards. When she dared to look him in the face, the compassion she saw there nearly made her start with the tears all over again. He needed to stop being so nice. Or maybe never stop.

He smiled, and then he tucked a tendril of hair behind her ear, the brush of his fingers so gentle it made her ache. It was nothing, and yet it felt like everything, because she'd never been touched like this before. She, the woman who gave her body too many times because she'd had nothing else to give, who used sex and beauty as bargaining chips, who had been tossed or discarded too many times to count… felt like a fresh-eyed innocent, discovering the wondrous joys of desire and love.

Ava licked her lips, looking up at him, waiting, *waiting.* Jace cradled her cheek with his palm and Ava closed her eyes. This was so perfect; she almost didn't want to risk ruining it with a kiss. With anything more that might morph into passion with all its expectations and demands. Because that was all she knew of passion.

Then her phone buzzed in her bag and, while she was tempted to ignore it, it also felt like an escape hatch from a moment that was getting too intense. Plus, very few people knew her mobile number.

She opened her eyes, edging away from him with a mumbled apology. "I should get this…"

"Okay," Jace said, easily enough, and he sat back.

Ava scrambled for her phone, frowning at the number she didn't recognize. "Hello?"

"Um, Ava? Is this Ava?"

"Yes…"

"It's Alice."

Chapter Twenty-Two

ALICE WAS WAITING for them at the petrol station just outside Wychwood-on-Lea, huddled by the pay phone, looking scared and miserable and very young.

When Ava had taken her call, Alice had asked, in a voice that wobbled all over the place, if Ava's offer of a place to stay was still going. Ava hadn't needed to think about it for a second.

"Of course," she'd said. "Where are you? Let me come get you." She hadn't needed to think about whether Jace would help her. Of course he would.

"And you question whether you're a good person," he said, in a lazy murmur, when Ava explained the situation and they started packing up, their date over before it had properly begun.

But perhaps that was just as well, Ava told herself as Jace drove back towards the village. She might be falling in love with Jace, but she still questioned whether she was ready for a relationship and all that it meant.

Jace pulled into the station's car park and as soon as he'd

stopped the truck Ava hopped out. "Alice," she called. "It's Ava."

Alice gave her a look of mingled relief and abject misery. "Sorry. I didn't want to bother you…"

"I want to be bothered. I told you to ring me anytime, and I meant it."

"Thanks," Alice whispered.

Ava looked at her critically, noting the tear on the hem of her t-shirt, the bruise on her arm. "Are you okay?" she asked quietly. "Do you need to go to a doctor's…?"

Alice looked startled, and then realization dawned and color flooded her face. "No. I mean… no. I went into the pub to ask for work because someone told me they were hiring, but they'd just hired someone. The landlord was nice about it, though."

"That would be Owen, and I'm afraid they just hired me."

"Oh, right. Well." Alice managed a shaky smile. "I left the pub and a few drunken blokes followed me. They started to get aggressive, and I felt a bit scared. I don't think they would have done anything, but…" She bit her lip while fury surged through Ava.

Being a young woman on her own sucked sometimes. The whole world sucked, when someone like Alice James couldn't feel safe even in Wychwood-on-Lea.

"I'm sorry about that," she said. "And something could have happened, you never know. I'm glad you called me. I only wished you'd rung sooner."

"I didn't want to," Alice admitted. "I wanted to sort myself out, but I haven't had much luck with that."

"You'll get yourself sorted," Ava said firmly. "You just need a chance." Alice was shivering even though the evening was warm, and Ava ushered her towards the truck. "Let's get you back to mine."

Alice glanced askance at Jace as Ava opened the door. "This is Jace," Ava said. "A friend."

"Hey." He smiled and waved.

Ava slid next to him on the bench seat and after a second's pause Alice climbed up, staying close to the window. Ava's heart ached for her.

"I don't have much in way of a bed or anything," she said as Jace started to drive off. In fact, she was woefully unprepared for a houseguest.

"I can sort that out," Jace said easily. "I've got a spare mattress at my place."

Ava shot him a grateful look and Jace gave her one of his old smiles, lazy and knowing. Her heart squeezed with the intensity of what she felt for this man, and she reminded herself that it was a good thing Alice had rung when she had.

Back at number three, Jace dropped them off and promised to return shortly with a bed for Alice. Ava unlocked the door and ushered her inside, conscious that now Alice was in her house, she wasn't sure what to do with her. How bossy to be. Alice seemed numb and shocked, standing in the center of the room and looking around as if she didn't know where she was or how she'd arrived there. Bossy it was, then.

"Maybe you'd like a shower or bath?" Ava suggested. "And something to eat? I don't have a cooker, actually, but the microwave definitely works."

"Oh." Alice focused on her, blinking and smiling slowly. "Yes, I suppose… I don't actually have…" She paused, blushing, and Ava silently filled in *anything.*

"You're in luck, because none of my clothes fit me at the moment so you can borrow them. I'm pregnant," she explained with both frankness and a touch of pride. "Almost thirteen weeks along."

"Oh. Congratulations."

"Thanks. Now there are clean towels in the bathroom, and I'll put some clothes in the spare room. What do you like to eat?"

"Oh, anything," Alice said quickly. "Really, anything at all. I'm not fussy."

I bet you're not. With a smile, Ava nodded towards the stairs and then headed towards the kitchen area to see what she could find.

It felt cozily and rather ridiculously domestic, making food for someone while the shower ran upstairs, especially considering all she was doing was heating some soup in the microwave and making toast.

While the soup was warming, Ava went upstairs and dug out some clothes that were halfway decent for Alice to wear.

She came up with a pair of skinny jeans and a top in flowing jersey that was rather low-cut but should be okay with a camisole underneath. Unfortunately her bras would swim on Alice, so she'd have to stick with the outer elements. Maybe they could go shopping tomorrow.

Although the more Ava thought about it, the more she wondered what she could do with Alice besides offer her a place to stay. She didn't have a lot of money of her own, and she was finding it difficult to get a job herself. Pregnant and virtually destitute, she wasn't the best choice for a fairy godmother. But she could offer a roof over Alice's head and food in her belly, which were two things Ava didn't think Alice had had lately. And Ava *wanted* to help Alice.

She left the clothes in the spare room, which was depressingly empty, and then went downstairs to serve up the soup and toast. By the time Alice came shyly down the stairs, it was on the table.

Ava turned to her with a smile, struck by how young she looked, with her pale hair brushed damply back from her pink, scrubbed face, and Ava's clothes hanging on her slender frame. "How old are you?" Ava blurted, suddenly realizing the potential dangers of sheltering a minor.

"Twenty-two."

Ava couldn't help but be skeptical. "Really?"

Alice sighed. "I know I look young, but it's true. I turned twenty-two a couple of weeks ago."

"All right, then." Ava gestured to the soup and toast.

"Dig in."

It didn't seem polite to hover over Alice while she was eating, so Ava busied herself in the kitchen, tidying away what few dirty dishes there were. After a few minutes, when she had no way to keep herself occupied, she made herself a cup of herbal tea and sat down at the table opposite Alice.

She did look absurdly young. Lovely too, with her roses and cream complexion, her pale golden hair, and her slender, almost ethereal figure. Having always been blessed—or cursed—with bodacious curves, Ava was ashamed to realize she was the tiniest bit envious.

"So what have you been doing for the last week?" she asked. "For accommodation?"

Alice slowly stirred her soup as she ducked her head. "This and that," she said, which sounded questionable. "I met some teenagers in the skate park and they let me kip in their parents' garage," she admitted with a grimace. "It was pretty awful, but I had nowhere else to go."

"Good Lord." Ava stared at her, appalled. "And what about for food? And clothes?"

Alice shrugged. "I had a rucksack," she said, "with some food and clothes. But I left it when I ran."

"Ran…?"

"From the blokes at the pub."

Fury beat through Ava's blood in a savage staccato. It was so bloody unfair, so *wrong*. "So you don't have anything?" she asked. "No belongings at all?" Alice shook her head.

"What have you been doing for the last few years, though?" Ava pressed. "Living in Witney…"

"I was living in a house funded by a charity for ex-foster kids," Alice explained quietly as she continued to stir her soup. "It's hard when you leave the system and there's no net, nothing, so they help you get a job, a place to stay. It's meant to be temporary, until you can support yourself."

"And?" Ava asked after a moment.

Alice shrugged. "My time was up. I'd been living there for three years, which is much longer than you're meant to. Della, the lady who runs it, had no choice but to give my bed to someone new coming through the system. From the government's perspective, I was sorted. I had a job and I'd aged out. She felt bad about it, but that's how it goes."

"So she just kicked you out?" Ava was even more appalled.

"She recommended some places for me to stay. I was working in a nursing home in Witney. I didn't do much, just serving meals and things, but I liked it well enough. The trouble was, it didn't pay enough for me even to get a bedsit, and you can't even get a bedsit unless you've got references and credit cards and things like that." She shrugged. "I've never even had a bank account."

"Why not? If you were working?"

Alice ducked her head. "I was paid in cash. I think the nursing home didn't have me on the books."

"But…" Ava was outraged, even though she knew she

shouldn't be. There were a million stories like Alice's, including her own. "Do you have any qualifications?" she asked.

"I was working towards a level 2 NVQ in healthcare, but I had to stop when I lost my job." And she'd presumably lost her job because she had nowhere to stay. The hopelessness, the *pointlessness* of it, made Ava burn inside with helpless fury.

A knock on the door put a stop to their conversation, and when Ava went to answer it, Jace was there, hefting a mattress.

"Thank you," Ava said fervently. "You're a star."

"I know," Jace replied with a grin, and heaved the mattress upstairs, followed by an ornate, Victorian-looking bedframe in several pieces and then, thoughtfully, a set of worn but clean sheets. Ava stood in the doorway while Jace put the bed together and Alice finished her soup and toast downstairs.

"So you've gained a stray," Jace said in a voice pitched low enough so Alice wouldn't hear.

"Crazy, isn't it," Ava answered. "Since I'm practically a stray myself."

"Seriously, though, Ava." Jace straightened, his dark eyes trained on her. "Can you afford to do this? Because you've got a lot going on in your life now."

"I know." It wasn't anything she hadn't already thought herself, and yet it still stung a bit. "But I've been selfish my whole life, Jace. I want to be different now."

"Selfish?" His eyebrows rose. "How so?"

"My motto has been to do what I have to do. Look out for number one. Get where I need to go no matter whom I need to kick or scratch or bite."

"Is that so?" He folded his arms, looking decidedly skeptical.

"I've been where Alice is," Ava said quietly. "Alone, afraid, with no choices, no resources. If I can help her just a little, and it probably will be just a little considering the state I'm in, then I'll feel better about her and better about myself."

He nodded slowly. "Fair enough."

"Thank you for everything." She nodded towards the bed. "And I'm sorry about tonight. Cutting things short, I mean."

"Another time." Jace gave her one of his old, glinting grins. "The music wasn't that good, anyway."

For a split-second she thought he might kiss her, but then he just waved and headed downstairs. When she followed, he was chatting easily to Alice, and then a few minutes later he was gone.

"Right." Ava gave Alice a bright smile. "Bed, I think, for both of us. In the morning we can figure out next steps."

The next morning, after Ava awoke, she found Alice sitting on the steps by the French windows into the garden, wearing Ava's clothes from last night, her hands clasped around her knees.

"Did you sleep well?" Ava asked, and she nodded.

"Yes, it was amazing. So peaceful, and such a comfortable bed." She gave her the quick flash of a smile. "It's so lovely here."

"Yes, it is, isn't it?" Ava braced one shoulder against the doorframe. "Where are you from, originally?"

"Oxford area, for the most part."

Ava raised her eyebrows. "For the most part?"

"In and out of foster homes since I was six."

"That must have been tough," Ava said quietly.

Alice shrugged. "I don't know much else, actually."

"Do you remember your parents?"

"Yes." Alice pursed her lips, and didn't say anything more. Ava decided not to ask.

"Why so many foster homes?" Ava asked. "If you were only six? Don't they try to put young kids in a long-term placement?"

"Generally, yes. But ultimately they want to reunite families, so I kept going back to my mum. It didn't work out so well, and by the time they figured that out, they needed to find another foster family." Alice shrugged. "People change their minds or their jobs, whatever."

It sounded awful. "And when you were eighteen?" Ava asked.

"I went into the house in Witney. I did a BTEC Level 1 in healthcare instead of A levels, which is how I got the job at the nursing home. I was trying to save money so I could get my own place, do some more training, but..." She sighed. "It got eaten up pretty quickly after I left the house."

"So how long have you been looking for a place?"

"About six weeks. I was trying to keep my job, and so I lived in a couple of different places for a while—a friend's flat, a youth hostel... but nothing really worked for long, you know? And then the money was gone, and the nursing home let me go because I was becoming unreliable—it wasn't always easy to get there on time from wherever I was staying."

"And you couldn't go back to this Della?"

Alice shook her head. "She had her hands full already."

And so she'd ended up on the street. Ava shook her head slowly. It was such a tragic story, and yet she wasn't even surprised. Alice was exactly the kind of person who slipped through the cracks, the kind the government let go because she seemed like she'd sorted herself, but when she didn't have a support network or a safety net it was no more than half a step to disaster. Ava knew that all too well.

"We'll figure something out," she said now, with more conviction than she actually felt. "Clothes and toiletries first, and then we'll think about a job."

"I don't want to take advantage," Alice said. She looked unhappy but determined. "It's not fair on you, especially in your condition."

"You mean pregnant?" Ava answered with a small smile

and a lifted eyebrow. "I'll survive, Alice. Don't worry about me. Let's focus on you."

They spent the morning going through Ava's clothes, figuring out what would work on Alice, and then Ava drove to Chipping Norton for basic toiletries and some underthings. Alice accepted this all with uncertain gratitude, and Ava knew it was hard on her to be in such a position of want and need. She didn't want to take Alice's pride—like she'd told Lady Stokeley, sometimes that was the only thing a person had left.

"Look, you can pay me back for this," she said when they were driving back to Willoughby Close. "I'm not so great with the cooking and housekeeping—if you can manage some of that, I'd definitely call us even."

"Okay," Alice agreed eagerly, and she took Ava at her word, and spent the afternoon cleaning the bathroom and hoovering. Number three had never looked so clean.

Sunday evening Ava took Alice over to Harriet's and introduced her, asking Harriet for some help with Alice's CV, or lack of it, which Harriet was more than willing to give.

"And I'm always looking for a sitter, if you're willing," she added. "Until you find a full-time position."

Alice agreed to everything, seeming overwhelmed by it at all, and Ava couldn't blame her. She'd swooped into her life like a fairy godmother, admittedly one that didn't have a magic wand or was low on fairy dust, but she was trying. And it felt good.

"Ava?" Alice called as she was heading up to bed that night.

"Yes?" Ava turned on the stairs; Alice had been pretty quiet while Harriet had taken her through the rudiments of making a CV, and it was impossible sometimes to tell what she was thinking, or if she resented Ava's bossiness.

"Thank you. For everything. I don't know what I would have done if you hadn't answered my call."

A warmth spread through Ava, as if she'd swallowed a spoonful of the sun. "I'm glad I did," she said.

Chapter Twenty-Three

AVA WAS FEELING buoyant as she drove up to Willoughby Manor to pick Lady Stokeley up for her treatment
the next morning. She'd left Alice deep-cleaning the fridge,
which didn't need it but she understood her new housemate
wanted to feel useful, and in that morning's post she'd
received a notice of her scan date in just three weeks.

Excitement and a little bit of nervousness fizzed through
her at the thought of seeing her baby in fuzzy black and
white on the screen, and maybe even finding out the sex.
She'd even toyed with the idea of asking Jace to accompany
her. Were they there yet? Maybe she should take that flying
leap of faith and see.

Lady Stokeley was more taciturn than usual as they drove
into Oxford, and it wasn't until they were well on their way
on the A40 that Ava twigged that something might be
wrong.

"Is everything okay, Lady Stokeley?" she asked. "Are you
feeling well?"

"I'm feeling fine," Lady Stokeley replied irritably. "And I

thought I told you to call me Dorothy."

"Sorry." Ava glanced at her uncertainly.

Lady Stokeley could be prickly at the best of times, but she seemed particularly sharp this morning. And she'd been quiet coming out of the consulting room on Friday. Worry cramped Ava's stomach. She'd been so busy with Jace and Alice and herself, she hadn't thought all that much about Lady Stokeley, except to drive her to and fro.

"How's the treatment been going, anyway?" she asked as she turned off the A40 towards the John Radcliffe Hospital. Lady Stokeley didn't answer, except to sigh. "Lad—Dorothy?" Ava prompted.

"The doctor says I have three more rounds," she said, her gaze on the passing view out the window. "Three more months."

It didn't seem like a full answer, but Ava didn't know what else to ask. Still feeling uneasy, she dropped Lady Stokeley off at the front and then went to park.

The appointment took longer this time, and sitting out in the waiting room, Ava started to feel even more worried, as well as a little panicky. She recognized a few of the other patients now, and they gave her some sympathetic smiles, as if they sensed her discord, which put Ava to shame. *She* didn't have cancer.

When Lady Stokeley finally emerged, she looked pale and tired but resolute. Wordlessly Ava followed her out of the ward, and then left her waiting on a bench downstairs while she fetched the car.

"Dorothy?" she asked cautiously once they were back in the car. "Was it… are you…"

"I'm just tired," Dorothy said, and she didn't speak until they were back in Wychwood-on-Lea.

Ava was just about to turn into Willoughby Manor's drive when Lady Stokeley spoke. "Would you… would you mind parking at the bottom of the drive? It's a beautiful day, and I'd like to walk to the canal."

Ava stared at her blankly. "The canal…?"

Lady Stokeley nodded to a set of wrought iron gates immediately opposite the manor's drive. "It's a public park now, but that woodland used to belong to my family. Well, Gerald's family. He sold it to the council in the 1950s, when it became too expensive to maintain, but I've always liked it."

"Okay," Ava said, and pulled the car off the road.

It was a pretty spot, a wide, leafy avenue of lime trees leading down to a dense woodland whose main feature were three spring-fed ponds, each one leading into the other by a series of narrow canals.

"They were built in the 1860s," Lady Stokeley explained as they walked slowly down the avenue. "A Victorian pleasure garden. It's all gone a bit wild now, but it was lovely, once."

Ava thought it was still lovely. They walked to the nearest pond and settled themselves on a bench by its still waters.

A few ducks paddled peacefully, and a small child on the other side of the garden tossed bread at them with her mother.

"They're the most overfed ducks in all of Britain, I should imagine," Lady Stokeley said dryly, and Ava laughed.

They didn't talk beyond that; the sky was hazy and blue, the sun filtering through the leaves and dappling the mulchy ground. Ava couldn't hear any traffic from the road, or anything beyond the twittering of the birds in the trees and the child's occasional laughter from across the pond.

"It looks as if the cancer might be coming back," Lady Stokeley said, her voice quiet, and Ava gave a start.

"Oh, Dorothy…"

"Not that it ever went anywhere, of course. My numbers looked good for a bit, as if I were responding to all this wretched chemo, and I suppose I was. But I'm old and it didn't last very long." She sighed and shook her head. "I never expected it to."

"So what does that mean exactly?" Ava asked after a moment.

She felt well and truly gutted for Lady Stokeley, and even for herself. She'd let herself be lulled into a false sense of security because of those ambiguous numbers that had been meant to be so good.

Lady Stokeley took a deep breath and straightened her shoulders. "I suppose it means I shall get sick and weak and die. How that happens, and how long it takes, remains to be seen."

"But if you keep with the chemotherapy, those numbers might improve again…"

Lady Stokeley let out a dry rasp of laughter. "I've seen enough in cancer to know once the numbers, whatever they are, start falling or rising or whatever they're not meant to do, your time is running out."

"Time is running out on all of us," Ava protested, and Lady Stokeley subjected her to a narrowed look.

"Perhaps, but it is running out a bit faster for me."

"What does the consultant say?"

"Oh, he wishes me to continue, of course. They always do. But life is not a sponge for me to squeeze from it its last bitter drops. I'll continue it for now, and they'll test again in a week. Perhaps we'll know more then."

"And it might be good news," Ava said with as much optimism as she could muster.

Lady Stokeley looked at her, seeming almost amused. "Perhaps. I'm not afraid of death, you know, Ava."

"I don't imagine you're afraid of much, Lady… Dorothy," Ava answered with complete sincerity.

"Oh, trust me, I am. I'm afraid of dying. The process," she explained. "It seems a nasty, messy business, but there's nothing to be done about that. And…" She paused, pressing her lips together. "I'm afraid of seeing my nephew Henry again, but I suppose I must, soon. I've put it off but I don't think I can much longer."

"Does he know…?"

"No, I haven't told him anything. It shall all be a shock to him, I suppose, but I suspect he'll recover quickly enough. I'll wait until I've had another set of tests before I say anything."

Ava wanted to ask about his relationship with Lady Stokeley, but she couldn't work up the nerve. It was clearly a deep and open wound, if Lady Stokeley dreaded the thought of even talking to him.

"I suppose we should go," Lady Stokeley said with a sigh and Ava took her arm to help her from the bench.

"Is there anything I can do?" she asked once they were back at the car. "To help…?"

"Thank you, my dear, but I don't imagine there will be much you can do. Once my nephew knows he will sweep in and start giving orders and making demands." Briefly Lady Stokeley closed her eyes. "And then what little independence I have had shall be gone."

She made him sound like a monster. If Ava ever laid eyes on Henry Trent, she'd half-expect to see horns and a forked tail poking out from beneath his City suit.

After settling Lady Stokeley at Willoughby Manor, Ava drove back to number three. Alice had left a note, saying she was walking Zuzu along with Harriet's dog, and the cottage smelled of lavender and lemon polish, and felt very empty. Funny, how quickly Ava had got used to living with someone again. Alice was certainly making herself useful, and Ava was glad of that, for Alice's sake.

Still, she had a couple of hours before she needed to be at The Drowned Sailor, and now that she was past that magic thirteen-week mark, she didn't feel as queasy or tired as she once did, and while her energy wasn't boundless, it was better.

After mooching around restlessly for a bit, she pulled out her tablet, fired up the search engine, and paused, her fingers hovering over the touch screen. She'd never got this far before. Hadn't dared. She'd told herself the past was better buried, that she was better off not knowing, not wanting. She didn't want to stir up that old, restless ache of need.

But now, thinking of Lady Stokeley, of Jace, of old wounds and half-healed scars, she decided she did want to know. At least she wanted to try.

Taking a deep breath, she typed in Stan Telford. Her father. Two million results appeared—Facebook, LinkedIn, White pages. Her heart nearly stopped at the sight of an obituary of a Stan Telford in Sunderland, but when she clicked on the link she saw it wasn't him. Wasn't her father.

She went through a few more links, but they were all dead ends, various Stans of various ages and occupations, none who looked or seemed like her father—although would she even know? She hadn't seen him in nearly twenty years. The last she'd known of him, he'd been living in Wolver-hampton, working as a plumber. But she'd heard from an old friend that he'd put the house up for sale, a few years after she'd left, before she'd lost touch with everyone from her former life. She hadn't learned any more than that, and she'd never tried to find him. Now she realized that maybe she couldn't, and the thought was a surprising, fresh grief, a new loss, and one she hadn't expected to feel.

She clicked a few more links, but nothing came up, and it wasn't until she'd reached the third page of results that she came across a photo from someone else's Facebook page—a darts club in Lancashire. The photo was fuzzy, taken in the dimly-lit backroom of a pub, half a dozen middle-aged men holding pints and looking red-faced and happy and a little drunk.

Ava squinted, peering at the image on the tablet, trying to enlarge it although even that was stretching her computer skills. Was that her dad? The picture had been taken two years ago, and it was hard to tell with the fuzziness of the photo, the gray hair and the paunch, if the man standing on the left of the picture, holding a pint and smiling happily at the camera, was in fact her father. Her Stan Telford. But the longer Ava looked at it, the more she was convinced it was, and the realization gave her a strange, sick feeling.

Abruptly she tossed the table aside, and then prowled around the house, even more restless, more unsettled, now that she'd looked.

After a few minutes of wandering through rooms, she decided to go to find Jace. He deserved to know about Lady Stokeley—and Henry Trent, for that matter, and she just wanted to see him. Maybe she'd even tell him about her dad, not that there was much to tell.

When she walked through the wood, however, and emerged in front of his cottage, she saw it was empty—something that made sense, since it was mid-afternoon on a sunny day and he was no doubt working somewhere on the estate. With nothing else to do and still feeling too restless to go back home, Ava decided to wander around, heading along an overgrown path that led from Jace's cottage towards the manor.

The path skirted the wood before ending at the border of the manor's terraced lawns, the grass jewel-bright and pristine. Jace did a good job; it looked as if each blade of grass had been individually clipped with a pair of nail scissors.

Feeling a bit nosy now, Ava skirted the terrace that extended from the back of the house, what looked like a thousand mullioned windows glinting in the sunlight, and started wandering through a set of small, ornate gardens, each one enclosed by a topiary hedge.

Jace had clearly been at work in some of the gardens, with freshly weeded flower beds and well-trimmed topiary sculptures, but in others she saw he hadn't yet been able to get to work. She wondered where he'd learned to garden—he'd said he'd grown up in Newcastle, and worked in construction.

It made her realize there was a lot she still didn't know

about him and, while she wanted to find out, could almost envision a future where she knew these things, she felt that familiar churn of uncertainty at all the future held—as well as all she'd left behind. It was as if she was suspended in mid-air, feet dangling and kicking, unable to go back—there was nothing to go back to—and having no way forward.

Willoughby Close had always been meant to be a stop-gap, a temporary measure. She couldn't afford it for more than a few more months, and what about when the baby came? *The baby.* Was she crazy, keeping this baby?

Ava sank onto a weathered stone bench in a small garden with a little fountain in its center, the water now stagnant, slimy and green. All around her, it was completely silent, without even the twitter or chirp of a bird. She felt, quite suddenly, like the loneliest person on earth, which was melodramatic and unreasonable, but she felt it all the same.

Maybe she was making too much of her friendship with Jace, because of the absence of other relationships in her life? She was already starting to depend on him—look at her now, going to search for him when she'd hit the tiniest bump in the road. A photo of her father, for heaven's sake, and she wasn't even sure it was him. But it had left her feeling uncertain, old emotions churning through her.

"Ava?"

And there he was, almost as if she'd conjured him from her mind, standing in the entrance to the sad little garden with its forgotten fountain. Jace wore a sweat-stained t-shirt and very dirty jeans, his hair rumpled and damp with sweat, mud smeared on one cheek and a spade carried over one shoulder. He'd clearly been doing some rather dirty work.

"What are you doing here?"

"Sorry, I know I shouldn't be." Ava tried for a smile. "I was looking for you and then I saw these little gardens and I thought I'd have a look. Do you think Lady Stokeley would mind?"

"I doubt it." Jace wiped his forehead with his forearm, his t-shirt lifting to reveal a tantalizing glimpse of his well-defined six-pack. "Is everything okay?"

"Sort of." Sort of not. She didn't even know what to say, how to explain everything she felt. Everything she was worried about. "Lady Stokeley's cancer looks to be coming back," she said quietly. "She told me today. They did some more tests and the numbers that looked so good a month ago aren't looking that way anymore."

"But if she continues…"

"I'm not sure she wants to continue with the chemo. I think she'd rather end her days in dignity, on her terms, not fighting for a few more days in the hospital, feeling wretched."

Jace absorbed that information without moving, but Ava felt as if she'd punched him.

He nodded slowly. "I expected as much, eventually. That's a little faster than I'd hoped, though. A few weeks ago you said they were talking about remission."

"I know." Ava paused. "She says she needs to call her nephew. I mean… Henry."

Jace's jaw tightened. "I know who her nephew is."

"I'm guessing he'll come here and sort things out. That's what she said, anyway. She talking about him giving orders and making demands."

"Right." Jace raked a hand through his sweaty hair, making it stick up on end. "I expected as much."

"What will you do?"

He glanced at her, his face expressionless. "When?"

"When Henry Trent comes."

"Stay low for as long as I can. When he has control of the estate, I'm sure he'll fire me." Jace shrugged. "And then I'll have to find another job."

Which wouldn't be easy at all. Jace's situation was even more precarious than her own. Life could be so *difficult* sometimes, one hard thing after another. But why should she ever expect things to be easy?

Ava sighed. "I don't want things to change," she said after a moment. "Not with Lady Stokeley, not with you, not with me. I wish I could stay at Willoughby Close forever, but…"

"You can't afford it," Jace stated flatly.

Ava shook her head. "Not for much longer. That ten thousand pounds is running out, and the money coming in just isn't enough. I'm starting to think I'm crazy, trying to keep this baby."

Jace hoisted his spade. "Something will turn up."

"Only if I keep looking." She paused, and then decided to plunge. "My scan is in three weeks, at Oxford. Would you... would come with me?"

Something flashed across Jace's face, so quick she almost missed it. Had she presumed way too much? She was asking him to accompany her to something that was rather intimate. "I mean, just as a friend," she hurried to explain, even though that wasn't quite what she meant. "It would be good not to go alone."

"Ava," Jace said, and there was a wealth of affection in the way he said her name. "I'd love to come."

Chapter Twenty-Four

TIME SEEMED TO speed up over the next few weeks, which as Lady Stokeley dryly remarked, always happened when you wanted more of it. Ava continued taking her to Oxford for treatment for the rest of the week, but on Friday she came out of the consulting room, smiled, and then gave a little shake of her head.

Ava's heart sank and she found she was fighting tears, which didn't feel fair because it was Lady Stokeley's life, Lady Stokeley's decision, not hers.

"Let's go have a cream tea," Lady Stokeley said once they were in the car. "At that little tearoom you dragged me to. The tea was decent, even if the jam was from a shop."

Ava nodded and drove in silence, not trusting herself to speak. To break down completely. A cream tea in the middle of the afternoon? Lady Stokeley had clearly made a decision.

Olivia greeted them with a smile, but sensing the serious mood, she put their cream teas on the table and left them to themselves, at a more private table in the back. Since Harriet's reopening event, the little tearoom had begun to attract more business. Ava was glad for Olivia's sake, but at the moment she wished the shop was empty as it usually had been, so she and Lady Stokeley could talk—and maybe cry—in peace.

"This is quite delicious," Lady Stokeley announced as she bit into a scone slathered with a generous helping of clotted cream. "Quite, quite delicious. I intend to enjoy every bite."

Ava nibbled at her own scone. Thankfully her morning sickness was mostly gone now but she had no appetite at the moment. Not when she knew, deep in her gut, what Lady Stokeley was going to say.

"So they did more tests," Lady Stokeley said matter-of-factly, once she'd finished her scone and then brushed the crumbs from her fingers. "And it's just as I thought. Those numbers, markers, what have you, aren't looking good at all. In fact, they're twice as bad as they were last week, so I think this is all going to happen quite rapidly." She almost sounded pleased about that fact, and Ava supposed she could understand that. Did anyone want to die slowly?

"I told the consultant I won't be coming back," Lady Stokeley said, her voice almost gentle, as if she thought this would hurt Ava more than it hurt her. "He understood and he didn't make a fuss or try to convince me to keep going." There was a warning in there, for Ava and everyone else, to respond in the same way. And so Ava tried.

With a sniff, she asked, "Did he say how long…?"

"No, doctors don't like to give dates. Weeks, months…?"

She shrugged. "No longer than that, I imagine, but we'll see. Today I feel quite well, actually." She smiled. "Tired and achy, of course, and sometimes I can't catch my breath. But really, all things considered, I feel quite well. In fact, I think I shall have another scone." With a smile, she lifted her hand to call Olivia.

Ava was still feeling heavy-hearted after dropping Lady Stokeley back at Willoughby Manor, with a promise to visit the next day.

"You don't need to keep tabs on me, my dear," Lady Stokeley had said. "I'm quite able to manage at the moment. And Abby comes to visit, as well as her mother and Harriet too. I have quite enough company."

Ava couldn't keep her voice from trembling as she said, "I want to come, Lad… Dorothy. If you don't mind."

"Of course I don't," Lady Stokeley said, and patted her hand.

Ava had to work that evening and, beforehand, she'd promised Alice she'd look at some online job postings with her. It was better to keep busy, and so after helping Alice trawl through various job postings—cleaning, waitressing, and working at an assisted living center in the next village— she took Zuzu for a walk and then went to Waitrose in Witney to stock up on food. Jace had delivered her new cooker a few days ago, and it was time to start learning how to make proper meals.

Over the next two weeks Ava did her best to stay busy.

She helped Alice with an online computer skills course, and then she decided she ought to take it herself and so she booked it in. Harriet and Ellie were both enthusiastic, and Harriet had even pushed the temp agency idea Ava had mentioned to her, despite Ava's insistence that she couldn't do something like that.

"Why not you? I think you're the perfect person. You've been in both worlds, haven't you?" Harriet pressed shrewdly. "Poverty and privilege—you can see both sides of the coin, Ava. Plus, you can come across as self-assured and charming when you want to." Ava laughed at that, and shook her head. "It's not as daunting as you think," Harriet insisted. "Take out a small business loan, start an office at home, get Olivia to run you up a website. Advertise in local parish magazines and newspapers, flyers in doctors' surgeries—that's it, really."

"That's it? And how can I place people in jobs when I can't even find one myself?"

"You start making connections, talking to people. Look at what you've done with Alice. In just a few short weeks she has far more confidence than she did when you took her in, and you've helped her prep for interviews, wear the right clothes, obtain the skills. You could offer a full service—not just a job placement, but a way to get the skills you need to get a job in the first place. You could run it as a not-for-profit, and get a grant from the council, even."

Ava shook her head, disbelieving, and yet Harriet's idea took tender root in her soul. She'd *love* to be able to do that for a living—help women in a way she hadn't been helped. She'd had to scratch and claw her way to survival, and she'd love to be able to keep other women from finding themselves in the depressing, dead-end circumstances she had time and time again.

But she couldn't see any money in it, and it felt far too overwhelming even to begin, no matter what Harriet said. She had no idea about loans or grants, websites or flyers. No idea at all.

Still, she felt inspired to do *something* positive with her life—and so she took a bunch of her designer clothes to a consignment shop in Oxford, and got a satisfactory amount for them all. She also traded her Mini in for a much less showy car—and seven thousand pounds, which eased her financial pressure considerably. On a whim, she booked herself for another online course, this one about starting a small business, though even that much felt like pie in the sky, but *still*. There was no harm in getting more information.

She visited Lady Stokeley every day, and was heartened to see her seeming well; those ambiguous numbers might be disappointing, but they weren't reflected in her health yet, and Ava was gladdened by that small mercy. Abby and Mallory were visiting her too, and Harriet and Ellie both stopped by on occasion, so Lady Stokeley was getting plenty of company just as she'd said, a thought which cheered Ava even more.

She only saw Jace a few times in passing, and they didn't go on any more dates, which was a disappointment. Sometimes Ava wondered if he was keeping his distance on purpose, or if he was just busy. It was high summer after all, and the gardens were running rampant. He had a lot of work to do, and yet...

They were closer than that, surely? Enough had happened for her to expect him to come around, ask her out again. Their one date had ended abruptly, and she'd been giving mixed signals, but *still*. They'd had something... or so she'd thought. Maybe she'd been wrong. Or maybe Jace was just busy.

A few times she'd chatted to him in passing, and she'd told him briefly about how she was pursuing the temp agency idea, and he'd been encouraging, smiling and nodding and telling her to go for it. But it hadn't felt as easy or natural as it had just a few weeks ago, and that worried her. Could he have changed his mind? She'd decided she was falling in love with him, and then he lost interest?

One summery afternoon a few days before her scan, Ava decided to bite the bullet and ask Jace out for a drink. She wasn't working that evening, and so, feeling rather wildly daring, she took time with her makeup and hair, wore her sexiest maternity top and skinny jeans and headed over to his cottage.

He answered the door looking wary, making her heart sink. Why the guarded expression? Weren't they past that?

"Hey, stranger," she said, echoing her greeting from when they'd first met, which felt like a lifetime ago. "Are you free? I thought you might like to go out for a drink with me."

Jace gave her an inscrutable look for a long moment, making Ava's heart start to thud unpleasantly. She'd hoped he would have jumped at the chance, or at least been mildly enthused, but he clearly wasn't.

"You really want to head over to The Drowned Sailor, considering you work there five nights week?"

"No, not particularly. I thought we could head out of the village. Go somewhere different." Her voice wavered a little because Jace didn't jump at that, either. "Jace…" Ava asked uncertainly, and he sighed, which was not a good sound.

"Okay," he said. "We can take my truck."

This wasn't going down at all the way Ava had planned. Hoped. She sat next to Jace in the truck while they drove to Burford in silence; they'd decided to go to The Angel, which was more like The Three Pennies than The Drowned Sailor, off Burford's high street.

It wasn't until they were sitting in the pub's beer garden, early evening sunlight making it feel drowsy and warm, with their drinks in front of them, that Ava found the courage to confront him.

"What's going on?" she asked quietly.

"What do you mean?"

"Don't give me that, Jace." Now that she'd found the

courage, she had quite a lot of it. "I've told you too much about my life, and you've told me too much about yours, for that matter, to just give me the cold shoulder now." She heard the hurt in her voice and she didn't care. "I've barely seen you in the last two weeks, and when I have it's only been to chat. I thought…" She gulped, hating how she was about to fling herself out there, but knowing she needed to. Knowing it was that important. "I thought we had something going on between us. Something starting, anyway."

Jace was silent for a long moment, gazing down into his pint of beer. Ava waited, her heart beating with painful thuds. She wouldn't prompt him. She wouldn't.

"Jace…" So much for that resolution.

"I don't want to mislead you, Ava," he said. Oh, crap. She really didn't want to hear that. "But I'm just not sure something between us is a good idea."

Ava stared at him, her chest so tight and painful, she couldn't speak. She felt a mixture of emotions—disbelief, and hurt, and also anger, because all along *he'd* been pursuing *her*. Mostly. And now *he* was backing off, as if *she'd* come on too strong?

"Oh, you don't, do you?" she said, and her voice sounded tight and cold.

Jace looked startled at her tone, and then resigned. "I'm not trying to do an about face or jerk you around…"

"Really?" Sarcasm. Dripping.

"Look, nothing really happened, right?" Color surged

into Jace's face as his tone sharpened. "You were the one who wanted to stay friends. I mean, let's be honest—"

"Honest? *Honest?* I was honest, Jace. I was painfully honest with you, more than I have been with anyone else in my life. And, yes, I wanted to be just friends, because my husband had died and I was afraid. I've never—" She drew her breath in sharply, not wanting to finish the end of that sentence.

Not wanting to admit it. *I've never felt this way before.* He didn't need to know that. Not at this unfortunate point, anyway.

"But things started to change between us. You admitted that much yourself. At that festival…" She trailed off, biting her lip, not wanting to show so much weakness and need.

How could she even be surprised by this? This was what happened when she started depending on people. When she started needing them. They let her down. One way or another, they let her down.

"I know," Jace said in a low voice. "I'm sorry."

Ava stared at him in despairing confusion. What was really going on here? Because she had the sudden feeling, sharp and sure, that Jace wasn't telling her everything. "Why are you backing away now, Jace?" she asked. "What are you not telling me?"

He stared at her, his face expressionless now, the angry color receding. "I don't have anything to offer you." He spoke so quietly, so sincerely, that Ava could only gape, the words whirling through her mind, barely making sense.

"You… wait. What?" she said stupidly, still staring.

"Ava." Jace leaned forward, his voice pitched low and vibrating with intensity. "I'm an ex-con. I'm about to lose my job. I have no savings, no house, even the truck isn't mine." He swallowed hard, the gesture oddly vulnerable. "I am the worst bet in the world for a woman."

"I'm not *betting.*"

"You know what I mean."

"I'm not sure I do." She let out an incredulous laugh. "If anything, I would have thought *you* were too good for *me.*"

Jace gave a sad little smile and shook his head. "Not a bit of it, Ava. You're a good person, even if you have trouble believing it. And you're going places. It wouldn't surprise me at all if you set up this temp agency, made a proper go of it. I'd just be a drag on you, unable to find a job, hauling my criminal record around with me. It's not worth it, for you."

"Shouldn't I be the one to decide that?"

"Sometimes the decision needs to be taken out of your hands."

She stared at him, taking in the obdurate set of his jaw, the determined glint in his eyes. He'd made up his mind and no amount of begging or pleading would make him change it. Besides, she had more pride than that. *Sometimes dignity is all you have left.* She wasn't going to get down on her knees and ask Jace to give her a chance. No way, not when he was presenting it as some act of kindness on his part. *Yeah, right.*

"So what is this?" she asked, keeping her voice as light as she could. "A breakup?"

"I'm not sure there's anything to break up," Jace answered. "We're friends, Ava. I still want to be friends."

"So why have you been ignoring me for the last two weeks?"

"I haven't been ignoring you. I've just been keeping my distance a little."

"And will you keep doing that? Or can we go back to the way we were, now that the message has been received?" Jace gazed at her for a moment, looking uneasy, and Ava let out a light laugh, or tried to. "I'm not going to play the desperate female, Jace, don't worry. That is so not my style." She flicked her hair over her shoulders, gave him one of her old Ava smiles, knowing and a little bit seductive.

It felt like slipping on a mask that no longer fit well—familiar but uncomfortable too. Painful. But damned if she'd let Jace see how he'd hurt her. *Gutted* her and there was nothing she could do about it. She knew that, and yet she still had to fight to keep from begging. *Don't give up on us.* No, she wasn't going to say that. Besides, Jace had been right; there wasn't an *us,* not really. They were friends, and they'd almost kissed. It was practically nothing. And yet it felt like so much.

"I know that you wouldn't be like that," he said. He looked unhappy but resolute. "I just don't want to…"

Lead her on? Give her false hope? Check and check.

"You won't," Ava said firmly, and then wondered if this was another type of begging. *Please, please stay in my life.* "But if it's going to make you stress, whatever." She took a sip of her drink, affecting a bored air. She was pretty sure Jace could see right through her.

"All right," he said after a moment.

Ava let out a careful, silent sigh of relief, despite the hurt still coursing through her. "So you'll still come to my scan next week?" she said, and could have cursed herself for sounding eager. But she needed him there.

"Yes, of course." He almost sounded affronted that she had to ask, which made Ava wonder.

Did Jace want it both ways? Well, as far as she was concerned, his I'm-not-good-enough-for-you speech was pretty darn lame. Paper-thin and flimsy. What guy thought that way, really? It had been Ava's experience that guys tended to think they were too good for her. And this time she wasn't going to take scraps or leavings. Damn it, she wanted a man who would fight for her. And if Jace wasn't it, then fine. She'd settle for being his friend—and she wouldn't beg or even ask for more.

Chapter Twenty-Five

O VER THE NEXT few days Ava catapulted into action. Some part of her had been waiting for Jace to saunter in on his charger and fix everything in her life. That was what she'd counted on before—finding a man to pay the bills, keep her company, make it right. Too bad it had never worked out for very long; even her marriage hadn't lasted.

But this time, she wasn't going to count on a man. She was going to make her own luck, forge her own future. And so, somewhat defiantly, she asked Harriet to help with a business plan for a bank loan, and had Olivia mock up a website for her potential temp agency, Fresh Start Solutions. It was all baby steps, because even Ava realized she couldn't just launch a business out of nothing. But with the money from the sale of her car, she had a little safety cushion. There was no reason, save for her own insecurity and fear, that she couldn't do this, or at least try.

She also took some personal steps that felt even riskier than starting her own business. She found a mailing address for the Stan Telford who was a member of the Lancashire

Darts Club, and wrote him a letter, asking him if he was her father. It was a short letter, but it contained some honesty that Ava hadn't felt ready for in twenty years. Telling him how his neglect after her mum had left had hurt. Wishing she hadn't lost touch. She sent the letter, telling herself not to get too hopeful. In some ways, it didn't matter so much whether he responded or not. It was more important that she'd written the letter in the first place.

She did an Internet search for her mother, but came up with nothing, something that didn't surprise her. Her mother had been a drifter, and was hardly one to have an Internet footprint of any description. Still, Ava tried, and she also thought about contacting her daughter, but that didn't seem fair. Her daughter had turned eighteen last year, and could access her adoption records if she chose to. If she wanted to find Ava, she could.

Ava decided to make it a little easier for her, though, and she set up a Facebook page with her maiden name, listing Wolverhampton as her home town and giving an email address. If her daughter decided to go looking, Ava would come up quickly in the search results.

And all the while, she tried to feel like her heart wasn't breaking, like just looking at Jace didn't hurt. The day of her scan he offered to drive her in his truck, and so Ava climbed in, her bladder uncomfortably full as per the instructions on her appointment notice, her heart racing.

"Are you going to find out whether it's a boy or girl?"

Jace asked as he pulled onto the A40.

"I think so. Harriet and Ellie have both offered me my pick of their baby clothes, and it would help to know which kind I'll be needing. Plus..." She let out a little laugh. "I want to know."

"Makes sense."

She glanced at Jace, trying to read beneath his easy expression, but he'd gone right back to being the sexy stranger with the lazy laugh—something that stung, because he'd been different with her once. It wasn't until he'd reverted to form that she realized how much.

They made small talk all the way to Oxford, something that irritated her because they'd moved so far beyond that, and then Jace let her off in front while he went to park. Ten minutes later, he strolled into the maternity ward, looking completely at ease amidst all the women in various stages of popping, hands complacently laced over burgeoning bumps.

Ava sat and tried not to squirm, because she might have drunk a tad too much water and the truth was she needed to go.

"Can't you go a little?" Jace asked when he clocked her fidgeting. "Just to relieve some of the pressure?"

She stared at him in disbelief. "Do you really think that's possible? Once I start to go, I'm going to *go*. There'll be no stopping me."

Jace's slow smile made her toes curl. Still. "That does seem like your personality," he said.

Ava tried to glower at him, but she couldn't. They'd been talking about her weeing, for heaven's sake, and it felt as easy and natural as so many other conversations they'd had. Why couldn't Jace see they could have had something special? Why couldn't he have fought for her?

"Ava Mitchell?"

Ava struggled to stand and Jace grabbed hold of her elbow and helped to hoist her to her feet. She was only a little over sixteen weeks pregnant and her bump was relatively small and neat, but she still sometimes felt like a whale.

The nurse smiled at them and then led them into a small consulting room with an examining table and an ultrasound machine. It wasn't until Ava was hoisting herself onto the table with Jace's help that she realized how it looked—as if Jace was the father of her baby. As if they were a proper couple.

And for one painful, breathtaking second, she wanted that more than she'd wanted just about anything in her life. She wanted it to be simple—her and Jace, a baby. A family. It seemed simple, in that second; it seemed *obvious*. This was how it was for most people in the world, wasn't it? They met, they fell in love, they had a child, they worked for that happily-ever-after, because Ava wasn't living in fantasy land. She knew it took work. She *wanted* to work. But Jace, it seemed, did not.

"So." The technician bustled in and took Ava's red folder of medical notes. "Seems like it's been smooth sailing so far?"

"Yes, for the most part," Ava answered.

Jace had taken a seat next to the examining table and sat there, looking alert but relaxed, typical Jace.

"And this is your sixteen-to-twenty week scan, to check on baby's health as well for any abnormalities?"

Ava tried not to gulp. "Yes."

"Brilliant." The woman gave her a reassuring smile. "Shall we get started, then?"

It had been nearly twenty years but Ava still remembered the feel of the cold, clear gel squirted on her soft belly; the technician always warned it would be cold but somehow it still came as a surprise. She remembered the firm, insistent press of the ultrasound wand, the technician's murmur that it might feel a little uncomfortable but it wouldn't hurt the baby. It was all the same. Except instead of Jeff, looking nervous and uncertain, it was Jace, looking relaxed and interested and making Ava want to cry.

Was he so relaxed because he wasn't invested, or because he was? Why, even now, was she second-guessing him, wishing things could be different when Jace had made it plain that they couldn't be?

"There we are," the technician murmured in satisfaction, and an image appeared on the ultrasound screen, in fuzzy black and white, looking a little bit like a child's drawing—head, stomach, skinny arms and legs poking out. Ava let out an incredulous laugh—she'd seen it before, and yet it was still so amazing. So wondrous.

The technician began to point out all the various bits and as she spoke the baby took an even clearer shape—eyes, nose, mouth. Fingers, toes.

"Baby is sucking its thumb," the technician said. "Can you see?"

"Yes…" Ava laughed, and then glanced at Jace, who was looking as amazed as she felt.

"Do you want to know the sex?" the technician asked.

"I think so, yes."

"All right. Let's get the important bits over with first, then." Ava remained still, her gaze transfixed on the screen, as the technician checked the internal organs—heart, lungs, liver, and the nuchal fold at the back of the neck. "Everything looks just as it should be," she said after several heart-stopping minutes. "And it's quite easy to tell the sex as it happens—perhaps you can see for yourself?" She shot a humorous look at Jace. "Daddy?"

"What?" Jace looked startled and Ava bit her lip, half-hoping he wouldn't correct the technician and plunge into awkward explanations about who he was. "Oh, right." He leaned forward and squinted at the screen, and then he smiled. "He's sitting like a bloke, isn't he?"

"Wait, what?" Ava struggled to peer at the screen and with a laugh the technician tapped the screen.

"Legs sprawled and one hand on his bits. Yes, I'd say it's a boy."

"A boy…" She hadn't expected that somehow. Somewhere deep in her heart she'd been thinking she'd have a girl, a do-over daughter, but this… this was a completely new fresh start. A boy. A son.

"Shall I print out some photos?"

"Yes, please."

A few minutes later the technician had left them alone.

Ava put the photos aside to wipe the gel off her belly. "Thanks for not making it awkward," she said, her head lowered, because she felt she had to say something.

"Awkward?"

"The daddy thing."

"Oh, right." He shrugged, his hands shoved into the front pockets of his jeans. "It was a natural assumption for her to make."

"I suppose."

"These are something else." He took the photos and studied each one in turn. "It looks like a proper baby."

"What are you expecting him to look like?" Ava teased, reveling in that he. "A frog?"

"I don't know. It's just…" He shook his head slowly. "I understand why people call it a miracle."

"Yes." And here she was, tearful again, for all sorts of reasons. She still wanted the happy ending, the simple family. Oh, well. Ava straightened and blinked hard, determined not to give in to her emotions. "Thanks for coming with me."

"I wouldn't have missed it."

She nodded and gave him an uncertain smile, unsure

how to navigate these moments.

"Do you need the loo?" Jace asked with a nod towards the bathroom and Ava let out a groan.

"Yes, rather badly." She hurried to the loo, closing the door, trying her best to wee as quietly as she could.

She thought she'd managed it until she heard Jace chuckle on the other side of the door. "Man, you really did need to go."

"Jace." She should have been mortified but somehow she wasn't; she was laughing. She washed her hands in the sink and then opened the door. "You shouldn't have been listening."

He raised his eyebrows. "How could I not? You were like a fire hose in there."

"*Jace.*" Laughing and feeling a *little* mortified now, Ava grabbed her notes and took the photos from Jace. Time to get going.

She'd just come out into the waiting room when she heard a sudden, sharply indrawn breath and looked up to see, of all people, Emma standing in front of her. Emma and her husband Jack, whom Ava had never had the privilege of meeting, holding a red folder just like Ava's.

And while Ava's gaze had dropped automatically to Emma's folder, so Emma clocked Ava's. Her shocked gaze narrowed as she took in Jace standing next to her, holding her elbow.

"You didn't," she said, the two words a hiss.

Ava stared at her blankly. Didn't what?

"You didn't," Emma continued in a louder hiss that managed to carry through the entire waiting room, "shack up with someone else days after my father died." She didn't phrase it as a question.

Emma, Ava realized in a daze, had made the same assumption as the technician, which was perfectly understandable, and yet—couldn't she have *asked?* Or at least lowered her voice?

"No, she didn't," Jace interjected pleasantly. "Not that it's any of your damn business."

Emma turned to him, her mouth dropping open in obvious outrage. Too obvious—Emma still was, it seemed, a drama queen. Only now she didn't have her father for an audience—there was no one to slide sideways glances to, to check that he was listening. That her tactics were working. "Who are you?" she demanded.

Jace kept his smile in place as he answered, "Like I said, none of your damn business."

"Jace." Ava tugged on his arm.

She didn't want a scene, and the truth, bizarre as it seemed, was that she felt sorry for Emma. At least a little bit. She'd been her Daddy's little girl and she was grieving him. Taking it out on Ava was probably a relief, like lancing a wound.

"Let's go."

Jace looked as if he wanted to argue, stick it to Emma a

few more times, but Emma was already quivering with determination to be the first to leave this unfortunate confrontation.

"Come on, Jack," she said, nose pointed firmly in the air, and she moved towards the waiting nurse.

Ava tried to ignore the curious stares as she walked out of the waiting room. So, that had been fun. Not.

"So that was Simon's sister, I'm guessing," Jace said once they were back in his truck.

"Yes."

"A piece of work."

"I feel sorry for her."

Jace let out a huff of disbelieving laughter. "You give everyone a fairer shake than you do yourself, Ava."

"So you've said." All the buoyant excitement she'd felt from the scan had now gone depressingly flat. Emma had ruined it, like someone putting a handprint in pristine, wet concrete. Her fresh start didn't feel so fresh anymore.

"Ava?" Jace put a hand on her shoulder, heavy and warm. "Don't let it bother you."

His sympathy stung, considering how he'd been keeping his distance before. Maybe she was the one who needed to remind him where they stood.

"I won't," she replied crisply. "And you didn't need to butt in and defend me, Jace. I can take care of myself."

Ava felt Jace stiffen, and then he took his hand from her shoulder. "All right, then," he said quietly, and started the truck.

Ava looked out the window, biting her lip and trying not to cry.

Chapter Twenty-Six

THOSE FEW SECONDS of interaction with Emma continued to bother Ava all through the next week. While working at the pub—she'd told Owen she was pregnant and he'd informed her, smiling, that if she worked up to her due date he'd be able to give her maternity pay, which was a relief—she thought of Emma. Filling out her business plan for this crazy temp agency idea, she thought of her. Walking Zuzu, chatting with Alice, visiting Lady Stokeley—all the time she kept thinking of stupid Emma.

It was annoying, because she didn't care about Emma, and yet the more Ava thought about Emma, the more Ava realized she needed to set the record straight, for her own sake as well as Emma's. Well, more for her own.

So, it happened on one Tuesday morning in early August, she found herself standing outside a comfortable cottage of Cotswold stone on a quaint lane off the high street, waiting for Emma to answer the door. She'd never been in Emma's house before, although she knew the address. She'd stayed in the car while David had run in to drop something off or give Emma a message. Now she steeled herself for the decidedly chilly reception she knew she was going to get. The box of macaroons from Olivia's, and the yellow babygro, probably weren't going to smooth things all that much.

The door opened and Emma stood there, dressed in expensive-looking yoga pants and a SuperDry hoodie, her blonde hair piled on top of her head with a clip, an expression of complete and utter astonishment on her face.

"Hi, Emma." Ava managed a rather determined smile. "Do you think we could talk?"

Emma thrust her face forward, so Ava had to suppress the urge to lean back. "Why," she demanded in her customary hiss, "should I ever let you inside my house?"

Ava tried not to sigh. "Doesn't all the indignation get tiresome sometimes, Emma?" she asked quietly. "I just want to explain about what you saw at the hospital. It's not what you think."

"Sure." Emma sneered the word.

Ava wondered why she'd bothered, and yet she was determined to persist. "And I also wanted to tell you the truth about your father and me."

"The truth?" Emma demanded, sounding suspicious, and Ava just waited. "Fine." She snarled and whirled away, leaving the door open for Ava to step through.

She came into a stone-flagged foyer, the walls Farrow-and-Balled within an inch of their life. Everything was studiously tasteful, from the framed watercolors to the rattan baskets that held high-end magazines, to the high-end knickknacks and the one black and white eight by ten of Emma and Jack on their wedding day; she was tilting her head up, laughing, while rose petals rained down.

Ava followed Emma to the back of the house and the enormous kitchen extension with floor-to-ceiling windows overlooking a surprisingly overgrown garden. Emma caught Ava looking and folded her arms, hunching her shoulders in self-defense.

"Jack works a lot and I don't like to garden."

Surprised, Ava looked at her, wondering what exactly had prompted that comment. Did Emma feel like she had to be perfect at everything?

"Your house is lovely," she said. "And your garden is too."

Emma chewed on her lip. "Why are you here?"

"This baby is your father's, Emma."

Emma flinched, her face draining of color, before she rallied, her chin thrusting in a way Ava knew well. "Sure it is."

"I suppose I can't prove it, now that he's dead," Ava said slowly. "But I'd do a DNA test if I had to. Which I don't"— she clarified tiredly—"because I'm not going to ask you or Simon for anything."

"Then why are you here?"

"Because, while I know you'll never like me, I want to

explain a few things," Ava said, her voice growing stronger. "For both of our sakes, but especially for mine."

"And you think I should listen to you?"

"Why wouldn't you? I know you think you've figured me all out, Emma, but you don't seem very happy about it. Maybe it will benefit you to listen. To see things from a different perspective, perhaps."

"And what are you going to say? That you *loved* each other?"

Oh, the disbelief. The scorn.

Ava kept her gaze level. "Yes, we did, after a fashion."

Emma snorted. Literally snorted. "After a fashion. Right."

"Look, I know you assumed I was only in it for the money, and in some ways you're right. At first, anyway." Emma's face twisted and Ava took a deep breath and kept going. "I liked your father, but I also wanted some stability—"

"A meal ticket."

"Is that so very wrong?" Ava asked quietly. The question reverberated all the way through her, the guilt finally falling away. "I was faithful to him, I did whatever he asked, I never complained about anything." She'd been his doll, more or less, to play with and put in whatever position he liked. But she wasn't going to be bitter about it, oh no. She was simply going to tell the truth. "I understand why you'd resent me, at least at first. I do, I always have. But it's *over,* Emma. He's gone and I didn't walk away with your inheritance or much of anything. I was a good wife to him, whether you believe it or not, and this is his baby. And don't worry." She held up a hand before Emma could protest; her mouth was already open, her eyes flashing. "I'm not going to make some case that this child deserves his inheritance too—yes, it's a boy." She lifted her chin proudly. "We'll be fine on our own. *Fine.* All I'm here to say is that I didn't deserve your hate. Not for five years. You could have thawed at some point, or David could have, for that matter."

"Don't blame him," Emma practically shouted, and Ava shook her head.

"I'm not. I'm not blaming anyone, not really. But he picked sides and he could have been neutral, or a referee. But he chose you, he always chose you, in a hundred different ways. Maybe that makes you feel better." Emma didn't reply and Ava continued, "I'm here because I wanted to set the record straight about this baby, and also about me. And if you want to have a relationship with your half-brother, if not with me, well, the door's open."

Emma's lip curled and she didn't say anything, and weirdly, Ava didn't even care. She hadn't come here looking for Emma's friendship. She'd come here simply to state the truth. To be free of the guilt and uncertainty that her marriage, her whole life, had been mired in.

"Goodbye, Emma," she said, and started towards the front door. "Oh," she added as she stopped and turned around. "Congratulations on your pregnancy. David mentioned that you and Jack had been trying for a while. I'm happy for you. Truly." She left the bag with the macaroons and baby gro on the hall table, next to the wedding photo. "Here's a little something for the baby, as well as for you. Enjoy."

Emma looked as if she were struggling between outrage and basic decency. Outrage, of course, won. With a tired smile Ava turned back to the door. She felt both weary and liberated.

"Ava." Emma sounded as if she were trying to contain some intense emotion.

Ava turned around and waited, still not hoping for much.

"Thank you," Emma said stiffly, and Ava smiled.

After five years of stifling, bristling animosity, a simple thank-you felt like a lot.

"You're welcome."

On the drive back to Willoughby Close, she wished she had someone to talk to, but unfortunately Jace wasn't an option. Ellie and Harriet were both at work, and she wasn't close enough with Alice yet to go through the whole sordid history of her marriage. Who, then?

The answer came quickly. Lady Stokeley. Dorothy. She'd listen, in her acerbic way, and she'd understand and offer some rather pointed wisdom. Ava bypassed the lane to Willoughby Close and drove up to the manor, the car coming to a sudden halt when she saw the forest-green

Jaguar parked by the front steps.

Ava didn't recognize the car, and yet she had an icy, sinking sensation that she knew whose it was.

She parked her car behind it and walked towards the front door. Her single knock went unanswered, and so, after a moment, Ava turned the handle and slipped inside. Despite the sunny warmth of the summer's day it was chilly and slightly damp in the dimly-lit foyer; Ava doubted Willoughby Manor ever warmed up.

"Lady Stokeley?" she called softly. Dorothy didn't mind her coming in unannounced, at least not too much, but now, because of that car, Ava felt nervous. Nervous and curious. "Dorothy…"

She crept towards the stairs, the ancient steps creaking under her footfalls. She'd just rounded the corner when she heard the cut-glass tones of the aristocracy, spoken in a deep baritone.

"Who the bloody hell are you?"

Ava froze like a rabbit in a snare, her wide gaze training on the man at the top of the stairs. He was surprisingly handsome, with piercing blue eyes and dark brown hair brushed back from a high forehead. He wore an expensive-looking suit in charcoal grey and had a mobile phone clamped to one ear. "Well?" he demanded.

"Where's Lady Stokeley?"

"None of your business, I should imagine."

Ava could already see why Dorothy hadn't wanted to call

her nephew. Ava planted her hands on her hips, determined not to cowed by this utter arse. "Then you imagine wrong. I'm a friend of hers, and I've been driving her to Oxford three times a week for the last month. So perhaps you could drop the regal snobbery, because you're not an earl yet, are you, Mr. Trent?"

Henry Trent's mouth compressed, his blue eyes flashing. "Actually, it's The Honorable Henry Trent, if you want to be technical," he informed her crisply. "Since I am not yet the earl. But you still have not answered my question."

"My name is Ava Mitchell, and I'm a neighbor. I live in Willoughby Close."

"Ah, a tenant, then."

Arse. "As well as a friend. I'd like to see Dorothy."

"Dorothy, is it, now? I'm afraid you can't see her."

Fury surged through her. "You're forbidding me—"

"No, I'm telling you she's sleeping," Henry Trent snapped. "Come back later, although you don't have much time—"

"What?" Ava nearly swayed where she stood. "You don't mean—"

"No, I don't mean she's about to die," Henry Trent replied irritably. "My aunt is far too stubborn to give up that quickly. But I'm transferring her to an assisted living facility closer to London."

"*What?*" Ava gaped at him for several seconds while Henry Trent strode down the stairs towards her.

"I'll escort you out."

"Why are you sending her to some *facility?*" Ava demanded as Henry took her firmly by the elbow and led her towards the front door.

"Because she needs more care than I am able to provide for her here."

"As far as I can tell, you haven't provided anything," Ava snapped, jerking her arm from Henry's grasp. "You didn't even know she had cancer until a few days ago, am I right?"

Henry Trent's eyes narrowed. "I have no intention of discussing my family with you, Miss Mitchell."

"Of course you don't." Ava fired back, disgusted by his highhandedness. "Have you even asked what your aunt wants before you stomp in and make all these decisions?"

"What my aunt wants and what is reasonable or feasible are two different things," Henry snapped. "Not, I shall remind you, that it is any business of yours." He wrenched open the front door and glared at her, leaving her with very little choice but to leave. And yet still Ava dug in.

"I don't think you're being fair—"

"And I don't think you're being very polite," Henry fired back. "Please leave my aunt's home."

She'd gone about this all wrong. She'd gone in with guns blazing and the result was warfare and destruction. She should have been self-effacing and apologetic, gentle and careful and damn it, why had she mouthed off to Henry Trent of all people? He'd never listen to her now.

He *wasn't* listening to her; in fact, he was steering her outside the house, but at least he went with her, closing the door behind him. Ava stood on the portico and tried desperately to think of a way to turn the conversation around.

"Please don't send Dorothy away," was as far as she got. Henry Trent just looked even more irritated. "Please," she said again. "She was afraid of this, afraid that you'd come in and call all the shots."

"Call all the shots?" One dark eyebrow arched incredulously. "You really have no idea what you're talking about."

"Don't I—"

"No," Henry said flatly. "You don't."

Ava stared at him in wary confusion for a few seconds. "Then perhaps you should tell me—"

"I have no interest in doing so. Good day, Miss Mitchell." He started to turn away and Ava grabbed his arm.

"Mr. Trent, your honorable however I'm meant to address you, please listen to me. I've spent a lot of time with Lady—Dorothy recently, and I know she wants to stay in her home for as long as she can. She'd hate being patronized in some care facility—if you know her at all, you know that. Please don't ship her off somewhere just because it's the easier option."

"For someone who has spent a great deal of time with my aunt," Henry replied icily, "you seem to be suspiciously uncomfortable with calling her by her first name."

"If you know your aunt at all," Ava returned, "you'd be

able to understand that."

To her amazement the very tiniest of smiles quirked Henry Trent's mouth, even though his ice-blue eyes remained hard.

"Perhaps," he acknowledged. "However, the fact remains about what is possible and what is desirable, and I am seeking the most expedient compromise."

"Expedient—" Ava repeated despairingly.

Henry Trent shook off her arm. "Now if you are quite finished—"

"Wait." The gruff voice had both stilling, and then Ava turned, her heart bumping in her chest, to see Jace striding across the lawn, looking grimly determined and frankly wonderful.

But Henry Trent… he couldn't know Jace was working here. In trepidation, Ava watched Jace approach, and then stunned realization dawn on Henry's face.

"You…"

"Yes, me." Jace spoke steadily, although Ava could tell he was both nervous and angry. "Your aunt gave me a job here after I was released from prison, as groundskeeper."

Henry shook his head slowly, completely disbelieving.

Jace continued, "But you should listen to Ava. She's brought more happiness to your aunt than all of us put together."

Ava doubted that was true, but she appreciated the sentiment, especially if it convinced Henry Trent. Although considering her recent behavior, she doubted it would. "She knows your aunt and she cares for her dearly, as do many of us who live on the estate. You'd be wrong to dismiss us out of hand."

"Would I?" Henry Trent still looked fairly poleaxed that he was looking at Jace. "Thank you for that ringing condemnation, especially coming from you." His mouth twisted. "You must surely know, Tucker, that I'd never listen to a word you had to say."

"That's not fair—" Ava began, and Henry Trent turned to her with a cold stare.

"You have no idea, Miss Mitchell—"

"Actually, I do." Ava threw back at him. "Jace told me."

Henry looked surprised and a bit discomfited, but then he shook his head. "This conversation is over. As for you"— he tossed towards Jace—"your services will no longer be needed."

It was exactly what Jace had expected, and yet so unfair. Ava watched in impotent fury as Henry Trent strode away from them and then climbed into his Jaguar and gunned it down the circular drive.

Ava's shoulder slumped. That had gone about as terribly as it could have. She turned to Jace, although to say what, she didn't even know. Thank you? I'm sorry? *I love you?*

But by the time she'd focused on where he'd been standing, he was already gone, a distant speck on the jewel-green grass, striding across the lawn, away from her.

Chapter Twenty-Seven

"I HAVE," AVA informed Alice that evening, wishing she could have a glass or three of wine to dull the pain of heartache, "made a complete mess of everything."

"You sound like me," Alice said with a shy smile.

They were curled up on opposite sides of Ava's sofa while twilight settled softly on the garden, violet clouds scudding across a darkening sky.

"You haven't made a mess of anything," Ava protested. "You were just given a very raw deal." She sighed and leaned her head against the sofa. "I, on the other hand, had a fairly decent chance to do something good and I cocked it up completely."

"Can I ask what this is in reference to?"

"Everything," Ava said with a long, defeated sigh. "Well, not quite everything," she amended. "But Lady Stokeley." Her throat went tight as she remembered how badly she'd handled that interaction with Henry Trent. And as for Jace...

Her eyes burned with unshed tears as she thought of how

he'd come to her defense, knowing it would cost him his job. Or had he figured his job was a lost cause? Either way, he'd been kind, kinder that she'd expected or deserved. She'd gone to his cottage right from Willoughby Manor that afternoon, but he hadn't been around. Had he already left? Was it all over? She'd gone to work a short while later and then Owen had taken pity on her and let her off at nine because she'd looked so knackered. She'd come back home and Alice had made her a cup of hot cocoa and now she was sitting here, stewing.

"What about Lady Stokeley?" Alice asked, and with a depressed sigh Ava explained the situation.

"I know she wants to stay at Willoughby Manor, if her nephew would just bend a little. She'd need a carer, I suppose, at least eventually, but I'm sure he could afford that..." She trailed off, blinking, realization dawning in a welcome rush. "Alice! You have some kind of qualification, don't you, a level two in healthcare...?"

"Not quite a level two," Alice returned cautiously.

"But still," Ava persisted. "You're experienced."

"Not actual *nursing*—"

"I don't know if she'd need nursing, at least not for a while. Just someone to be around, make sure she's comfortable, give her her pain medication..."

And now her throat had gone too tight for Ava to speak. She hated thinking of Lady Stokeley dwindling away to death. She'd miss her when she was gone. She'd miss her so much.

"Can you think about it?" she asked Alice. "We could go visit her tomorrow, if you think you might be up for it."

Alice hesitated, and then nodded. "She might not like me, though," she warned, and Ava laughed.

"I'm sure she will," she said. "Even if she acts as if she doesn't."

"And what about this nephew? He sounds fairly awful."

"Let me take care of him," Ava said, with far more confidence than she felt.

Ava's insides juddered with nerves as she walked up the drive with Alice the next day. Thankfully, there was no forest-green Jaguar parked in the drive and so she relaxed a little bit as she came up to the front door. She looked around for Jace, hoping he might still be there, but she didn't seem him anywhere.

"Ah, Ava. I was hoping you'd stop by." Lady Stokeley opened the door, looking, surprisingly, like a picture of health, at least for a woman of eighty-six. She was dressed in her customary twinset and tweed, although she'd swapped her usual Uggs for a pair of orthopedic sandals.

"Lady... Dorothy," Ava exclaimed. "I'm glad to see you looking so well."

Lady Stokeley arched an eyebrow. "I am not quite at death's door yet. Approaching the threshold, perhaps, but not quite yet arrived." Ava smiled at that, and Lady Stokeley ushered them both inside. "But who is this?" she asked, and

Ava introduced Alice.

Ava made tea while Lady Stokeley took Alice out to the terrace. Ava felt remarkably cheerful, all things considered, and she chastised herself for half-expecting to find Lady Stokeley chained to her bed by her evil nephew.

"I thought you might come by," Lady Stokeley said as Ava brought the tea tray out onto the terrace.

It was sunny enough, with a few clouds scudding across the sky, but the slight nip in the air reminded Ava that it was August, and not high summer anymore, at least not in England.

"Did you?" Ava sat down and started to pour the tea.

"Yes, I suspected Henry put your nose right out of joint," Lady Stokeley said with both a smile and a sigh. "He mentioned that he'd met you, and also that he found you singularly unpleasant."

"Ah. Well. It was somewhat mutual, I'm afraid."

Lady Stokeley's eyebrows drew together as she shook her head. "I am afraid, my dear, that you have completely misunderstood my relationship with my nephew."

"What?" Ava's cup clattered in its saucer. "What do you mean?"

"It is not, as you seem to think, one of enmity," Lady Stokeley said gently. "However, it is far too complicated to explain to you now. Suffice it to say, I am willing to go along with Henry's plans. I knew when I rang him that he would have some, and he would put them in motion the second he could."

"But... but..." Ava was practically spluttering. "I thought... I thought you wanted to stay in Willoughby Manor?" Had she got it *completely* wrong?

"Oh, I do." Lady Stokeley assured her. "But I recognize how difficult that will be for Henry, and even for me." She sighed again. "At some point, I have to relinquish my independence. I accept that."

She seemed remarkably peaceful about the concept. Ava hesitated, unsure whether to introduce a new possibility at this point. But it had felt so *right* for Alice to take care of Lady Stokeley. She couldn't just let it go without saying anything.

"Actually," she said, "I have a proposition for you."

Lady Stokeley raised her eyebrows. "Go on."

Quickly, Ava outlined the basic details of who Alice was and the qualifications she had. "You could keep your independence for a while longer, and your nephew wouldn't have to worry," she finished, although privately she doubted that Henry Trent would worry. "But only if you want to, of course. If you think staying at Willoughby Manor a bit longer would be a good thing..."

"Of course I think it would be a good thing," Lady Stokeley replied with some of her usual acerbity. "I doubt my nephew will, however."

"Does that matter so much?" Ava asked cautiously.

She knew how she would answer, but Lady Stokeley's

relationship with Henry Trent seemed a bit more complex than she'd realized.

"I'm not quite certain," Lady Stokeley said after a moment. She seemed lost in thought, her gaze distant, her lips pursed. Then she roused herself and turned to look at Alice.

"My dear, are you quite sure you want to spend your days looking after an old woman and then watching her die?"

Ava blinked at that plain speaking, but Alice, to her surprise, nodded. "I'm quite sure, Lady Stokeley. I nursed my gran when she was ill, and I think it was the most important thing I ever did. I don't regret a moment of it."

Ava hadn't known that. Where had the grandmother fitted in with the flitting about foster homes? Alice's answer seemed to satisfy Lady Stokeley, though. She nodded and smiled.

"Very well, then. I'll inform Henry of the arrangements."

"Do you think he'll..." Ava hesitated, trying to find the most diplomatic way of speaking. "Resist?"

Lady Stokeley chuckled. "Oh, certainly. Henry resists most things as a matter of course. I'm afraid power goes straight to his head. He's just like his father in that regard, alas." For a moment Lady Stokeley's face was drawn in lines of sadness and memory, but then she snapped her gaze back to Ava and gave a small smile. "But I will insist, and therefore I shall prevail." She glanced shrewdly at Ava. "Now was there someone else you wanted to ask me about?"

"Jace," Ava said quietly. "Has he left already?"

"Left? I shouldn't think so. I told Henry Jace must stay, and he agreed with me."

"He—what?" Ava blinked, wondering if Henry was schizophrenic. Or something.

"Not at first, of course," Lady Stokeley continued. "But he came around. My dear, Henry always acts first and thinks later. He blusters and fumes and then later he realizes he was wrong, although, being a man, he never quite admits it." She sighed. "Jace's position is secure as long as I am alive, and I hope afterwards as well, although, of course, I have no power to enforce such a thing."

Ava felt the familiar burn behind her eyelids. She hated talking about Lady Stokeley's death as if it were simply a matter of time, and not much at that.

"Don't worry," Lady Stokeley said as she reached over and patted her hand. "And go after that man, for goodness' sake."

"You mean…"

"Yes, I mean exactly that. Or should I say, whom."

Ava began to blush. "I didn't realize…"

"That I noticed? I think nearly everyone would, although admittedly, I can be quite astute about these things." Lady Stokeley gave her a smile of such affection that it took everything Ava had not to start blubbering.

"I'm not sure he…" she began, sniffling, and Lady Stokeley reached over again and squeezed her hand, her bony fingers curling over Ava's for a few lovely seconds.

"And I am quite sure that he does."

Later that afternoon, dressed in a summery maternity dress belonging to Harriet, her heart pinned to her sleeve, Ava walked over to Jace's cottage. She'd run through various openers, but nothing sounded or felt right. How did you convince someone that you thought he loved you? It felt arrogant and foolish and frankly pathetic, and yet she thought of Jace striding across the lawn to confront Henry Trent, and her heart ached with love.

Just like with Emma, she had things to say and she told herself it didn't matter if the person listening didn't respond in the way she wanted him to. Admittedly, she wanted him to a lot.

She wanted him to sweep her up in his arms and kiss her senseless and tell her he couldn't live without her. But if none of that happened, so be it. She was going to say it all anyway, because she'd lived too long ducking the worst-case scenario, keeping her cards close to her chest and her heart firmly off the table. It was time, whether she felt ready or not, to put it all out there.

But, when she got to Jace's cottage, it was empty, the windows dark, the place seeming desolate. Even so, Ava knocked on both the front and back door and waited around for a good fifteen minutes. No one came to the door or through the path in the wood.

"Major buzzkill," she muttered, the pre-confrontation adrenalin still racing through her. She'd expected to see him.

She'd been counting on it, because that was what was supposed to happen, in movies and romance novels and all the rest. Cue the crescendo and… curtain. Too bad real life wasn't actually like that.

She walked back through the wood slowly, the sky beginning to cloud over as a chilly breeze swept through the trees. The stretch of sunny, warm weather looked poised to be over, right at the start of the summer holidays. *That's life for you.*

The first drops, big and heavy, were starting to spatter as Ava rounded the bend to Willoughby Close—and stopped in her tracks, because Jace's truck was in the courtyard.

"Jace!" She practically screeched his name as she started to run, afraid she'd miss him.

Needing to see him. He was standing in front of her door, hands thrust into the pockets of his jeans, an expression on his face like he wasn't sure he should be there. Oh, she loved this man.

And suddenly it seemed so easy. What was she afraid of? That he might say no thanks? He already had. She had nothing left to lose; her heart was already gone.

"Jace!" she screeched again, and he turned, his eyebrows snapping together as he caught sight of her.

"Ava! Are you okay?"

"Yes, of course. Why?"

"Because you're screeching like a banshee."

"That's because I wanted to see you." She was also grinning like a fool. "I had something to tell you."

Jace looked wary. So far, there hadn't been any about-to-kiss-her-senseless signs, but so what? It didn't matter. She wouldn't let it.

"What is it?" he asked.

"I love you." The words spilled out, an overflow from her heart that she couldn't have kept in a second more. "I love you. I should have said it before, when you tried to shut me out. I went into self-defense mode instead, because I didn't want to beg. I've begged a lot in my life, and I've taken some pretty crappy deals, because I didn't think I deserved or could get more. But that's over. I'm different now, and I'm stronger." She took a breath, trying to slow down because her words were all jumbled together, and as for Jace...

She couldn't tell what he was thinking at all. "I love you," she said again, because that seemed like a good thing to keep on repeating. "And I think you love me." She thrust her chin out, bolshy now. Hell, yes! "You don't want to admit it, because you're afraid I'll start to resent you somewhere down the line, when we're struggling with money or you can't get a job or whatever crap is thrown our way." Jace looked surprised at that, and Ava knew she'd nailed it. He simply hadn't expected her to guess.

"But I won't resent you, Jace," she said quietly, trying to take her time now. "The only thing I'll resent is if you walk away from us out of fear. I've made so many decisions, *big* decisions, out of fear, and I don't want to do that anymore. I don't want you to, either."

"Ava…"

No, she wasn't ready to be let down gently, or even at all. Not yet. Not until she'd said everything.

"I'm not done." She cut him off, practically snapping. "I've got more to say. I love you." There she went again.

Jace's mouth quirked, just a little. "I got that part."

"I didn't want to say it before because I wanted you to fight for me. No one's fought for me, ever. David—my husband—he slighted me in a thousand different ways and I didn't realize it for a long time, because that's what I was used to." The tears were coming. They were in her throat, behind her eyes. And this time she let them fall. "But then I realized you *have* fought for me. In so many ways, you've fought for me, whether it was listening to me or holding my hands or even cleaning up my puke—"

"Technically," Jace said, "you didn't actually puke. It was more just some nasty spit."

"Still," Ava said, laughing even as tears streaked down her face. "*Still.* I won't resent you, ever, because of who you are and how much I love you, and how much you love me, because you do, whether you realize it or—"

"I know," Jace said quietly, and Ava stared at him, her face tear-streaked, rain falling, and her heart suspended in her chest like some fragile glass orb, something that could fall and shatter at any second, or float right up to the sky like a balloon.

"You do?" she whispered.

"Yes, I do. That's what I came here to say, but you beat me to it. I love you. I'll say it a few more times, since you got so many in. I love you, I love you, I love you, Ava Mitchell. So much."

Ava let out a shaky laugh and wiped her cheeks. "I could hear that one more time, actually."

Jace laughed and then, finally, thankfully, he reached for her, pulling her into his arms like she'd always belonged there. "I love you," he murmured against her hair. "I freaked out, I admit it, because I saw how your life was coming together—your friends and your job and your confidence. Ava, you've been amazing, coming into your own strength, and I was so afraid I'd just bring you down. But that's not even what I was afraid of most. Like you said I was afraid of you realizing it and resenting me. Hating me."

"I wouldn't," Ava answered, the words utterly heartfelt. "I won't."

"I believe you. At least, I'm going to make myself believe you. Because I'm still a bad bet, Ava, and it's selfishness that has me here at your door, pure and simple. I'm too selfish to let you go. I want you too much."

"That's all I want, Jace. For you to want me the way I want you."

"I do."

She rested her head against his shoulder, the rain falling

steadily now, but she didn't care. The moment was perfect. Her heart felt like it could explode out of her chest, a confetti of joy raining down.

"Then maybe," she said after a moment, tilting her head to gaze up at him, "you should kiss me. Finally. Because I've been waiting for this kiss for a long time."

"So have I," Jace said, his whiskey eyes glinting with emotion, and then he finally did what she'd been longing for him to do.

His lips brushed hers once in a sort of hello, and Ava answered on a sigh. Jace's hands tightened on her shoulders and he deepened the kiss so it became everything all at once—an invitation, a promise, a seal. And Ava answered it with her heart and soul, all that she had. She gave it all to this man who loved her.

After several blissful but not long enough moments Jace broke the kiss and lifted his head. "We have an audience."

"Do we?" Ava asked, blinking, dazed. Harriet, Ellie, and Alice were all standing in their doorways, each of them looking thrilled. Ava laughed and leaned her forehead against Jace's shoulder. "That's okay."

"You sure you don't mind?" Jace asked in a low voice. "About... about me?"

"What is there to mind?" Ava demanded. "I love you, Jace. All of you. Every bit. I'm not just taking the good without the bad. You can't cherry pick the bits of the person you love."

"But…"

"No buts." She put her finger against his lips, smiling when he kissed it. "No buts anymore, about anything. There's just this. Us." And then she kissed him, and it was just as sweet and wonderful as the last.

There was going to be a lot more where that came from, Ava thought as Jace put his arms around her. There was going to be forever.

The End

The Willoughby Close series

Discover the lives and loves of the residents of Willoughby Close

The four occupants of Willoughby Close are utterly different and about to become best friends, each in search of her own happy ending as they navigate the treacherous waters of modern womanhood in the quirky yet beautiful village of Shipstow, nestled in the English Cotswolds...

Book 1: *A Cotswold Christmas*

Book 2: *Meet Me at Willoughby Close*

Book 3: *Find me at Willoughby Close*

Book 4: *Kiss Me at Willoughby Close*

Book 5: *Marry Me at Willoughby Close*

Available now at your favorite online retailer!

About the Author

After spending three years as a diehard New Yorker, **Kate Hewitt** now lives in the Lake District in England with her husband, their five children, and a Golden Retriever. She enjoys such novel things as long country walks and chatting with people in the street, and her children love the freedom of village life—although she often has to ring four or five people to figure out where they've gone off to.

She writes women's fiction as well as contemporary romance under the name Kate Hewitt, and whatever the genre she enjoys delivering a compelling and intensely emotional story.

You can find out more about Katharine on her website at kate-hewitt.com.

Thank you for reading

Kiss Me at Willoughby Close

If you enjoyed this book, you can find more from all our great authors at TulePublishing.com, or from your favorite online retailer.

TULE
PUBLISHING